INVASION

ALSO BY SCOTT JAMES MAGNER

THE FOREWORLD SAGA

Hearts of Iron

Blood and Ashes

THE TRANSGENIC WARS

Homefront

The Homefront trilogy:

Invasion

Landfall

Beachhead

The Reclamation's End trilogy:

Starfarer's Legacy

Red Genesis

Black Destiny

THE HUNTERS CHRONICLE

Seasons of Truth

Empire of Night

Crusade of Shadows

INVASION

A NOVEL OF THE TRANSGENIC WARS

SCOTT JAMES MAGNER

ARUS
Entertainment

www.arusentertainment.com

FOR ONKEL SVEN. NO WORDS I CAN EVER WRITE WILL PAY MY DEBT TO YOU, OR FILL THE HOLE YOU LEFT BEHIND.

(Partial Transcript)

CHAIRMAN DAVIS:

WE'RE LOOKING FOR A LITTLE CLARITY HERE, DR. HARRISON. YOU SAID in your report that the Transgenic virus was a part of the natural course of human evolution, but in your testimony today you are indicating otherwise. Were you lying then, or are you lying now?

(silence of approximately 12 seconds)

Nothing to say, Doctor?

(further silence of 10 seconds)

DR. MICAH HARRISON:

I have a great deal to say, Mr. Chairman, but I'm trying to figure out exactly which parts of my study your aides decided to misinterpret. If they had read the entire report, they might have gleaned the relevant words, rather than just the ones you wanted to hear.

DAVIS:

Please, enlighten us. And don't be afraid of the big words. We're all intelligent people here.

HARRISON:

With respect, sir, there are no words big enough for what's been done to us.

DAVIS:

To us, Doctor?

HARRISON:

If you, or your lackeys, had actually read the report, instead of the summaries meant for exobiology students, you'd already understand my position. But for the record, and to dispel the confusion you yourself have now injected into the issue, I will state definitively that the human race has not evolved as a result of contact with the virus.

DAVIS:

So you are reversing yourself then!

HARRISON:

Hardly, sir. Evolution is a long, chaotic process of genetic mutation in living creatures. Over time, favorable mutations are more likely to survive and reproduce. What's happened-what's happening-to the human race is not evolution. It is a biological attack by an unknown factor.

(*silence of approximately 20 seconds*)

SENATOR CLARK:

Doctor, are you suggesting . . .

DAVIS:

Preposterous! In over two hundred years of space exploration there has never been any conclusive proof of . . .

(general shouting, gavel pounding)

Order, order! Doctor Harrison, please explain yourself!

HARRISON:

Again, I refer the committee to my study. Evolutionary mutations are a response to environmental factors or species imperatives. They do not occur in adult organisms; nor could random chance produce mutations like functional body parts. Additional arms and legs, third or fourth eyes that can read radio waves, that sort of thing. And evolution certainly does not produce these results essentially overnight in widely separated populations and genetically diverse individuals.

The Transgenic virus, as you name it, affects—is affecting—specific portions of the human genome. In fact, it might be more accurate to say it targets them. It transforms a normal human being into a fully functional member of another species.

No technology we possess does this. No process we have can stop or reverse these mutations, nor can we explain why some people are affected and others are not. Moreover, we—

(gavel pounding)

DAVIS:

Doctor Harrison! This is a serious inquiry, not a . . . a . . .

HARRISON:

What it is, sir, is the end of the human race. Ladies and gentleman of the committee, I cannot stress this point enough. The virus is real, and did not originate on this world. The more planets we explore, the more likely it is that we will find other organisms like this one, which will have similar interactions with our biology.

No sir, the virus is not evolution, but it's foolish in the extreme to assume the evolution of our species has ended. It will happen, must happen because of the virus. It's inevitable.

Superior forms of life now inhabit this planet with us, and there's a clear pattern for what happens next. Like our own species displaced those that came before us, we will eventually give way to these new forms of human.

DAVIS:

Unless we take steps to stop it. Quarantine the infected, limit new exposures . . .

HARRISON:

Steps? Steps? Mr. Chairman, every man, woman and child on this planet is infected. For now, most of us have not expressed any effects. But our children, and our children's children, will quite literally see things we cannot imagine.

You can attempt containment, but you will fail. You can hound and harry and treat your children like animals, but in the end you will only destroy yourselves.

CLARK:

Doctor, for the benefit of those who have not read your study and are watching these proceedings, how would you recommend we proceed?

HARRISON:

With patience, Senator. This is all so new, and there's so much we do not understand. In time, we'll learn to manage the effects, perhaps even guide them. But the one thing we must not, cannot do is act out of fear.

DAVIS:

And why is that, Dr. Harrison?

HARRISON:

Because for now, they still remember being human. And there's one thing that children, animals, and all living things have in common.

When threatened, our transformed descendants will defend themselves . . .

16 JULY, 2640 OER

JANTINE

As suicide missions go, thought Jantine, *this one could do with a bit more excitement.*

Maybe it was the lack of activity, or that she and her team had no way to alter their course through hyperspace. Maybe it was that she really didn't understand their mission, or that despite their training her team seemed ill-suited for it.

Maybe if they'd given us a proper spaceship, instead of stuffing a bunch of mods barely old enough to leave the crèche into a cargo container and firing us into another dimension. But three weeks of travel for what might only be seconds of activity makes even the best of us a bit restless.

"Malik, time to insertion?"

Her second-in-command's face glowed in the light of his computer screen. She and Malik were alone, but he made a point of looking around before answering.

"Fifteen minutes less than when you last asked. Three hours, twenty-five minutes, and odd seconds remaining. You should make the call."

Malik was right, of course. The others needed to prepare as best they could. But delaying the call meant she could push back the reality of their mission a short while longer, and savor what little life she had left.

Jantine got up from her chair and stretched, careful not to extend her arms all the way and touch the fabric of the temporary shelter that served as their command center. She'd made that mistake on their first day out, and Malik had barely made it outside with the portable terminal before the tent collapsed around her. Everything about this mission was temporary, including its personnel. But Jantine couldn't fault the Alphas for their accommodations. After all, why spend money on equipment you'd never need again?

"I need to take a walk. Give a shout if something happens."

"Will do, boss."

Jantine shut down her own computer. It was a near duplicate of Malik's, built into a carrying case of ballistic plating and powerful enough to run an entire city if necessary. But instead of scanning the not-landscape of hyperspace for threats as her second-in-command did, her daily routine consisted of comparing crew readiness reports and preparing training schedules.

My first command, and it's like I never left the training center. Reports for everything, including how many reports there are.

Closing her eyes and twisting so as to not touch the sides of the opening, she eased herself out of the tent. It was one of many tiny exercises she'd assigned herself every day to keep sharp, and her engineered body was as responsive as ever.

As Betas, Jantine and Malik were the finest soldiers the Colonies could produce. Her specialty was operational command, and he was designed for tactics and interpersonal relations. Physically, their strength and speed were nearly matched, but despite a higher combat aptitude she'd never been able to best him while sparring. Malik always found a way to win, no matter how hopeless the situation was.

Eyes still shut, she let the red glow on the other side of her lids move her dark-adjusted eyes back to normal. When she opened them, the simulated light of the cargo container came at her from every direction, banishing shadows and approximating the ground-level light of their destination. If the surface currently serving as a floor weren't darker in color than the walls around them, the appearance of their camp would be even more surreal.

At present, her command consisted of a handful of tents and a few dozen crates of equipment neatly arranged on the deck plating—everything they'd need if the mission lasted longer than a few seconds after landing. Only her combat team and the support crew were awake during this phase, and a group of them were far enough away at the other end of the container that the gently arcing floor put them above her.

The remainder of her people were in cryosleep in a second container, waiting for Jantine to make the most important decision of her young life. Of everyone's lives, really, but the responsibility was hers. She'd been training for this moment almost since she took her first steps, and it still didn't seem right to her.

A dozen mods, with the weight of the worlds on our shoulders. And only half of us have military training. Me and Malik, Katra, Jarl, and the Deltas. What were the Alphas thinking?

About half the support team civvies were watching Crassus and Artemus walk through their paces under Katra's watchful eye. Unlike the Gamma's subtle genetic advantages, there was no mistaking the Deltas for baseline humans. Almost four meters tall, their extra arms and hardened gray skin were easy indicators of their primary function as combat infantry.

Both mods were carrying an unpowered squad weapon in the upper set of arms, and deflection panels in the lower. By the looks of it, Katra had them executing a defensive sim, projecting holographic opponents directly into their eyes. The Gamma's fair hair was a shade lighter than Jantine's, but she had a similar lanky build.

The speed at which the Deltas moved was impressive, and the civvies watching them seemed a bit confused as to what they were actually doing. To Jantine's trained eye, the Deltas were adjusting to incoming fire from imaginary combatants, moving the barriers in front of simulated beams and bullets that would otherwise make sticky paste of the unprotected scientists and technicians sitting behind them. The audience was an unknowing part of the training exercise, and in the long run, the most important part of their mission.

Assuming, of course, that we survive the landing. And then make it out into the open. And then find a place to defend. And then...

Three hours, twenty-some minutes. She needed to make the call.

Jantine thought about keying into Katra's sim, and giving the Deltas some real opposition. Not physically—either one could rip her apart if she let them get close enough—but strategically. Katra's sims were straight out of the training manuals. Although the Gamma was a talented instructor, she didn't have the right mindset for improvising a chaotic battle—Katra and Jarl were combat infiltrators, not leaders.

Speaking of whom...

The hairs on the back of Jantine's neck stood up, and her senses went into overdrive. She bent her right knee and kicked out with her left leg, while at the same time tasting the air around her for some hint as to Jarl's direction of attack. She smelled nothing but the sterile blandness of recycled air and the slightly greasy feel of tent material.

Jantine rolled forward when she hit the ground, adjusting for the curving surface of the container. But her maneuver came to an abrupt halt when her back slammed into something that shouldn't be there, and she knew she'd guessed wrong as to Jarl's location.

Again.

Before she could twist away, strong hands pulled her arms behind her back and the full weight of her opponent pressed her into the floor. She scissored her legs in an attempt to get free, but Jarl was a heartbeat faster, and locked one of her thighs behind one of his knees.

"Stabby Stabby. Dead."

Jarl's throaty whisper was close enough to her ear that she could feel his breath moving across her skin, and still she couldn't smell him. He held her down long enough for her hypothetically slit throat to bleed out, and then pulled her to her feet.

When she looked at him, the dark outfit Jarl was wearing told her how he'd done it. Instead of the non-descript brown coveralls the rest of the team was wearing, he'd somehow fashioned a spare shelter into a flowing garment that not only broke up the lines of his body, but allowed him a full range of movement. She'd smelled a tent because she was attacked by one, and the knowledge made her smile at her earlier thoughts regarding Gammas not being able to improvise.

"How long?"

"Two hours. Malik spotted me when I came inside, and scored a kill. So I waited for you to come out instead."

Damn. Should have thought of that. Make the score: Jantine, 0; Malik, more than 0; and Jarl, 37.

Jantine gave Jarl a small bow and ducked back into the tent. He'd heard Malik's timetable announcements and knew as well as she did where the mission stood. It was time to make the call, and prepare for the rest of her life.

She didn't bother sneaking up on Malik—his senses were better than hers, and he'd likely heard everything that transpired outside. Malik's intense focus on the screen in front of him didn't blunt his perceptions of the world around him, and this heightened awareness was one of the many reasons she liked working with him.

Settling back into her chair, she spent some time looking at Malik's face in the dim light of his screen. It was similar to her own, but with enough differences to mark him as belonging to another crèche.

Betas were bred to serve, be it as officers, underlings, ambassadors, or teachers. Gammas like Jarl and Katra were carefully designed tools meant for a specific task, but Betas were the ones qualified to use them. Most of the team outside were Betas, as were about ten percent of the sleepers in the second container. But before partnering up with Malik, she'd never really considered what it meant to just like somebody for who they were.

And she did like him. His casual efficiency at everyday tasks, the way he kept her on track, and the occasional smile that escaped his inbred professionalism. If she didn't know better, Malik could almost pass for an Alpha, but they were far too valuable to send on a mission like this.

Jantine saw a slight movement of Malik's left eye before he spoke, the only acknowledgement he ever gave that he noticed her scrutiny.

"Are you ready?"

The implications of those three words were almost too much for Jantine to handle. Malik knew the most likely outcome of their mission, and the prospect of permanent exile on a hostile planet should they survive it didn't seem to bother him. He only wanted to know that she was prepared to command him to his death when necessary, and was more than capable of activating the container's destruct sequence if she was not.

Because a Beta who would not do her duty was as big a threat to the Colonies as the enemy, and Malik would certainly do his. The rest of the team would never know it had happened, and their mission would disappear from the universe as if it had never launched in the first place.

"Yes. Open a channel for me."

Malik nodded, and mumbled a phrase that both disarmed the destruct system ready to burn them to ashes and activated the communications array. As a result of her choice, life in the containers would become interesting over the next few hours.

The next words Jantine spoke to her team would pale in comparison to the message she was about to send, possibly the most important words ever spoken aloud since humans first went out into space. She knew the message so well she could recite it in her sleep, and she would deliver the words of the Alphas to the universe without a single change.

"It's ready, Jantine."

Jantine was still watching Malik for some sign that he returned her almost-affection, and was surprised when he turned his head to look her in the eyes. It had been eighteen days, seventeen hours and thirty-seven minutes since they'd been sealed into the container and fired into hyperspace, and in all that time Malik had displayed nothing but perfect Beta obedience and efficiency. But as the last day of their lives slowly counted down, she saw in his eyes how much he'd wanted to not activate the destruct sequence, and in his smile how happy he was to be alive for just a little bit longer.

Malik gave her a nod, then rose and left the tent. Jantine pulled his portable unit over to her, placing her palm on the scanner and verifying her willingness to die for the Colonies.

"This is JTN-B34256-O. Streamship 7 is a go. Time to insertion is three hours, ten minutes, twenty-six seconds. Message begins.

"This is JTN-B34256-O. In accordance with Interstellar Compact and the Magellan Accords, I state now for the record that my actions are mine and mine alone. I hereby declare myself free of the tyranny of the Outer Colonies, and ask that my actions be viewed in the context of the greater good.

"On March 17, 2640 OER, I commandeered the freighter *Argo* and killed its crew, appropriating its cargo of workers and colonists for my own use and freeing them from lives of genetic servitude.

"Do not attempt to find us. Do not attempt to reclaim us. We are armed, we are free, and will defend ourselves to the utmost of our abilities.

"You have been warned..."

ANDREISON

INSTEAD OF BREAKING his hand off at the wrist, Sub-Lieutenant Marya Andreison swiveled her chair to dislodge Lieutenant Mitchell Williams' grip and leave him floating helpless for a few seconds. There was never a good time to deal with this sort of thing, but the cramped confines of Forward Sensor Pod Alpha were one of the worst places she could think of to fend off unwanted advances, especially with the chair's safety harness restricting her movements.

Williams either didn't take the hint, or chose to ignore it. Anchoring himself against the pod's hatch, he put on his best approximation of a seductive smile.

"Come on, one drink. I'm just trying to get to know you, that's all."

Williams had been trying to get to know her for weeks now, ever since Marya's transfer aboard. Her wedding rings, her rank, and her clear disinterest weren't the deterrents they should have been, and her service record meant any waves she made now could wash her right back to monitoring deep space communications from a planetside observatory instead of doing the same duty aboard a Redstone dreadnaught.

Most of *City of Lights'* other officers left her alone; a stint in a military prison, however unjustified, left a stain on an officer's career that took years—if not decades—to fully erase. But as a section head, Williams—in theory—had legitimate reasons to talk to her. About hydroponics and power allocations, anyway, neither of which had anything to do with her current assignment.

Just another few months in grade, and I can either retire like Deb wants, or transfer somewhere where a pig like Williams can't affect my destiny.

"So, what do you say, Marya? Are we going to be friends?"

Ok. That does it.

Marya turned her head away, not bothering to hide her contempt. Williams' smile was still in place, and she knew she'd lost a few points by rising to the bait. But his too-smug face was very punchable, and his signature stale sweat plus depilatory odor was particularly offensive today. She triggered both the security monitors and a portable data recorder before speaking, so this time at her disciplinary review there would at least be some record of what had happened.

"No. We're not." *My friends act like human beings, and leave me alone when I ask them to.* Marya was biting back a lot of comments like this lately, and each one moved her a little closer to her Deb's way of thinking.

"Not only would my wives not approve"—*of me slumming it with the worst the Fleet has to offer*—"but I have a lot of work to do this shift. I'm still cleaning up the mess this section was in when I came aboard. There is a lot of space to monitor, Lieutenant."

Marya activated a holo display with her left hand, making a point to flash her rings at him again as a miniature representation of *City of Lights* coalesced in the air between them.

Williams' smirk twisted into a scowl. "You should start making friends instead of mistakes, Andreison. No one wants you on this ship, and if you ever want out of this hole," Williams said, waving a hand through the display to indicate the cramped compartment—"you'd better come around to the right way of thinking."

Marya surged against her harness, fists and teeth clenched. Like many would-be and unwanted suitors, Williams was convinced that he was the right man she'd always been yearning for. And like some of the others who wouldn't take no for an answer, he was about to lose a few teeth.

But before she could release her harness and add another black mark to her service record, a buzzing alert pulled her attention back to the board. It showed an imminent hyperspace emergence, and the schedule floating next to it showed no ships due to arrive for at least a day.

"Get out or strap in, Williams. I don't much care which."

Technically, protocol demanded she close the hatch immediately and jettison the pod regardless of his decision, but the thought of being stuck in a sensor pod with Mitchell Williams' infamous wandering hands and too-ripe stench was more than Marya could bear right now. As he scrambled back through the access tube to the ship proper, she triggered the pod's ejection sequence, taking no small amount of pleasure from the panicked look on Williams' face through the closing airlock as she launched herself into space.

Once she was surrounded by nothing but stars she put him out of her mind and focused on the task at hand. Marya's hands flew through holos and established a tight beam link with *City of Lights'* main array. Once the two systems were talking to one another, she commed the control deck.

"Ships, Andreison. Hyperspace emergence detected at 0339 ship-time, no scheduled arrivals. I repeat, no scheduled arrivals. Hostile incursion protocols engaged."

"Confirmed, Andreison. We're on lockdown. Good hunting."

Commander Phillips sent a telemetry packet back through the link before signing off, indicating the rest of Marya's team had launched and the dreadnaught's weapon systems were powering up.

As a widening cloud of information formed around *City of Lights,*

Marya watched the rest of the battlegroup come to life. Missile tenders, attack cruisers, and courier ships arranged themselves in a standard defensive formation, waiting for Comms division's pod crews to give them something to shoot at.

With the press of a button, any one of her three dozen specialists could focus the entire battlegroup's destructive power on a single target, in addition to serving as a remote communications hub almost impossible to detect by an opposing force. Marya's slowly tumbling electronic coffin was even darker than the space around her, completely undetectable even by her own people until she reopened communications with the rest of the battlegroup.

When no ship presented itself after a minute, she craned her neck to peer out the pod's tiny porthole for some indication of what was going on.

Where are you, my unannounced friend?

For any other officer, scanning the blackness of space visually instead of studying her readouts would have been a waste of time. But thanks to a training accident at flight school, Marya's eyes were artifical, supported by a neural mesh and a series of cybernetic implants that allowed her brain to process the greatly increased input they provided.

On most days, the constant barrage of sights, sounds, and smells she registered every waking moment required the extra computing power they'd shoehorned into her head just to stay sane. But today, it meant that in addition to recording the micro-expressions of lecherous hydroponics officers, she could use her extra visual range to detect the rippling of space preceding a hyperspace corridor.

The chance of her pod being aimed in exactly the right direction during emergence were infinitesimal, but as the seconds ticked away she could already imagine Williams spinning this incursion to Captain Maddsen as an alert invented by an incompetent ground officer who had no business serving with the "real" Fleet.

Come on, give me something to work with. I need a win here...

Depending on its speed and configuration, it could take hours for a ship to successfully transit a corridor, and Marya rechecked her board after a few more minutes without an incursion. Only the weirdness of space-time allowed gravitic sensors to detect one before it actually occurred, and even her enhanced eyesight couldn't find something that wasn't there.

Unless...

Marya pulled up the readings again, searching not for data on what had caused the alert, but instead for the alert itself. Once she found the waveform that triggered her sensors, it was the work of a moment to replicate it in her display.

Instead of seeing violent crests and troughs representing an object's arrival propagating back through time, she saw what appeared to be a gently curving modulation that shouldn't have tripped the sensors at all. There just wasn't enough energy to distort local space, yet here she was, waiting for something—or someone—to pop into existence.

She magnified the waveform as much as the holos could display, then set her artificial pupils to maximum dilation. To her surprise, the smooth lines became a rapidly oscillating waveform of irregular amplitude, something very few objects in the universe produced naturally.

Marya stared at the sequence for a while before she realized it was repeating. She played it again, and after verifying the pattern, she keyed up a decryption algorithm in hopes the pod's data core could make some sense of it. Something about it just read wrong to her, and a minute later her suspicions were confirmed.

It's not a ship, it's a transmission. But how? And more importantly, why?

Marya wasn't sure what to do with this new information. If she was right, there would be no ship, and the exercise was over. But a Fleet transmission would have come through by courier pod and uploaded itself to the encrypted FTL comm network. Whatever it was she'd just decoded didn't originate within the solar system or the corridor colonies.

And that means gennies, something else I don't need in my life.

All of her training, all the Fleet's preparation, had been aimed toward this exact moment. But despite that legacy, her hand hesitated over the transmit icon.

Maybe it's a mistake. Maybe it's a test. But can I, or the human race, afford to be wrong?

Marya's pod tumbled through space while she deliberated, still scanning the cosmos for something that would explain her current situation. Her breathing echoed back to her from a thousand irregular surfaces, and every few seconds she caught a whiff of Williams as the air circulators did their best to scrub his presence out of existence.

The universe is running a special on crazy shit that comes out of nowhere today, wrapped up in a shiny package and secured with a big, fat, gennie bow.

No one else on her team was likely to identify the waveform for what it truly was, and Marya was self-aware enough to admit that coming from her it would be viewed with derision and scorn.

But no one else on my team can do the things I can, and none of them can do what needs to be done.

Marya undid her safety harness, and let the pod's rotation lift her out of her chair. She floated above the console, the flashing red icon daring her to take action as she stared at the readout representing a human voice. She thought about her wives—Deb down on Earth, and Mira on *Valiant* somewhere else in the system. She thought about how nice it would be if their children lived in a world where they weren't the latest data points in a 400 year-long war.

In the end, it was her daughters that made up her mind. If she didn't retransmit the message, Marya would never be able to describe her time in service to them without feeling shame.

I miss you, kittens. Momma Mar will be home soon.

Marya checked that the recorders were still active, then swiped a hand across the holo to activate the Fleet emergency channel. Eight ship captains and thirty-six tumbling communications specialists listened along with her to the message she'd decoded, a woman's voice with more confidence than Marya had felt since launching from

City of Lights. She hugged herself as the words echoed around the pod, and wondered how long it would be before the shooting started again.

"This is JTN-B38726-O. In accordance with Interstellar Compact and the Magellan Accords..."

MALIK

Malik stepped out of the tent, wary of another encounter with
Jarl. The Gamma rarely tried an ambush twice in the same cycle, but
Katra once told him that in training, Jarl was known to attempt
touches at any time.

*It's a good command. A bit small, but with a bit of luck we'll have
everything we need for success down on the surface.*

Malik did a quick scan of the immediate area, then moved himself
into the open. The scattered tents of their encampment cast no
shadows to speak of, and if Jarl was lying in wait he'd shed his tent
camouflage in favor of something even more inventive.

*He'll probably try for someone inside a tent next. It's no use stalking
Katra, she's far too good at this, and he knows not to bother her while she's
running sims.*

And the Deltas don't care in any event.

At the other end of the container, Katra and the Deltas were
performing for a nearly full audience. Only the Omegas were missing, but their translator Doria was front and center with a huge smile
on her face, as always. The other civvies were watching with a
mixture of concern and confusion on their faces, but Doria was just
relaxing and enjoying the show.

Perhaps it was her empathic abilities that made the difference.

Malik wasn't exactly sure how it worked, but she seemed to get more enjoyment out of life than anyone he'd ever met.

Malik started walking toward the group, looking around for the Omegas. The shape and size of the container were such that to really conceal oneself took a great deal of skill and ingenuity, so the two hulking mods must be engaged in some private project inside their shelter tent.

The Transgenic virus hadn't done humanity any favors overall, but compared to the base stock the Omegas' appearance was truly alien. For reasons lost to time, the hulking pair looked even more extreme than did the Deltas. Instead of gray skin and extra arms, their skin was a vivid orange, and they were almost half a meter taller. Their broad faces had extra pairs of eyes, and a double set of ears on each side of their heads.

In contrast, their mouths were comically small. Again for unknown reasons, the Omegas had very different respiratory systems than other mods, one that allowed them to work in a variety of hazardous conditions, including the vacuum of space. As a result, though they understood language well enough, their mouths and throats couldn't form responses in normal frequencies. Rather than use translation devices, they preferred to communicate with empathic facilitators like Doria.

Responding to his thoughts, Doria turned and looked at him. Her knowing smile hinted at a lifetime of other people's secrets, including his own.

Without saying a word, Doria patted the space beside her and then turned back to watch the Deltas. Malik walked up and took the place she'd indicated, interested in what she might have to say.

"They're designing." Doria's whisper was unprompted, but Malik knew her well enough to know she was answering the questions most people asked her when she was sitting alone: "Where are the Omegas?" and "Is everything okay?"

While Malik wasn't particularly worried about the Omegas, he always felt a bit frustrated that the other mods defined Doria by her association with the Omegas instead of engaging her on her own merits. She was funny, intelligent, and insightful—all traits a trained medical specialist needed. But despite her easygoing nature, since she was "the voice," she tended to give status updates instead of greetings.

Just like the rest of us. Until long after landing, anyway. There won't be much time for casual interactions until we're fully established and out of danger.

"Anything in particular?" As he spoke, Malik kept his eyes focused on Katra rather than the Deltas. She had a look of intense concentration he rarely saw in a Gamma, and he wondered if something had gone wrong with the training simulation. But Doria's next words made him forget all about that.

"They won't tell me. They usually don't if the project is going to take a while. They don't want to burden us with disappointments."

Malik now gave his full attention to Doria. Rather than sputter out the words of his many questions all at once, he waited for the Gamma to continue. She'd turned to face him, and the warmth of her smile was all the communication she deemed necessary. When she didn't speak, Malik was ashamed that right now he was treating her just like the rest of the mods did.

Doria's hand came up and caressed the side of his face. The gesture was so unexpected that the only thing Malik could do was cover it with one of his own, and continue looking into her eyes.

"Thank you. For acknowledging it—most people don't bother. It's all right not to know how to react around an empath. It's also okay to ask questions if you have them, I don't mind. The Omegas don't think on the same timescales as we do, or about the same sorts of things."

Malik reluctantly pulled her hand away from his face, but didn't want to let go of it. Somewhat surprised by his reaction, he kept holding her hand while considering his next action, and decided a full conversation on this topic was probably a good idea.

Malik rose to his feet, and Doria came up with him without any urging. She cocked her head toward the tents, then slipped her hand from his.

In another community, the pair's departure might have been met with raised eyebrows and hushed whispers. Both Malik and Doria were healthy and mature, and given the probable outcome of the next few hours no one would fault them for seeking some comfort in sexual activity. But the very nature of this mission required the team's members remain professional at all times, and Doria's role as a counselor put her off-limits in any event.

Besides, she's not the one for me...

Malik followed Doria to her shelter tent. Ducking his head to step inside, he saw the same basic camp furniture he had in his own tent, although Doria had arranged it into a much more comfortable space. Where Malik, Jantine, and the other combat mods had set up their quarters in nearly identical fashion based on years of training and discipline, Doria's personal space was an organic extension of herself.

Unlike the command tent, Doria had opened up all the ventilation flaps to let in air and light. Her gear wasn't set up based on how fast she could exit the tent in an emergency, or with an eye to where her weapons were stored. Instead, Doria's layout invited him to sit down and relax for as long as he wanted to visit.

"I don't usually see people here like this, but you and Jantine are always welcome." Doria waved him to one of the chairs and sat down facing him half a meter away in the other. Malik noticed that she'd chosen the one that kept her face fully visible in the tent's half-light, while he was more in shadow.

How does she do that? Always coming up with the right thing to do or say?

"I can't read minds, not exactly. Empathic communication is more about predicting behavior than telepathy, but you're very easy for me to read. You and Jantine are so used to command that people do what you want them to as a matter of course; it's almost like working with Them."

When Doria said the word like that, Malik knew she meant the Omegas. They had designations like every other mod, but since there was so little cosmetic variation among them they decided to embrace their similarities and rejected individuality altogether along with their names. Over time, a skilled observer could tell them apart, but even through intermediaries like Doria, few mods tried to engage them in conversation.

"Um, thank you. But...you do communicate directly with the Omegas, right?"

"Of course. I was bred for it. They have wonderful minds, and their desires are very easy to sort out. I use words and terms I'm familiar with, and they guide me to the right meanings. It's functionally the same thing."

Malik tried to keep the confusion off his face, then remembered that with Doria it didn't matter. If she really could interpret his emotions, she'd know better than he what he wanted to say.

Doria smiled, and leaned forward to rest one of her hands on his knee. She gave it a gentle squeeze, then sat back in her chair. The slight disturbance in the air as she did so carried a scent to him from deeper in her tent, something spicy and soft and full of mystery. He was just about to comment on it when she continued.

"There aren't a lot of us in the Colonies. Part of it is that the Omegas live very long lives, and prefer not to deal with our chaotic personalities. One, maybe two Gammas like me can support an entire community. For the most part they do their own thing, and they don't need facilitators to communicate with one another. And like you, people generally understand what they want on the little stuff."

"Why don't they cover this during education?" Malik was genuinely curious now, and leaned forward slightly to hear Doria's response.

"They do for some. But I don't know how to use the weapon your hand just went to, or how Jarl got so close to you before you realized he was there." Doria's smile didn't falter, but her gaze shifted to a point just over Malik's shoulder. "Oh, sorry, you hadn't figured it out yet. Not consciously anyway."

Malik's eyes widened as a strong hand squeezed his shoulder. He didn't turn his head, but instead looked down at his right hand, which was indeed curled around the handle of his sidearm.

I wonder which of us he came for?

"Jarl, if you'd like to join us I can sit on the cot." Doria gestured to the side, and cocked her head slightly before continuing. "We're talking about the Omegas, who are impressed at how quietly you moved around in their shelter. They want me to let you know that watching you has helped them with their design problem for the Colony's outer defenses, and that you're welcome to try and kill them again any time."

Malik felt the hand leave, and this time did turn to look. Jarl was back in his normal coveralls but had dusted his skin with some kind of dull powder. Given the visual range of the Omegas, it was likely something meant to change his skin temperature.

"No, I'm good. Malik, Boss says to call a meeting."

Jarl was speaking to Malik, but the Gamma's eyes never left Doria. Malik wasn't sure if his expression was one of disappointment or admiration, or some mixture of both.

Doria would know, of course, and Malik decided that was what was bothering Jarl. Empathics made an infiltrator's job a lot harder, but at the same time they gave him a reason to do it.

"Thanks, Jarl." Malik saw that the infiltrator was waiting for further orders, and continued. "Get cleaned up, and meet us in the group tent in…let's say twenty minutes."

That should be more than enough time for you to prepare your next "surprise."

Jarl nodded, and left without saying another word. On the way out he didn't bother with stealth, and his shoulder somehow brushed the tent's entrance flap. It cut off some of the outside light as it fell into place, and Malik turned his attention back to the ever-smiling Doria.

"That was well done, Malik. Whether you realize it or not, you can read people too. I think it's a part of your training as much as your mods."

Doria's face softened after she spoke, and Malik tried to imagine what it would feel like to do what she did. Jarl and Katra were easy enough to understand, and Jantine…Jantine was different in her own way. She wanted some kind of reaction from him whenever they spoke, and half the fun of his day was finding ways to almost give one. But the civvies didn't have a lot in common with the combat mods, and he didn't expect that to change after landing. JonB was an excellent example of how the two groups were just...different.

But then there's Doria...

Malik decided to switch topics. He'd come here to learn more about Doria, but they'd spent most of the time talking about the Omegas or himself.

"Why did you do that? Ask Jarl to join us?"

"Because he wanted to. He wants to understand you, much like you're here trying to understand me. You see him as more than a killer, and he's not used to that in a commander."

Malik sat back in his chair, trying to process what Doria was saying to him. He hadn't thought about it in exactly those terms before, but it seemed that Doria knew his mind better than he did.

"Are we all that obvious?"

Doria paused before answering. When she did, her voice was a bit softer than before, almost childlike.

"No. Like I said before, I can't read minds. Not exactly. But you and Jantine see us—Gammas, I mean—not just as tools for a specific job like other Betas do. We notice. And you in particular are...special. I sometimes can read a bit more from you than the others."

Now Malik was truly at a loss for what to say. After almost three weeks of close contact with them, in the last few minutes he learned more of what it meant to be a Gamma than he'd thought possible. He didn't feel special—he wasn't sure exactly what he was feeling.

Is there a word for this? Maybe it's what Jarl was feeling. Something between disappointment and anger. Not toward myself, or the Gammas. But towards our society as a whole maybe? I don't know, and that's...

He hadn't seen Doria move, but suddenly she was next to his chair and that same spicy-sweet smell came with her. He found himself on his feet, and as soon as he was standing Doria was crushing herself to him in a fierce hug. Her left cheek was pressed against his, and the warmth of it was as unexpected as the words she was whispering in his ear.

"Don't think like that. Never like that. It's all right, you've done nothing wrong. It's all right, it's all right…"

The words trailed off in his ear, but Malik felt Doria was still speaking to him somehow. He could feel her jaw moving against his own, and small puffs of air were tickling his skin.

Unsure of what to do, Malik put his arms around Doria and just held her. He tried not to think about the mission, or his orders, or anything at all but her in his arms. In that shared moment he was as much a part of her world any of the objects around them, but it couldn't last. He knew what was expected of him outside the walls of the tent, and though his body was certainly interested, he couldn't help being who he was.

I'm a Beta. And Doria is not the one for me.

They stood there in silence for several minutes, until Doria relaxed her arms around him. He let his hands fall away from her back, and before she pulled away she surprised him one last time by turning her head and kissing his cheek. It lasted only for a moment, but in that time Malik's universe contracted to the few square centimeters of his body still in contact with her warmth.

Doria moved a short distance away, and took a moment to compose herself with her head turned to the side. When their eyes met again her smile was back in place. Malik didn't know what to say, but he was sure she understood. He watched her eyes in the shadows for a few long seconds, and then said the only thing he could.

"I should go tell Carlton and Harren to prepare a meal. I…I'd like to talk to you again sometime, but I don't think we'll have a chance before landing. Would that…would that be all right with you?"

Malik was almost disappointed at the speed, and professionalism, of her response.

"Yes, of course. I'll see you at the meeting, Commander."

Malik nodded, and turned to leave. Out of respect he waited until he was outside to smooth his coveralls, biting down hard on his emotions as he realized that no one would be looking at the entrance to Doria's tent.

It may be all right, but after we land things are going to be different for you, Doria. I can promise you that for sure.

Malik pulled out his handheld and keyed in a general meeting call. He had fifteen minutes now to prepare for the next phase of the mission, and the rest of his life would just have to wait.

KOŁODZIEJSKI

FLEET CAPTAIN HORACE Kołodziejski was not happy. A very junior third shift officer had set a new course while he was asleep, putting *Indomitable* a few billion kilometers away from the search grid he'd authorized for *Valiant*.

Wherever Captain Aloysius Martin and his battlegroup were hiding, it wouldn't be near Mars, the most heavily monitored part of human space. And as much as Horace wanted to return home, there was work to be done.

"Who is the captain on this ship, son?"

His words had the desired effect, and every eye in the command center turned toward Horace and the object of his disappointment—Sub-Lieutenant James Edward Carter III, a well-placed political appointee who was one of the few Earthers who'd made it through his screening process.

I should have known Carter couldn't cut it, but his father is a necessary ally on the Reclamation council.

For now.

"Y-you are, sir." Carter looked like he was about to vomit, so there was at least one thing about him to which Horace could relate. In fact, Horace had been in the process of doing just that when he learned about the course change, and had pulled himself together specifically to come to the command center and give the boy a dressing-down.

These new meds may be doing me more harm than good. Which makes it even more important for us to get back on course.

"My specific instructions were, 'Stay close to the Home Fleet, and find me that ship.' Maybe that means something different on Earth—which, by the way, is where we should be heading right now. But on this ship, mister, when I give an order, I expect it to be carried out. Set the course, clean up this mess," he said, waving a hand at the bulb of coffee and half-eaten meal packet sitting on the arm of his command chair—also in defiance of his orders, "and leave the pit. You're done here."

To his credit, Carter said nothing while keying in the course change. A nav holo showing the correction appeared over the heads of the suddenly busy crew, who were in reality just as much to blame as Carter for their current location.

A problem for another time, but one I should have expected when packing my ship with political opportunists. They let his name override their judgment, when they should have informed someone immediately when he fucked up.

Carter collected his unauthorized meal, took one last look around the command center, and departed. Horace arched an eye at the pair of armored troopers by the hatch, one of whom fell in behind Carter as he began his walk of shame.

But Horace had no time to savor the sight as another spasm hit and he fell unceremoniously into the command chair. The pain was getting worse, and if there was any food left in his system he'd definitely have spit it back up.

Helpless as a fucking child. This can't continue.

Horace had closed his eyes against the pain, and opened them to a half-dozen expectant eyes. Hopefully they'd taken his weakness for disgust, but they were definitely waiting for instructions.

"Helm, come about to the new course, cruising speed. Mr. Julian?"

"Sir?"

"Welcome to the big chair. You'll complete the remainder of third shift, and continue on into first under the supervision of Commander Annahko when she arrives. And I do hope you don't disappoint her; I want no more surprises for the next few hours. Mr. Calas?"

"Sir!" Bob Calas was the officer who'd alerted Horace to the unauthorized course change. Calas was another opportunist, but instead of Carter's ineptitude, Calas was a model officer, and from a high dome family. One of his trusted Loyalists, Calas noticed the error when he reported early intending to install new search parameters for Captain Martin and his battlegroup. Caroline Annahko was the third member of his inner circle, and she was more than capable of overseeing first shift while Horace crawled back to his quarters to die.

"Resume the search pattern once we're back in cislunar space. I want good news this morning. How long until our next secure window?"

"I make it…six hours, sir."

"Good. Notify me when we're in range, I want to talk to Echo Base as soon as possible."

"Understood, sir."

Horace took a firm grip on the chair's arms, leveraging himself up with as much grace as he could muster without betraying any weakness. Even in *Indomitable*'s relatively forgiving simulated Martian gravity, he was barely able to stand without screaming.

Seventy-five paces back to my quarters, three to the sanitary sink, and then a short crawl back to my rack. That's not too much to ask, is it?

"Carry on, people."

A chorus of *Sirs* followed Horace out the hatch, a decided improvement from the hushed silence marking his entrance. As soon as it was shut, his trooper escort moved quickly to assist with an arm under his sagging shoulder.

"Thank you, Daniel."

Daniel Tepes was part of Horace's permanent retinue, and technically wasn't a member of *Indomitable*'s crew at all. As such, the trooper was privy to some, but not all, of Horace's medical issues, and like Horace came from one of the oldest Martian families.

"Just a few steps more, sir, and I think we'll be fine. Do you have any additional instructions for Andrew?"

Horace held on to Tepes as they walked, considering possible future uses for Sub-Lieutenant Carter.

I need Carter II's vote on the Fleet appropriations mandate, but his son isn't worth recycled piss. Dumping him off on another captain would be better than shooting him, and only slightly more paperwork. But it will only postpone the problem, and if this morning is any indication he might cause more trouble down the line. Until I can be absolutely sure of his father's loyalty to the cause, I need to keep a careful eye on him.

"No. Tell Collins to keep young Carter in his quarters until further notice. I'll think of something."

"Of course, sir. You always do."

Sixty-eight, Sixty-nine, Seventy...

Damn.

The corridor curved slightly away and to the left, with the hatch to the captain's suite within view on the long wall. But he wasn't the only officer with quarters on this deck, and the sound of ship boots walking toward them echoed around the curve.

"A moment, Daniel."

"Of course, sir."

Unlike the romanticized version of Fleet ships paraded in front of the sheep on Earth, the floors, walls, and ceilings of a Redstone dreadnaught were covered with magnetic grating designed to aid transit in emergencies. Catch rings were placed every ten meters, and he used one to steady himself before the unknown officer came into view.

Luckily, it was Commander Caroline Annahko. Like most of *Indomitable*'s crew members, she had the lanky build of a Marsborn, supplemented by Fleet-mandated full-g workouts. Despite the early hour, her uniform was neatly pressed, and she looked as if she'd stepped straight out of a recruiting poster instead of being rousted from her rack just minutes before.

Annahko's eyes narrowed slightly, taking in Horace's own hastily assembled attire. From any another officer, Horace would take it as a challenge. But from a friend, he took it for what it was—concern.

"Captain."

"Sorry to have woken you early, Commander, but we had a bit of trouble on third shift. Calas will brief you in the pit."

"Understood, sir. We can handle things today, while you figure out where our quarry is hiding."

A sudden spasm turned his smile into a grimace, and Horace gripped the ring tighter to avoid falling. He saw the edges of Caroline's smile harden, and nodded to buy himself a moment.

How much do you know, Caroline? How much can I tell you, before your love for me is overridden by our oaths to the cause?

"Thank, you, Commander, I may do just that. Join me for tea later?"

Annahko's face relaxed somewhat, and she gave him a slight bow before answering.

"Of course, sir. I'd be honored. I'll send an update when first shift comes online. If you'll excuse me, I should check in with Lt. Calas as you suggest."

"Until then, Commander." Horace returned the bow, using the motion to ride out another spasm. The sooner he could get back to his quarters and plug himself in to a diagnostic scanner, the better.

Annahko continued on around the curve, and as soon as she as out of sight Horace felt Tepes' armored arms encircle him.

"I've got you sir. We're almost there."

The last few steps were pure agony, but once he was inside his quarters, safely away from prying eyes and with the sound filters engaged, Horace finally let out the scream he'd been holding in for the last twenty minutes.

"It's not fucking fair!"

He pounded the wall above the sanitary sink, repeating the words until he collapsed in a trembling heap, too wasted to even cry. He felt his bowels loose, and the sour odor of his own filth filled the compartment, kicking off another round of dry heaves.

It's not fucking fair. I'm only fifty-seven, I'm supposed to have more time. Another hundred years, at least. Not half as many days.

Where are you with my test subject, Aloysius? Do you know what you've done to me?

Would you even care if you did?

Horace didn't know how long he huddled in pain before noticing the alert light on his desk. He tried to push up from the deck to answer it, but after several unsuccessful efforts decided to stay put.

Fuck it. One of the benefits of being captain is that people work on my schedule, not the other way around. Besides, not even I want to see me like this.

Horace searched the sleeves of his tunic for a clean spot, then used it to wipe his mouth before answering. He took a few experimental breaths, then raised his wrist comm to his lips.

"Go for Horace," he whispered, wincing at the sound of his own voice. Annahko's reply seemed booming in comparison.

"Sir, I have a priority comm from *City of Lights* on Alpha channel, coded eyes only. Shall I put it through to your terminal?"

Horace eyed the compartment's combination desk and table just a few meters away, wondering if he could clean himself up enough to sit at it without assistance.

"What's our communications delay?"

"Mr. Calas puts it at three light-minutes, and closing."

Fucking Carter. We can't use FTL comms without alerting Valiant *as to where we are, and he's put me across the solar system from our strongest ally.*

Perhaps I should have him shot after all.

"Send an acknowledgment with your code, then put it through. I'll be ready for the reply."

"Understood, sir. Command out."

Horace spent one of his six minutes of waiting gathering his strength, and another getting out of his soiled uniform and shoving it into the recycler. He stumbled into the sonic shower as two more ticked by, then downed a stim cocktail as he pulled a mess tunic over his emaciated form and sat down at his desk.

Hell, for all I know, Markus Maddsen's not wearing pants either.

Keying in his personal code, Horace saw the elfin features of his oldest friend contorted into a frown.

Looks like I'm not the only one having a bad day.

"Horace, we've got a situation here I think you should know about..."

Mindful of the delay, Horace listened to *City of Lights*' captain's report without interruption, followed by the intercepted transmission. Neither did much to improve his mood.

"You're certain of this, Markus?"

Five minutes and fifty-seven seconds later, Maddsen's response only fanned the flames of his anger. Bad enough to feel and smell like shit, but having to wait to hear his worst fears confirmed was a special kind of agony.

"I have my doubts, sir. None of my techs can replicate the signal on their own, but following Andreison's work they say it's genuine.

"From what I'm told, she ran a ton of analysis on the signal before relaying it, and even more since. Wherever it came from, it's not one of ours, and the voice markers are consistent with gennie accents on file."

Fucking gennies. They pick now, of all times, to return from exile. And we have no idea where they are, or what they're planning.

An abdominal spasm hit as he was about to speak, and Horace hit the kill switch just in time to avoid transmitting the image of him spewing a thin spray of yellow bile all over the desk. As it was, he barely got to the sanitary sink in time to spit up some more, along with some dark blood.

You'll be waiting a few more minutes for my response, Markus. Hopefully I'll live through them.

Following another round of cleanup, Horace returned to his chair, drawing out his response with strategic pauses to keep his gorge down. Something about Maddsen's message was bothering him, and he couldn't quite place what it was.

Could be anything, really. It's too soon to tell what's going on.

When he felt he was presentable again, Horace plopped himself in one of the compartment's two chairs, triggered the holorecorder, and sent a response.

"Andreison. Sounds Earther. If you haven't already, isolate her, and clear the ship of people we can't trust. We may have to tip our hand earlier than expected. Also, stay on the line for new search parameters. Bob's got some ideas that may flush Aloysius out of his hidey-hole sooner rather than later.

"I'll have more for you in a few hours, when we can talk face to face. Horace out."

After typing a quick message to Lt. Calas, Horace slumped in his chair while he worked through the possibilities. To save time, he clamped a diagnostic cuff over the paper-thin skin of his left wrist, and let it sample his blood.

Five more hours until I can transmit these results to Echo Base, and another five until I can talk to Markus in real time.

Horace didn't need the scanner to tell him he was dying. He could feel it in every cell of his being, endured it every second he was awake. His body was betraying him in every way possible, and now, when every minute counted, the enemy he'd been preparing for his entire life was almost upon him.

The gennie transmission is problematic, but at this point it's containable. We can still manage the flow of information, use it to our advantage. If word gets out, Aloysius Martin and whoever else is on his side will turn our planned war of extermination into a diplomatic exercise that celebrates those mutant freaks, instead of ending them.

And for the good of the human race, we definitely need this to end.

ANNAHKO

TEA WITH HORACE Kołodziejski was one of the many rituals that defined Commander Caroline Annahko's life, and one of the few opportunities the two officers had to enjoy each other's company.

Both officers knew that life in the Home Fleet meant life on ships, and for the scions of Mars' most prominent families, a very public life at that. She and Horace had met as teenagers, and thanks to the repeated urging of their parents, remained together ever since. But unlike most celebrity pairings, they had genuine affection for one another, and their almost-romance was the highlight of every conversation Caroline had had with her mother over the last 15 years.

But today, their midday meal seemed forced, and Caroline couldn't put her finger on why. Until recently, they'd enjoyed the kind of physical relationship that was only possible through years of familiarity and a thorough knowledge of one another's needs. Their time as lovers ended when she came aboard as his second-in-command, but in private they could be themselves again, free of regulations and responsibilities.

"Can I get you anything else, Commander? You seem a bit

distracted." Horace's words weren't warm, and to Caroline's practiced ear seemed a bit distant. His voice, his manner, almost everything about the man she loved was still the same, but for the last few weeks Horace had been moving through his life as if it was about to end.

And we're both too proud to do anything about it.

Caroline placed her teacup on the table, trying hard to keep her eyes on Horace's face. Any time she could spend with him was time well spent, and she was already avoiding conversations about how he had barely touched his food, his drawn face, or the faint smell of bile in his quarters that even Fleet standard cleaners couldn't remove.

"I'm fine, Horace. Just thinking about mother. She sends her best, as always."

The lie nearly burned her tongue, and Caroline's collar was suddenly far too tight. It didn't help that Horace's quarters were uncomfortably warm, though the captain seemed unaffected by the heat. For their private meal, he'd chosen a basic blouse with no rank or boards, immaculately pressed as always. In contrast, Caroline felt ridiculously over-dressed in her ship's duty uniform, with its polished insignia, service ribbons, and badges.

It looks brand new. Definitely not what he had on this morning.

Earlier in the corridor the distance between them seemed greater than ever. She'd wanted to rush to his side as he sagged against her cousin Daniel, but even with their history Horace would never have allowed it. He would have waved away her assistance, and she wouldn't be here now.

And I do want to be here, Horace. Never forget that my place is by your side.

Caroline didn't think this morning's unfortunate course change was what had turned his mood so sour, though resolving that issue was a burden she'd gladly take off his shoulders if he'd let her.

"If you'll permit me, Horace, I was also wondering if you'd allow me to deal with Carter while you focus on more important things. I can think of a few creative punishments that won't get back to his father."

At the mention of the hapless Earther's name Horace's eyes lit up, with a hint of a smile to follow. But even though she could hear joy in his next words, it somehow failed to join the rest of his face.

"No, thank you Commander. I have him contained for now. He's a nuisance, but like most Earthers he's more inconvenient than dangerous. I think we can leave him where he is until we get back to Echo Base."

Horace's eyes narrowed, pulling his lip up slightly into a sneer that had Caroline wondering if he already had something in mind for the boy who'd ruined his meticulously planned search for Aloysius Martin and *Valiant*.

Running that pompous ass to ground is something I probably want as much as Horace does. He's been blocking Marsborn appointments to the Academy for years, in favor of Earther proles and station trash. Drumming him out to the Fleet for treason is in everybody's best interests.

And if it makes Horace happy, so much the better.

Although she didn't know all Horace's reasons for pursuing Martin across the Home System, or really any details of the numerous projects he had in motion, she knew Horace would never do anything against the interests of Mars. Even his frequent visits to Earth's moon were in service to a greater cause: developing weapons to defend the worlds against an inevitable gennie invasion.

For now, seeing him happy was all she wanted from the universe. And as for her own needs, she at least had some hope that their relationship would revert to its previous status at some point.

Even in this private, unguarded moment, there was less of the real Horace Kołodziejski on display than she would have liked. But it was still Horace across the table from her, still the man she'd followed out of the high domes into the Fleet, and whom she'd follow anywhere in the universe if only he'd ask.

Neither officer had been back to Mars in years, and despite her mother's frequent urging, her inevitable marriage to Horace had stalled completely when she joined *Indomitable*'s crew. She still loved him, and although she was sure he returned her feelings, his insistence on protocol and propriety went over and above Fleet standards.

These stolen moments are all we can have together.

For now.

"Are we abandoning the search, then?" She sipped the last of her tea, eyeing both the kettle and Horace's half-full cup.

"No, we're closer than ever. I can feel it. Now that we're back on course, Bob's new algorithms should do the trick,"

Caroline reached for the kettle, topped off both their cups, and set it back on its magnetic holder. She wanted time to continue her examination of her best friend, but there was only so much she could do over the rim of a cup. As she'd noticed earlier, Horace was thinner than ever, and despite Daniel's subtle assistance in the corridor she had the distinct impression that he was far worse off than he projected.

What's wrong, my love? What are you keeping from me? I don't think I've ever seen you so...small.

Never a big man, over the past few weeks Horace had become almost skeletal, and their infrequent embraces hinted that the rest of his body was similarly diminished.

Horace's eyes met hers, and Caroline was only able to hold his gaze for a few seconds before turning away. Even in his current state, Horace's will was barely contained by his body, and her heart beat faster imagining his hands on her skin. To avoid blushing, she turned her attention to his quarters instead, praying she'd have the strength to look away a second time.

Horace's—*no, he's the Captain now, and I have to accept that's his role in my life if this is going to work*—quarters were spare and spotless. There was no art on display, no personal items secured to bulkheads. There was absolutely nothing out of place, and if the Captain wasn't showing up in fresh uniforms every day she'd suspect he wasn't spending much time here at all.

Further, the cleaning products she'd detected upon entering had been put to excellent use. Few officers adhered to the sanitary regulations as fiercely as Horace. Few Earthers, anyway. On Mars, children were taught from an early age that an unsecured compartment meant death in an emergency. Caroline kept her own quarters in a similar state, not only because of regulations, but on the off-chance Horace might visit or ask to share them.

"Caroline?" It took her a second to process that Horace was speaking, and another to realize he'd asked more than one question while she was looking around his private space. She returned her attention to his face, aroused as always by the intensity of his gaze. Her breath caught in her throat, and another moment passed before she could find her voice.

He's so...

I...

"I'm sorry, Captain. What was that?"

"Have you given any more thought to succeeding me as *Indomitable's* captain? Once we find Aloysius, I plan to transfer my command to Echo Base, and I can't think of anyone else who'll treat her the way she deserves."

"Sir, I..." The prospect of not seeing Horace every day was disturbing, but command of a dreadnaught was something she'd wanted from the first time she and Horace had snuck into the shipyards and roamed the half-finished corridors of *City of Lights*. Technically her oath had been to command that vessel, but as Horace intimated, *Indomitable* was indeed the finest ship in the Fleet.

"You're ready, Caroline. You were ready when you came aboard, and this will allow me time to...there are things I must tend to sooner, rather than later, if our lives are to continue as planned."

Caroline searched Horace's face for any clue that their real relationship was about to resume, and his eyes drew her into a virtual embrace she had no intention of leaving. Horace was smiling now, but it seemed forced, and she had the distinct impression that if she pressed the issue of their marriage, he might pull even further away.

"I'd be honored, sir. More than honored, blessed."

"Then it's settled, then. I'll make the arrangements."

Caroline couldn't help but feel she'd just been dismissed, and stood up. Horace rose in response, and for a moment she thought he was going to move forward and embrace her. She took half a step toward him, lips parted, heart racing. But if Horace shared her growing passion, if he had any emotion left for her at all, he was hiding it well.

Instead of an embrace, he held out his right hand. Not knowing what else to do, Caroline took it in a loose, but still professional handshake. Horace's grip wasn't exactly limp, but neither was it strong, and after a perfunctory shake he broke contact.

"Congratulations, Captain-designate Annahko. I'll forward my recommendation on to the Fleet Council during our next session. Now...if you'll excuse me, there are a few things I still need to do this shift. Thank you for a lovely meal, and even better conversation."

Not knowing what else to do, she gathered up the remains of her meal—and the barely picked-at food in front of Horace—and placed it into the bag she'd brought it in.

"Thank, you, sir. I'll see you later at the Senior staff briefing, yes?"

"Of course, Caroline. I'm looking forward to it." This time Horace's smile appeared genuine, but she could sense something else behind it, something she couldn't dwell on without losing herself completely in his eyes.

Caroline searched his face one more time for something, anything, to guide her emotions, but found nothing. She managed to pull herself away from his intensity, and lurched toward the compartment's out hatch without completely losing her composure.

Once safely on the other side, Caroline pressed herself against the bulkhead, eyes closed as she took long, deep breaths.

Did I do what you wanted? Is there anyway I can even know what that is anymore? I should never have agreed to your proposal. We're both professionals, we could have stayed as we were. Life could be so much better for us now, if only you'd let me back in.

"Caroline?"

Horace?

Caroline opened her eyes. It wasn't the captain addressing her, but her cousin Daniel, dutifully standing guard across the hatch from her.

Once upon a time, before the Kołodziejskis came into the picture, she and Daniel were to be paired off to preserve their line. But to cement their alliance, Daniel's line was traded to Horace's family for a majority stake in Dome 3, and an enduring dynasty was formed.

With his armor on and faceplate sealed, Caroline couldn't see Daniel's eyes, but her memory was sufficient to summon up his face as he spoke.

"Is everything all right, Commander? You seem...bothered."

Horace's words, Daniel's voice. Am I so transparent?

Caroline moved closer to the armored form of her cousin, careful neither to stand directly in front of the hatch or obscure his lines of sight. Even now, dome discipline was ingrained in them both, and the first rule was always to keep the corridors clear in case of an emergency.

She glanced down the gently curving arms of the corridor to see if anyone else was about, then settled in next to Daniel against the bulkhead. She took a moment to compose herself, but as this seemed more a matter of family than protocol, she decided instead to bare her heart.

"No, Daniel, it's not. I can't...seeing him like this is killing me. I feel...I feel like we're drifting away on a frayed tether, and soon we're going to snap. Is there anything you can say, that you're allowed to tell me about what's going on with him?"

She kept her voice low, staring into his mirrored faceplate as she spoke. He gave no acknowledgment, but she knew his helmet pickups caught every word. She also knew Daniel would keep her confession a secret, but that same trust meant he'd probably keep Horace's as well.

Daniel's reply was slow in coming, but when he did speak it made her blood run cold.

"I can't, Commander. I'm sorry, But I think...I think if something's going to happen, it has to be soon. We may not...no, I've said too much. I'm sorry, Caroline. So, so sorry."

Caroline's heart skipped a beat, and she pressed herself harder against the bulkhead. She wanted to sink down to the floor, to curl up against the thought of a universe without Horace in it. She wanted to tear off Daniel's faceplate and slap his pity away. She wanted to rip the ship apart with her bare hands until she found a way that would keep Horace by her side forever.

But that's not a luxury I have, now is it? I'm an officer and a Marsborn, a high dome woman who's not allowed any personal pain. The Iron Princess reborn, I have to be perfect.

Just like Horace.

Caroline stood up straight, and put her hand on Daniel's armored shoulder. He moved a gauntlet to cover it, and the two stood like that for a while while *Indomitable* thrummed around them.

Two lost souls uncertain of what to do, or how to save the man they both loved.

JANTINE

"...AND THAT'S WHERE WE STAND. I KNOW IT'S NOT A SURPRISE TO ANY OF you that we'd be considered rogue agents, but I felt you should know that we are now officially at war with the human race."

Jantine scanned the faces of her team, looking for any signs of dissent brought on by her revelation. She expected none—even the civvies had volunteered for the mission—but other than Malik and Jarl none of them had known about the destruct sequence before just now.

The crew—if they could be called that—of Streamship 7 was gathered in the large tent they used for communal meals. One last round of tasteless nutrient wafers and a speech before dying was all she had to offer her people, and now she'd given them both.

Sitting on chairs, crates, and deck plating, both the combat and support teams were silent. Everyone but Malik seemed to be waiting for more information, though no one wanted to be the first to ask. Even the Deltas and Omegas squatting in the back seemed ready to say something, though it was hard to tell with the Omegas.

Doria looked enough like Katra that they could be crèche-sisters, at least while seated. But the contemplative Doria rarely spoke out in a group meeting. And when she did, it was to relay any concerns the Omegas might have. Jantine could see her throat pulsing as she subvocalized her thoughts, but whatever communication she was having with them wasn't meant for the entire team.

The message she'd sent was pure diplomatic fiction, but it was a carefully scripted and executed one. The Alphas needed to disavow their actions, and Jantine and her team, along with the three hundred sleepers in the other container, were a small price to pay to give plausible deniability to the other Streamships.

The real ships. The ones that might actually survive their missions.

Surprisingly, the first person to speak was Katra. She wasn't the most intelligent Gamma Jantine had ever worked with, but Katra was definitely one of the more perceptive.

"Did the words mean anything, other than as a cover story? Are we actually free?"

Interesting. Wasn't expecting that at all.

Jantine looked at the other mod's face, searching for her real questions. The answer to both her spoken ones was *no*, but at the same time a solid case could be made for *yes*. They really were disavowed, and since the penalty for going rogue was death, being condemned as rebels wouldn't mean all that much in the end.

After a few seconds, Jantine decided Katra was more afraid of not having a command structure than anything else. It was unlikely she had any truly treasonous thoughts, and could be counted on to do her duty.

"It means we have a mission to carry out, and a license to do so as we see fit. We know the target planet has Colonial sympathizers, and whether or not we get down safely, my broadcast will tell them that at least we tried. But our priority is still to establish a secure base, and cycle the sleepers as fast as possible. We'll deal with any political ramifications once we complete that objective."

Katra nodded, and Jantine was about to dismiss the team when JonB spoke up.

"When you say 'get down safely' does that mean you don't expect us to?"

JonB hadn't made any friends since coming aboard, even among the other civvies. His pessimism always seemed out of place in a scientist, and Jantine hoped that if—when—they landed, one of the sleeper Betas would be a better fit to act as her chief science advisor. It's not that she disliked the dark-haired mod, but she'd rather deal with someone she felt a real connection to as her civilian liaison, instead of someone assigned to her by the Alphas because he did well on tests.

"It means that right now, I'm in command of twelve mods and not a lot else. We've got exactly two buttons left to push that can control our destiny, and a whole bunch of hopefully empty space between us and our objective. Once we jettison the hyperdrive module and re-enter normal space, the best-case scenario has us a few hundred million kilometers from the planet, and on target. If all goes well, Malik will orient us and start our burn accordingly."

Jantine tried not to think about how insane it was to be traveling through space—hyper- or otherwise—without any way to change their destination. The cargo slug the containers were attached to had no maneuvering thrusters, no navigation sensors, and worst of all, no weapons.

Not that any were necessary. The slug itself was a weapon, a mass of rock and iron moving at relativistic speeds. Aimed directly at a planet, it was so potentially destructive that until now the human race had avoided using anything like it in five centuries of space travel.

Jantine's team was another kind of weapon, also meant to be fired and discarded after use. According to the Alphas' plan, her crew container and its twin containing the sleepers would detach from the slug as they approached the target planet. Their projected insertion point was far above the plane of the ecliptic, so slug itself would go on traveling into interstellar space once the containers were away. If the plan worked, they'd come down intact on gravity buffers, blast their way out into sunshine and clean air and start killing anything that moved while the civvies and Omegas started building them a stronghold.

If. Lots of ifs. But the Alphas had big brains, and they said it would work. So Jantine believed it would too.

Mostly.

"Carlton, Harren, are you ready?"

The civvie Betas actually were crèche-sibs, and responsible for reviving the sleepers as soon as it was determined safe to do so. Unlike JonB, they were open and jovial, and tended to finish one another's sentences.

"You bet, Boss. Find us a spot to work in, and we'll get the job done."

Harren nodded at Carlton's words, and she knew they'd get it done. All of them would, even JonB.

We have to be more than our numbers. At least for a little while.

"Then that's all for now. We've got a little more than two hours until the transition. I want our camp broken down and final readiness reports in one hour."

And with that, the meeting was over. Jantine stood as the crew filed out, running a hand over her jumpsuit in search of crumbs. There were none, but generations of Betas before her had done the same thing after a meal, whether or not they were in the field. It was the little things that got you killed. Even though they would likely be dead soon anyway, there was no reason to abandon discipline.

Carlton and Harren were hanging back from the others, and it took her a moment to process that they were waiting for her to exit the tent. This space needed to be collapsed as well, and since the team had already eaten there was no need to leave it standing.

Jantine picked up several crates to carry outside. Everybody helped on this team—there were no ranks or egos to interfere. Jantine was in command, Malik backed her up, and everybody else did their jobs. Jarl would likely assume command if both of them were incapacitated, but given how few combat operatives they had it wouldn't be for very long.

Out in the too-white light of the cargo unit, Jantine watched the camp collapse around her. As each gray-green shelter came down, the mission got more real. They were going to invade an inhabited world, establish both an initial base and a hidden colony, and then defend them to the death with only the barest hope of support from the local population.

No problem. Yet.

Jantine had dealt with her own gear right after she'd made the call, so she had time now to circulate and talk to her people one-on-one. For her first conversation, she selected Doria and the Omegas.

The trio was securing the other team members' crates as they were assembled, in preparation for a hard landing. There was no guarantee Malik could get them down in the same relative orientation they had now, and to power the external buffers he'd need to kill the internal gravity.

Watching the Omegas work filled Jantine with something akin to the wonder the civvies felt when Crassus and Artemus ran sims. There was no wasted movement in their activity—just a quiet grace she wished she could emulate.

Jantine was a hair slower than most other Betas, a bit more awkward and unsure of her body. But her mind worked much faster than she could explain to the others. She could see each Omega's actions for the poetry it was, knew exactly how much force they were using, and how much they were holding back.

Doria knew. Doria knew everything, though she rarely let on. Her empathic mods let her speak for the Omegas, but they also gave her unparalleled insight into the mental health of all the team members.

Doria didn't look up from her handheld when she spoke, continuing to catalog the mission's supplies. The Omegas had seen Jantine approach, and likely had relayed that information to the Gamma through their link.

"They really like you. They want me to make sure you understand that. They're sorry you're so sad."

Sad? I'm not...

"You're not like the other Betas, and they know it. You're special, but alone."

Jantine stood silent, unsure of exactly how, or to whom, she should reply. Doria tapped out something on the handheld and then turned to look at Jantine. As if sensing the nature of her conversation, the Omegas turned away to wait for the next crate. Jantine knew they could hear every sound in the container if they wished, but also that they understood the other mods needed privacy now and then.

"It's okay, the damper is running. We're as alone as you need us to be."

Doria waved a hand toward a pair of chairs that had yet to be stowed, and smiled. Jantine returned the expression, and took one of the offered seats.

"Is this an official session, then?"

"If you'd like. The chairs are here for everyone, and I expect you won't be the last visitor we have over the next hour. What we're doing isn't...small."

Jantine nodded, as much at Doria's phrasing as the words themselves.

"No—no, it's not. You were communicating with the Omegas during the meeting. Is there something they want?"

"Katra asked more or less the same question they had, and you answered it well enough. They wanted to be sure the team understood the full meaning of the message. But they were more concerned about you than anything else. Like they said, you seemed sad."

There's that word again.

"I'm fine, really. This is a big thing. An impossible thing, if you think about it. Everything has to go exactly right for this to end well, and so little of it is in our control."

"And the Omegas know that. We all do, even JonB. But we volunteered for a one-way trip knowing we might not even make it that far. The Alphas could have picked anyone for command. They chose you, and that's enough for us."

Jantine exhaled, pushing herself back a bit into the chair and wishing it were a warm pile of blankets she could hide in until the mission was over. It wasn't sadness the Omegas felt in her, but doubt. She could admit to herself, if not to Doria, how overmatched she felt for what was to come. Why she'd delayed making the call for so long, when she knew she had to do it from the moment the cargo slug launched.

The Omegas are perceptive, and they talk to Doria. But can the others figure it out?

Jantine was older than Doria by a couple of years, but she'd spent those years absorbing tactics and history, while Doria had spent almost all of her time since leaving the crèche listening to people's problems. It made the Gamma seem so much older and competent by comparison, even though Doria was among the physically weakest mods on the team.

"Thanks. And let them know I appreciate their concern, will you? I know that I wasn't all that approachable in the command tent."

"I will." Doria smiled and gestured toward the Omegas. "And don't worry about the Builders. They're the most well-adjusted among us. They don't worry about the same things the rest of us do in the Colonies. To hear them tell it, they've been preparing for a mission like this for a very long time, almost since the exile."

Jantine took pause at this, trying to remember exactly when the Omega line stabilized. It was one of the last mods to really distinguish itself from the baseline, the first expressions arriving a good fifty years after the Gammas bred true. The Omega community adapted well to life in the Colonies, and were full partners in the Accords. Jantine couldn't imagine a society without Omega architects and builders, where artists made music and drew pictures with senses designed for one planet only.

If any of us could plan on that scale, it would be the Alphas. But the Omegas might be capable of it as well. They build great things. Would a shaping a society be any different than planning a city? If only we—I— knew them better.

Jantine started to stand, but Doria's hand came over to rest on hers, and despite the seeming kindness of the gesture Jantine tensed up.

"It's important to them that you understand. It's all right if things go wrong. They are here to help you, and are ready to do whatever you need them to do. All you have to do is ask."

Something in Doria's eyes made Jantine wish for the blankets again, along with a big bowl of something warm that didn't come out of a tube. There was a meaning in the words that was pure Omega, layered and nuanced and beyond the understanding of most mods. Doria herself might not really understand the message she was delivering, but Jantine suspected she did, and that the Gamma was frightened by it.

The peaceful, gentle Omegas were ready to fight and die at her command.

Doria's hand withdrew, and Jantine watched the other mod's smile settle back in place.

"I understand." Jantine wanted to say more, but those two words were all that seemed appropriate. She'd answered their question, now she had to make sure the Omegas never needed to fulfill that promise of sacrifice. Instead she nodded to Doria, and walked away from the staging area.

She didn't need to check her handheld to know how much time there was to insertion, but she'd need to talk to every member of the team like this before Malik pushed the button.

And if everyone uses their time to tell me how much faith they have in me, I sure hope we live long enough for me to thank them properly down on the surface.

ANDREISON

PUNCHING commands into the makeshift workstation she'd set up in the cramped confines of the aft head, Marya's frustration with the battlegroup's repeated delays in getting her back to *City of Lights* was almost as great as with whomever had sent the gennie signal that landed her in this mess in the first place.

This grand tour of the Fleet's least-maintained ships isn't making things any easier. Even if they're going to bury this incident—or me, for that matter—there should at least be some chatter on the network.

What's taking them so long to make up their minds? It's not like I'm going anywhere.

She'd needed a data core with more power than the one in her head to continue her analysis, and the triple redundancies built in to shuttles this old meant any control panel wired in to the shuttle's environmental control systems gave her, and more importantly, her implants, almost unlimited access to the vessel's systems.

Which was why, at first, setting up shop here seemed like the best possible location. But retasking the panel also shut down the environmental systems in her compartment, and every missed maintenance cycle and improperly disposed-of waste product was readily apparent to her heightened senses. And since her eyes and headware could communicate directly with the main data core through the panel, she'd elected to work in darkness rather than identify the source of the smells.

Besides, watching my decryption algorithms chew on the gennie transmission won't make the work go any faster, and time is apparently no longer of the essence.

In the nine hours since she'd discovered the transmission, Marya had run this exact analysis a dozen times as she bounced between shuttles, missile tenders, and courier ships, and the only thing that ever changed was the quality of the equipment she had to use.

The two hours in her pod waiting for retrieval were by far the most productive, and while she was there Marya had run a few other tests to determine the transmission's actual source. But despite the considerable processing power of the pod's systems, Marya still couldn't explain how it even existed, or why it had registered as a hyperspace event.

That's the thing that bothers me most about this whole deal. Clearly this JTN-B34256-O wanted her message to be heard, so why did she try so hard to hide it? And why make up a vessel registry at the same time? None of this makes any damn sense.

In the pod, Marya had searched for signals with similar profiles to the gennie message, but just didn't have access to enough data. The main core on *City of Lights* would have what she needed, but with every passing hour the signal itself degraded as it passed through the solar system, and her original recording was confiscated along with the pod by the retrieval team.

Good thing I've got multiple backups, and they'll have to kill me to get the one inside my head. But if I'm right, the entire Home Fleet needs to be on alert, and these silly transit games need to fucking stop.

The next few hours after retrieval were spent shuffling from one vessel to another, all of which had bullshit reasons not to take her directly back home. In theory, this was the last one, but she didn't put it past her fellow officers to take her once more around the solar system.

Just after stepping onto CL-3011 for what was hopefully her last shuttle ride of the day, Marya had given the hard-suited escorts she'd picked up three transfers back some alone time in the airlock, and used the few minutes of freedom it gained her to reprogram the shuttle's navigation system to run her decryption software.

Marya's original plan was to access the data from the flight deck, but one look at the hatchet-faced pilot running through her preflights put an end to that one before it even began. Her next best choice was a small conference area just back from the flight deck, but for some reason all the comms gear had been ripped out of the workstation, ultimately forcing Marya to hack her way in from her current location to continue her analysis.

Not the most glamorous workstation I've ever used, but it's what I've got. At least I don't have to touch anything in here, and my headware's doing most of the work.

Just when she thought she was getting somewhere, an insistent knock at the hatch brought home the reality of her situation.

"Sub-lieutenant, are you about finished in there? We're on final approach to *City of Lights*."

Well then. Looks like playtime's over. Thought I'd have a few more minutes before they found me.

Counting herself, there were four people on the shuttle, which was two more than it needed for a milk run between capital ships in the safest sector of human-controlled space. It was a man's voice, which meant it was one of the two otherwise interchangeable troopers assigned to her after she'd spent a little too much time in the *Volga*'s computer core. The data worm she'd planted to search for other gennie transmissions was virtually undetectable, but the hash she'd made of their encryption protocols had earned her a couple armored, and heavily armed, new friends.

"Cool your jets, trooper. Just freshening up, be done in a moment."

Marya busied herself with re-assembling the terminal as quietly as she could in the near-darkness of the head, then washed her face in the sanitary sink as the environmental systems came back online. Her headware accepted the hand-off from the navigation core, which also told her that they were on final approach to *City of Lights*.

The overhead panel flickered to life as she finished, revealing a few new lines in her already worn face. Marya didn't think of herself as particularly attractive, but her third generation spacer genes gave her face just enough exotic features that the Mitchell Williamses of the worlds usually marked her as a potential conquest before they even bothered to learn her name.

Funny how I never have that problem with the women in my life, but I guess I'm just lucky that way. When I met Mira, she cared more about my life in space than how I looked, and when I met Deb…

Deb fell for me long before I realized how truly special she was, and long after my eyes were gone. So any beauty I now behold is all because of her.

Thinking about her wives made Marya stand up a little straighter, and she caught herself smoothing down her jumpsuit at the thought of seeing them and the girls again. But the moment came to an abrupt halt when the trooper's gentle knocking escalated to pounding on the hatch.

"Ma'am, I'm going to have to ask you to leave the compartment. It's time to go."

Biting back what she really wanted to say, Marya prepped herself for yet another unwanted encounter with the Fleet's least-elite.

"Give a girl a minute, will ya? It's not just zip up and go in here, you know!"

Marya let him puzzle on that for a few more seconds, then triggered the hatch and stepped through into the dimly lit corridor.

She nearly caught a gauntlet in the face, but slid past the trooper's aborted knock as he fell forward into the head. Although he had remembered to keep his faceplate blanked in true fascist fashion, he'd neglected to set his boots or switch on either chem lights or shoulder beacons to maintain a combat advantage.

Pathetic. You wouldn't last five minutes in one of Mira's squads, which is probably why you drew the short straw and were assigned to me.

"Look, if you had to go that bad, why didn't you just go in the suit?"

She wasn't sure which whether this one's name was Harris or Hardoway, but at the same time she really didn't care. This whole situation was a clusterfuck, and she didn't have time for new friends.

Besides, at this point, I really don't give a shit. Neither one of these morons knows his ass from a hole in the ground, and since only one of them came to claim me whatever he wants can't be that important.

To his credit, the trooper recovered quickly and spun around to face her. But he still hadn't engaged his magnetic boots, which gave Marya one more opportunity to humiliate him. Since he was in an unbalanced stance half in, half out of the hatch, she grabbed his helmet and planted a kiss in the middle of his faceplate. As expected, he took an involuntary half-step back, coming up hard against the sanitary sink and bending backward until his helmet smashed into the metal mirror above it.

Furious, he moved to draw the induction pistol fastened to his chest plate before Marya put her left hand on top of the holstered weapon.

"Relax, Sunshine. Nothing in there is worth losing any sleep over.'

The trooper shoved his left gauntlet in front of him to fend her off while his right continued toward his weapon, but from his position he had no real leverage. His head was bobbing, though, and Marya had the distinct impression he was calling his partner for assistance. So instead of reminding him why drawing an induction pistol in an enclosed space was a bad idea, Marya stepped to the side and triggered the hatch.

It slammed closed just ahead of his outstretched hands, and for good measure Marya scrambled the lock code in time to the sweet sounds of muffled screams and trooper Whatsisname's furious pounding on the other side of the hatch.

Right. That was stupid, on both our parts.

But it sure was fun.

Marya wasn't sure whether it was her meat brain or its silicon enhancements that brought the shuttle's layout to mind, but after so many years of coexistence inside her skull she often found it hard to tell them apart. Either way, she used the knowledge to plot the quickest path to the starboard airlock and the approaching crossover to *City of Lights*.

It was the same portal she'd use to board the shuttle, and still mostly intact after the troopers had forced their way out of the airlock. She judged it still usable, but took some of the forty seconds she'd estimated until her escorts arrived to run a quick diagnostic.

In theory the outer doors wouldn't open unless *City of Lights* had a hard seal, but given what she'd gleaned about CL-3011's maintenance schedule over the last few months, Marya didn't want to risk it. As she worked, she noted that it had been less than twenty minutes since she'd come aboard, making this leg of her voyage home by far the most eventful.

Judging the airlock safe and functional, she stepped inside and closed the doors behind her just as her trooper escort arrived. Seconds later, the compartment shuddered and her stomach lurched as the shuttle's gravity switched over to the much more powerful field generated by the capital ship on the other side of the outboard hatch.

Every passing second brought a new sound and vibration, until finally the green lamp was lit, verifying a strong seal. Marya reached back and triggered the airlock doors leading into her ship, smiling slightly at the continued pounding on the ones behind her.

Cool air rushed past Marya into the airlock, bringing the smells of the Home Fleet's newest warship along for the ride and marking the end of her long journey back home.

Every ship had its own particular blend of recycled odors, but *City of Lights* was *her* ship, her first real posting in years. Marya had lived in space for most of her life and there still wasn't anything like coming aboard a Redstone dreadnaught. Something about it almost made her forget about why there was a pair of armed and armored goons rushing through the now open airlock behind her on the shuttle, and a second set of guards on the other side of the transit tube.

A tantalizing mix of rice, sweat, and conduit lubricant like no other. Catch me, I might swoon.

Home, sweet-stinking home. I think. It was a few hours ago, now I'm not so sure. Who knows what the universe has in store for me next.

Marya didn't have long to wait, as one of the troopers in front of her stepped into the airlock, turned slightly, then waved her forward.

"Sub-Lieutenant. If you'll come with us, please."

The trooper's tone wasn't just polite, it was pre-arrest, formalities-must-be-observed-capital-letters Polite. Marya had heard it far too often from station security growing up, and enough times since leaving the Academy to know that something interesting was about to happen.

Marya tried to scan their chest plates to get an idea of who she was dealing with, but apparently whoever was making them dance had some idea of her capabilities. After weeks of near-constant contact, her eyes—and the tech backing them up inside her reinforced skull—weren't connecting to the *City of Lights* data core.

And since I'm the officer in charge of granting or revoking that access to 95% of the crew, the kinds of somethings waiting for me on the other side of the airlock are rapidly narrowing to a set of outcomes I'm sure I won't like.

"Of course. Thanks for the ride, boys. It's been a real slice of life." Marya skipped forward through the airlock and grabbed the nearest catch ring, then turned to give her guards on the transfer shuttle a one-fingered salute. The new troopers from *City of Lights* were careful not to point their weapons directly at her, but the way they held them close was enough to command her attention.

"This way, ma'am." Trooper Starboard took one hand off his weapon and waved her down the corridor, subtly tightening his grip on the stock and keeping his finger near the firing studs. Marya's eyes recorded every move he made, and the tactical computer inside her head added helpful green lines describing his mass, a balance profile, approximate reaction times, and an estimate of how long his suit had gone without proper maintenance based on its outward appearance.

Marya felt one of her special headaches coming on as the data jumped back and forth between her meat and silicon brains. She closed her left eye briefly against the onslaught, mainly to avoid collecting a similar threat analysis on Trooper Portside.

The software that ran her prostheses was a mix of the stock code that would have her running into walls if someone sneezed, and a modified sensor suite she and Deb had put together as their first real collaboration. It was much better at dealing with the constant barrage of information coming at her through her eyes, but didn't do much of anything about her enhanced brain's ability to process every sound, smell, and errant breeze of which most humans were blissfully unaware.

It's an okay trade off, in the long run. I don't even miss sunrises anymore.

Much.

Despite their enforced anonymity, one thing Marya did know as soon as she stepped through the airlock was the direction the trooper indicated was nowhere near her quarters, and she had no intention of sitting through yet another session of questioning without a fresh shirt. So instead of bargaining with them for a few minutes to change, Marya started walking in the opposite direction, smiling at the sounds of their pursuit echoing past her down the corridor.

"Ma'am. Ma'am!"

Marya kept walking, turning her head just enough to swivel her left eye in the trooper's direction, while keeping her right fixed firmly ahead. It had been a hard trick to master after the operation, but over the years she'd done it enough times that it was almost as natural as blinking had been before the accident.

Almost.

"Try and keep up, fellas. My quarters are this way."

The trooper stopped in the middle of the corridor, and Marya knew she'd scored a couple points with her googly eye trick. But the second trooper kept right on coming, pausing for only a second to smack his partner's helmet as he passed.

"Ma'am. I'm going to have to ask you to come with us."

Trooper Two's—*Starboard, I think*—voice had a bit of an edge to it

Mayra didn't care for. Although whoever had given hem their orders may have outranked her, these two certainly did not, at least until such time as they formally arrested her.

And I'd love to see you two assholes try.

Marya stepped up her pace a little, turning down the corridor leading to her quarters just ahead of the trooper's outstretched gauntlet. The air shifted flavor slightly—residential scrubbers did a much better job of cleaning the air than those in the main access corridors. It was still the same atmo, just a bit less machine shop and socks, another distinction that was lost on most of her crew mates.

As the officer in charge of Comms division, Marya's quarters were located closer to the skin of the ship—and its airlocks—than those of the command crew, who typically had their quarters within a hundred meters of the command center proper. Marya and her shift leaders needed fast access to the pods and the main observation lounges, as well as the planning spaces they shared with the fire control teams.

When she passed compartment AC215, she caught a glimpse of Mitchell Williams inside, wildly gesticulating and sporting a lopsided smirk she meant to slap completely off his face before she left *City of Lights* for good.

She must have lingered on his hate-twisted features a bit too long, and Mitchell's smile widened as he made eye contact not only with Marya, but also the armored guards just behind her.

Well, shit.

The true significance of AC215 was that it marked the home stretch to her rack, now only fifty meters away and on the outside curve. She had clear sight lines down both ends of the corridor, and she estimated that she had enough time to key in her personal code before the troopers caught up with her.

Come on, come on...

The hatch hissed open, and Marya was inside as soon as there was enough space for her muscular frame. Sadly, her troopers were literally right on her heels, and the hatch closed behind them.

Marya's normal state of hyper-sensory hyper-vigilance kicked into overdrive now that she had no clear exit from the compartment, and she had to stop herself from charging Trooper Portside as he began poking at objects on her suite's workstation.

Give me five minutes alone with that thing and I'll be running this ship. Give this yahoo five years and he might figure out how to turn it on.

"Sub-lieutenant, what is the purpose of this unscheduled visit to what I assume are your quarters. Commander Phillips is waiting for us."

Ethan? What's he got to do with this?

"Maybe the air in your suit is scented with lilacs, but I've been up and running for the last twenty hours and need a change of clothing."

Marya moved to her bunk and activated its privacy screen, a shimmering, decidedly aftermarket curtain of alternating light that completely obscured her from the other occupants of the compartment. It wasn't a physical barrier—not even Deb had worked up a forcefield that small yet—but it did hide her for a few seconds from both the troopers and any remote voyeurs piggybacking their feeds.

"Ma'am, Commander Phillips's orders were quite clear. You're to come with us to Interview 7, at once."

Behind the screen, Marya looked around at her available clothing options. In her haste, she'd forgotten that her dress blues were draped across her workstation chair on the other side of the compartment. Fresh back from ship's laundry, she'd hadn't stowed them before her shift, and to get them she'd have to cross into the trooper's reach and likely endure yet another pat down.

The fate she'd narrowly escaped by booting Williams out of the pod had come back to her five-fold as she transferred between vessels, each search more humiliating than the last.

Instead, she pulled a mostly clean mess tunic from her hutch, wincing at the noise her ribbon board and its accompanying medal made as it hit the side of the rack. She used the next few seconds to transfer the portable data recorder from her jumpsuit to her boot, making it that much harder to find in case her escorts decided on another search. The real data was secure in her headware, but a lot harder to share in front of a board of inquiry, which is where Marya assumed this was heading.

She looked longingly at her spare flight suit, worn-thin in all the right places and far too complex to slip into with two armed troopers just a few meters away. She'd thought to do a full wardrobe refresh, but had lingered too long on Mitchell Williams' smug face and whatever story he'd been concocting in her absence to keep the troopers on the other side of the hatch.

No use crying about it now, I guess. If we're going to do this, let's do it.

"Ma'am, I really must insist..." Starboard's voice through his speakers trailed off, and she had the distinct impression it was because someone else was talking to him.

Marya pulled on the tunic, fastening the side belts into some approximation of propriety. Almost as an afterthought, she reached beneath her pillow and retrieved the letter Deb had given her when she shipped out, a ridiculously sentimental gesture which made Marya love her all the more. She read and reread it every night before sleeping, and right now she needed the reassurance of her wife's presence, even if only secondhand.

Folding the letter into one of the tunic's pockets, Marya disengaged the privacy field. The trooper just on the other side was already stepping across where the luminous barrier had been, and nearly caught an elbow to the helmet for his impatience. Even in an officer's suite, there wasn't a lot of room between the bunk and the walls, and suit of powered armor took up almost all of it.

"All right, cowboy, all right. I'm as pretty as I'm going to get. Lead the way." Marya gestured towards the out hatch, watching her reflection in the trooper's mirrored faceplate. When he didn't move out of her way, she snapped her fingers in front of his helmet.

"Hey. Are we doing this, or what?"

The nameless trooper tried to bat away her hand, but Marya dropped her arm just in time for his slap to carry him out of position and shift his center of balance. Marya used the moment to slip past him on his right, bumping him as she did and using his imbalance to nudge him face-first into the wall. It wasn't enough to do any real damage to anything other than his pride, but it did open up enough room for her to reach the hatch. Portside didn't seem nearly as committed to hassling her, and made no move to stop her as she opened the hatch.

Marya paused before exiting her quarters, mulling over her options. Despite being a relative newcomer, she knew *City of Lights* intimately, and there were a half-dozen routes to Interview 7 from her location. Half of them involved moving back the way they'd come, which no doubt was how Starboard planned to take her. But their limited interaction so far told Marya that what that particular trooper wanted was the least important thing in her universe right now, and the first chance she had to get rid of him was one she'd be happy to take.

But instead of a well-timed escape, an armored palm hit the center of her back hard enough trip her over the hatch's frame into the corridor. She stumbled to a catch ring as she heard him say, "Get a move on, convict. No more games."

Ah, so that's how it's going to be.

All right, asshole, I'll play. But first we'll have to set some ground rules.

Marya tightened her grip on the catch ring, scanning one side of the corridor with each eye to get a sense of her available space. Trooper Starboard took a step toward her and Marya straightened up and squared herself against him, arms loose and at the ready. Her eyes were already marking spots for her first blows, and her legs tensed for her initial charge.

The worst part about fighting someone in armor was the complete lack of visual cues. Academy instructors had been remarkably unhelpful on this topic, and most of what they had to share involved wearing a suit yourself and carrying a big fuck-off gun.

Marya had discarded all of her official training years ago, relying instead on the hard-earned street smarts of the ancient gunny in the cell next to hers. The scrappy sergeant had more than earned his place in the stockade, but he'd been happy to share what he'd learned from a long career of bad behavior.

The only problem was, every one of his techniques started with letting your opponent take the first shot.

And even Smitty would run from this one. Too many variables, not enough advantages.

Until Starboard made his move, Marya would be on the defensive, with nothing to rely on but her gut. It looked like he was planning to slap her around a bit more instead of shooting her, but she had no way of knowing for sure, and going for his pistol opened her up to all sorts of disciplinary measures she didn't even want to think about right now.

Don't do it. Don't do it...

Marya wasn't sure if the words were meant for herself or her erstwhile opponent, but a second later Portside ended the fight before it began by putting a hand on his Starboard's shoulder and pushing him to the side.

Marya took a step to her right just in case, turning her back to the empty corridor they'd come down only minutes before. Portside shifted to block her view of Starboard's chest, obscuring the induction pistols on both men's breastplates and triggering another round of combat calculations Marya wished she could turn off, or at least dial back. But her blood was already pumping in anticipation of what could be either the last fight of her career or her life, until Portside turned around and unblanked his faceplate.

"Stand down, Sub-lieutenant. Let's not keep Commander Phillips waiting any longer than we have to."

Marya felt a trickle of sweat gather over her left ear, and willed herself out of both fight and flight states. After the day she'd had she was absolutely ready for a good brawl, but now she'd be the aggressor, and that never looked good on securecams. She shook out her hands, stood up a little straighter, and nodded in response.

"Of course. Lead the way, Trooper...?" Not being able to access the core for his name was almost as infuriating as being stuck in corridor with two armed enemies and no way to summon backup, but neither problem had an immediate solution.

"Hartley, Ma'am. And we really should be going."

Seriously? Another H name? BuPers must be ordering them from some goon catalog.

Marya shot a glance over Hartley's shoulder at Starboard, but still couldn't get a read on his intentions. The last thing she wanted to do was turn her back on the man right now, But Hartley had given them both an out, and she had every intention of taking it.

Okay, Hartley. You bought yourself and your partner some politeness points. Hopefully they'll be enough to keep us going until you can hand me off to whomever is holding your strings.

Turning around, Marya settled on the longest possible route to Interview 7. It annoyed her to no end to leave her quarters unsecured, but if she was right, the recorder in her boot and Deb's letter were the only things that mattered right now.

Okay, let's go give another fucking deposition. Because I'm sure that's going to be a barrel of laughs for everyone.

KOŁODZIEJSKI

AS THE SECONDS ticked down to proper alignment of the communications array, Horace smiled, though no-one was in his quarters to see it. He was still dressed for tea, though Caroline had taken the remains of their meal with her when she left. The meds he'd taken afterward softened the edges of his pain, but in truth her company did more to settle his nerves than anything else he'd tried in the last few months.

Although he'd hand-picked her for his command, she'd already earned her place aboard *Indomitable* through hard work, not favoritism, and her willingness to suspend their relationship while serving together meant the worlds to him.

She's still interested, I can tell. But I can't trust my body right now, and there's no telling if this disease will spread. Once this is over, once I have a cure, we can finally formalize our arrangement.

The transfer would be hard on both of them, but when the Loyalist plan came to fruition, Echo Base and Project Chimera would be a much more important part of the System Defense Force.

Located under Luna's northern magnetic pole, the base was the most heavily classified research facility in the home system, and the only place where he could conduct his experiments into ending the gennie menace once and for all.

And it should be coming into range right about...

Unlike the sub-lieutenant he'd replaced, Carl Julian was an able officer who could follow instructions. When his comm buzzed, Kołodziejski answered without hesitation.

"Yes, Mr. Julian?"

"I have Echo Base for you, sir."

Good lad.

"Thank you, lieutenant. On our current course, how long can you maintain secure transmission?"

Kołodziejski had already calculated the window to the second, but given the problems they'd had already today, he welcomed the additional confirmation. Plus, it was another teaching moment for Julian and the rest of third shift, who were still on duty to make up for their earlier lapse.

"I can maintain a secure channel for a bit over twenty-nine minutes, sir. Longer if we slow our acceleration to half."

Close enough, I guess. And unless there's been a breakthrough of some kind, longer than I'll need.

Kołodziejski put the diagnostic cuff on his wrist and synced it to the desk's systems. There was only one person in the universe who could make sense of the readings it was collecting, and that individual was about to receive them through a network of perfectly aligned—and perfectly secure—FTL communications pods.

"Maintain course and speed, lieutenant. I'll need full use of the main array for the next ten minutes. I will signal you when I'm done."

"Understood, sir. Transferring control to you...now."

Kołodziejski slotted his command key into his desk, then entered his override code. All of *Indomitable*'s systems were now slaved to his workstation, instead of just the titular control he held as captain.

He would have preferred to do this during third shift, when most of the ship was asleep. But the unexpected course change put them too far from the pods during the usual window, and only now could he securely transmit the bioreadings that could end his career.

The next code he entered shut down Echo Base's non-essential systems, and gave him complete control of the rest. Although his standing orders kept the base on communications blackout, there was always someone who found a way to circumvent security protocols.

Sorry kids, you'll need to wait a few minutes to get all the latest gossip from Earth.

Kołodziejski had spent the hours before his tea with Caroline alternately formulating response plans for a gennie incursion or trying to keep down enough food for his body to function. Sleep was almost out of the question, though he did try. Ultimately, the fear of missing this communications window was enough to keep him awake, despite the toll it was taking on his body.

Okay. Let's get this over with.

Within a minute, the face of Doctor Thomas Watson appeared over Kołodziejski's desk. He was wearing his ridiculously oversized lab coat again, and over his shoulder Horace could see the pictures of Earth the doctor insisted on hanging in his office. From the angle of his face, he was leaning back in his chair, another needless extravagance on the moon.

"Hello, Captain. How are we feeling today?"

The same thing every time. As if you didn't know already from my scans.

"I feel like shit, Watson. These new meds aren't working, unless your intent was to liquefy my guts and set my nerves on fire."

Watson's eyes narrowed in the holo, but he kept smiling. Looking at him now—and feeling the way he did—Kołodziejski wanted to punch him in his too-white teeth. Instead, he straightened up in his chair, adjusting the lines of his uniform as he did.

Just because you've gone soft, doesn't mean I have to be.

Watson had an Earther's wide face, exacerbated by years of living on the moon. He also had the dark skin and quasi-African ancestry common to the North American Reclamation. Not that that was unique to Earth—far from it. Most Marsborn carried at least a few of the same genetic markers, but Watson in particular came from an Old Earth family who fancied themselves pure, and had resettled that continent once it was declared safe.

Like the distinction means anything. Plus, most Earthers are genetic freaks, and never leave the gravity well.

"These side effects are to be expected, Captain. We're fighting not only the Transgenic virus, but also your own immune system. And from the look of these latest readings, we may be losing both battles."

Tell me something I don't know, Earther.

"How long, Watson? How long until you make me a cure? I'm no doctor, but I can still count, and my numbers have been steadily climbing since we last spoke."

Watson's smile went from pleasantly wide to a tight-lipped frown.

"You know I can't answer that, Captain. I'm nearly out of samples taken from your gennie test subjects, and this base is set up for weapons development, not the kind of biometric analysis I need to run. I can work up more treatments to slow the virus' progression through your system, but I can't reverse the effects. And yours is one of the few Marsborn families that still have Simak Syndrome, which complicates matters. If you'd just let..."

Kołodziejski's nostrils flared, along with his temper. He leaned forward to intimidate Watson, then remembered the actual distance between them prohibited a physical display from having any lasting effect.

Smug little bastard. Should have left you in the gutter where I found you.

"Don't say it, Doctor. You know that's not an option for me, no matter how many times you suggest it. I'm not going to let you put any more of that gennie filth in my body. And as to the facilities on Echo Base, the virus *is* a weapon. One that's been used on us!"

Watson's expression hardened further, and for the first time since they'd met the Earther actually showed some backbone.

"Frankly, Captain, I'm not sure you have a choice. It's not the T-virus that's killing you, it's your ridiculous adherence to genetic purity. Sure, a transgenic expression would land you at a desk instead of commanding dreadnaughts, but you'd still be alive. Isn't that better than the alternative?"

Would you be this cocky if you weren't billions of kilometers away? I'm not at all sure this newfound bravery suits you.

"No, it's not, and you know that. I'm—we're fighting a war out here, Doctor, and this disease is the enemy. Your job, your one reason for being, should be to cure it. Instead, you want to make me worse, and in the process take away all the things that make me who I am. Well I won't have it, Watson. Not one bit of it!"

Kołodziejski was shouting now, and the effort made his head pound. A sudden spasm of pain made his left eye twitch, and he was sure that Watson was enjoying the show.

"Look, Captain—Horace, you have to meet me halfway. I'm just a doctor, not a miracle worker. And you're not giving me a lot to work with. You won't tell me where you were exposed to the virus, and the only link I have to its origin were the test subjects, one of whom is dead and one of whom you're chasing throughout the system, along with most of the research we conducted on her.

"The Transgenic virus isn't some chemical imbalance I can fix with a few pills. Right now, every cell of your body is trying to adapt itself to function in an unknown biosphere, and your intestinal flora are mutating to supply those cells with what they need to survive. A modified transgenic therapy is the only realistic treatment option. Controlled exposure will not only cure your Simak Syndrome, but it will also move you to the human baseline, thereby stopping..."

Kołodziejski slammed his palm down on the desk, cutting off Watson's explanation.

"Earth baseline, Doctor, and as you are so fond of pointing out, I am not from Earth. Simak Syndrome is not a disability, it's who I am. Marsborn, and proud of it."

Watson's smile was gone now, and the Earther leaned forward in his chair before speaking.

"No, Captain, it's who you were. The virus is correcting the underlying defects in your genetic code, which tells me among other things that you did not find the test subjects on Mars. Or while breathing a Martian atmosphere, for that matter."

Horace clenched his jaw tight, not sure exactly which insult to hurl at the smug image in front of him.

You dare! I own you, gutter rat. Everything you have is because I thought you were useful to the cause, and you dare to insult me like this!

"My family is the reason there is a human race at all. After the war, after humans on Earth destroyed themselves, it was Martians who provided resources, Martians who developed the technology to feed a dying Earth. You owe your life, your freedom, to me and mine, and I'll thank you to remember that!"

Watson sat up straight, and the holorecorder on his end dutifully zoomed in on his face. Being forced to view a close-up image of his subordinate's face only made Kołodziejski angrier, as did his doctor's next words.

"No human is truly free, Captain, but I'm sorry if I offend. I'm only trying to get across the seriousness of your condition. You have an unknown, aggressive strain of the Transgenic virus, and our current efforts to stop it are killing you.

"Those are the cold, hard facts, and every minute we debate them is another minute closer to your death. I can't stop you from killing yourself with ignorance, although I will keep trying. If you want to live—on any planet—you'll accept the therapy I'm offering. If not, I recommend you move to artificial blood until you can get back here for another round of trials, and make whatever arrangements you need to for your funeral."

Kołodziejski fell back in his chair, overcome with emotion. His skin itched, his hands shook, and if he had a pistol at hand he'd have fired it at Watson's holographic head by now.

"You and I have very different definitions of what it means to be human, Watson. And I'm not exactly sitting on my hands out here. I will find Captain Martin—and our missing gennie-and you will find me a cure. These are the facts with which you should concern yourself, and no others. Am I clear?"

You're fucking dead, Watson. As soon as I get a cure, you're fucking dead. I'll finish what that bitch started, and...

And...

Kołodziejski couldn't help but smile, as he put all the pieces together. Some part of his brain must have made the connection hours ago, but seeing it all in place for the first time made him truly happy for the first time in weeks.

"Do your damn job, Doctor Watson, or I'll find somebody else who can. And my first call after I dump you on that backwater planet you call home will be to that firebrand lieutenant you've been hiding from for the last few years."

Watson's jaw dropped, as the utter hopelessness of his situation sunk in. Kołodziejski was the one who truly held all the power in their relationship, and no amount of self-righteous scientific posturing would change that.

"I'm s-s-sorry, Captain. I'll...I'll g-g-get back to work right away. B-b-but I do need more samples."

Horace's lips pulled back in a predator's smile.

"You'll have them, never fear. Transmit the specs for the blood replacement, and signal me when you're done. You have...eight minutes left to comply. I don't think I need to tell you again what happens in nine."

Kołodziejski terminated the call, still smiling. He'd found the leverage he needed to properly motivate Thomas Watson to find a cure, and the Earther would either deliver or die trying.

I'll need to find some way to thank Markus for giving it to me. And myself, for that matter, for ordering him to sequester Sub-Lieutenant Andreison when I did.

ANDREISON

MARYA HATED interview rooms almost as much as she'd hated her prison cell back on Earth. The two were inseparable in her experience, and she didn't think telling her story yet another time would make it sound any better, even to a supposed friend.

It's the chairs, really. I think they make them extra uncomfortable just for the occasion.

Commander Ethan Phillips was the one asking the questions on the other side of the table, looking sharp in his dress blues as always. He hadn't graduated at the top of their class, but he'd certainly learned how to navigate the command ladder in the intervening years. Not only did he outrank her, but he had more ship ribbons than Marya was likely to earn during what was left of her career.

Hell, the "clerk" in the corner has more than I do. And a clean tunic to boot.

The woman in question was wearing a standard duty uniform with a communications insignia, but Marya had made a point of memorizing every face in her division when she took over, and this was a new one. Which meant despite her apparent familiarity with a holorecorder and pad, she wasn't normal crew.

And given how crisp and clean her uniform is, she's possibly not Fleet at all.

Starboard and Portside—*no, Hartley*—were standing behind her with their backs against the bulkhead. They definitely knew what they were doing, and despite Hartley's earlier kindness neither man made any attempt to hide what they thought of Marya.

This can all go so very wrong.

"Is there any possibility this is some kind of hoax?"

Phillips' question called Marya back to the immediate problem. They were over an hour into the interview, and so far they'd made no progress whatsoever. Ethan either didn't understand, or didn't care that the worlds were back at war, and now was apparently suggesting that the transmission hadn't even happened at all.

I've got a recorder in my boot and half a trillion credits worth of cybernetics in my head that say it did, so what's really going on here?

Mayra squinted, searching his face for some sign of amusement. If there was a joke involved in all this, she certainly didn't see any humor in either the transmission, or the hours she'd spent shuffling through airlocks on the way back to *City of Lights*.

Ethan was a good officer, just woefully unqualified to interpret the data in front of him. Always had been, even at the Academy. Marya wondered if Ethan had worn his blues just so he'd look better on the holorecord, but the thought of her only friend on *City of Lights* throwing her to the wolves to get another promotion was almost too much to bear.

Taking a deep breath to push down her fear, Marya readied her response. If all she had to defend her actions were words, she might as well pick the right ones.

"No, sir. The transmission is real; it just makes no sense. We've never seen a naked waveform make a hyperspace transition before, which implies a level of technology far beyond our own. Anything coming from one of our ships or a corridor colony would have a transponder signal, and..."

"Andreison, that's not why we're here." Phillips' interruption was punctuated by a chopping hand gesture, and Marya thought she read a hint of resignation at the corners of his eyes. "I'm not talking about the signal. I'm talking about you."

"Sir?"

"Just listen to yourself for a minute. Setting aside the source of the signal—and I have to be honest here, a signal no-one else detected, and no-one else can replicate—you broke protocol by transmitting an unknown, possibly dangerous message over an open channel. Even if—especially *if*—it's real, there could have been a data worm in the transmission. Or a signal to some kind of sleeper agent. Did you even think about the consequences before you transmitted, or is this another one of your famous 'snap judgments?'"

Marya's lips parted momentarily, then she closed her mouth to deny the suddenly attentive clerk the satisfaction of seeing her speechless. The woman had stopped tapping on her pad, and was now leaning forward, staring intently at Marya.

Who the hell are you, lady? And what's got into you, Ethan? You're the one who fought for me to be assigned to this ship. You're one of the only people who stood by me after...

Marya felt herself gripping the cold metal arms of her chair and forced herself to relax. Trying not to think about the mystery clerk, she focused instead on Ethan's hairline, where a tiny bead of sweat was forming over a rapidly pulsing blood vessel. Marya relaxed her jaw and widened her eyes, instructing her implants to take in his whole face at once.

A swarm of reticules only she could see formed around his eyes, mouth, cheeks, and ears, but Phillips met her gaze with an expression she didn't need algorithms to read. It was the same fear she saw in the mirror most mornings, the inescapable certainty that no matter what she did, today was the day that everything would come crashing down around her.

Jesus, what do they have on you? Marya's pulse quickened thinking about what they'd threatened her friend with, and the artificial chill of the interview room grew a little more intense. Phillip's eyes darted towards the nameless clerk and her guards, and for a fraction of a second Marya's implants picked up a pulsating glow in the back of his eye. He turned his head to the left, and she saw it again, along with a dim flash against the inside of his ear.

Marya closed her eyes, her mind racing.

Keep it together, Mar. It's not Ethan doing this, but it's you they're doing it to. And you have to get through this interview before you can do anything about it...

"Sir, the Magellan Accords clearly state that any unscheduled contact with the Outer Colonies must be reported immediately, and the author of that transmission clearly identified themselves as a gennie. Comms Division's mandate is to detect and warn the battle-group of imminent threats, and I was the only person with the ability to do that. Judgment is not the issue here, sir. It's whether or not we're ignoring a declaration of war!"

Phillips was slow in responding, further cementing in Marya's mind that he was speaking someone else's words.

"Sub-Lieutenant Andreison, your ill-considered—and illegal—actions have cost this battlegroup—no, wasted—an untold number of hours and credits searching for your mystery gennies, with nothing to show for it but forty-five seconds of unverified transmission about a ship no-one has ever heard of."

"That doesn't mean it's not a real threat, sir. And with respect, even if I am wrong this battlegroup can use the practice! This is the first contact of any kind we've had in the last few weeks, and what are we looking for out here if not this?"

Marya knew the words were a mistake as soon as she said them aloud. Ethan's face drained of blood, and he swallowed hard before continuing, eyes darting to the side again.

"Given your past history, sub-lieutenant, and in light of other complaints made against you by your fellow officers, you leave me no choice but to take immediate disciplinary action."

Shit. Wrong words.

"Pursuant to Fleet regulations, you are hereby relieved of duty until the captain makes a determination as to your suitability for command. Troopers, please escort Ms. Andreison to her quarters, and see that she doesn't get into any more trouble on the way there."

The pleading look in Ethan's eyes told Marya this was the best she was going to get out of the situation, though being summarily dismissed—by proxy, no less—angered her almost as much as the eager looks of the two goons moving toward her.

This won't stand a formal review, but what choice do I have at the moment?

She made a show of straightening her tunic as she stood, and turned away from Hartley's outstretched hand. She walked all the way around the table, continuing her internal record of the proceedings by focusing on Ethan's face, making sure to capture as many details about the nameless clerk over his shoulder as she could.

You're not the one pulling the strings, but I'll bet you know who is, don't you? And once I figure it out, you're all going down.

Starboard and Hartley double-timed it to catch up as she as she moved to the hatch and waited for it to cycle. Marya was sure that given the chance they'd be more than happy to follow through on Ethan's unspoken order to restrain her if necessary, and since her career was probably already in tatters, that suited her just fine.

Go ahead, boys, try it. You have no idea just how much trouble I can cause, especially now that I know the rules of the game.

ANNAHKO

1300 SHIP TIME, **SDF** *INDOMITABLE*

THE OFFICER'S mess was more crowded than usual when Caroline arrived for lunch, an unfortunate result of the extra shifts the Captain had ordered this morning. While she couldn't fault Horace for keeping third shift on as punishment, the command center wasn't the only section affected by his orders.

Now both third and second were jostling for position among the increasingly crowded tables, with first due soon after. The stewards were working double-time to keep up with their requests, and the smells of a dozen different regional Martian dishes combined into a sweet melange that drowned out *Indomitable*'s usual actinic odor.

Caroline wasn't particularly hungry, and was looking for companionship more than sustenance. As *Indomitable*'s second-in-command, she had access to a private wardroom, but today she needed the sounds of other humans to distract her from her thoughts.

Nothing about this deployment is going right, and if Daniel is correct soon all the things I love about this ship will come crashing down around me. I need to know what I'm dealing with, and I need to know it now.

As she approached, one of *Indomitable*'s junior pilots caught Caroline's eye and waved her over. The pilot had high dome features like herself, and that fresh-from-the-Academy gleam in her eyes that probably annoyed everyone around her on a regular basis. Caroline smiled at the memory of her long-ago middie cruise, and how hard it had been for Cadet Annahko to make friends amongst *Valiant*'s mostly Earther crew.

I loved that ship too, and one of the few officers who reached out to me on that trip was Aloysius Martin. Now we're hunting it—and him—through the system for reasons I neither know nor understand.

But in the end, all I really need to know is that it's important to Horace. And as always, that's good enough for me.

The young woman smacked the cadet next to her, who shot her a look of mock pain and a smile that said they were more than just friends. Caroline remembered the first time Horace had looked at her like that, lost in the lines of her face and trying to work up the courage to talk to her as their parents looked on.

I could barely stand to look at him then, still hurting at Daniel's sudden departure, angry at Mother and Da for promising me to a stranger three years younger than me with funny eyes and pale skin.

But when Horace finally found his words, they were like full sunshine on the plateau, and before a month passed I made sure he knew he was mine.

And now, now all we have left are memories...

Whoever the boy was, it was a couple of seconds before he registered what—or rather, who—his lover was pointing at. He swallowed hastily, choking a bit on his sandwich as he gathered up his meal to make room for Caroline.

Caroline's smile widened, and she nodded in acknowledgment of the respect her fellow Marsborns offered. She waved the cadet back into his seat, then signaled to the nearest steward for her meal. The rest of the table's occupants either shifted away from her and the cadets or moved to another table, giving Caroline a double space in which to sit opposite the pair.

Caroline didn't remember the cadets' names at first, her brain still reeling from the morning's events. But their crisply pressed jumpsuits still had factory creases, and like most juniors they were still wearing Academy-issued name patches under their wings.

Of course she's a Tepes. I'll ask Daniel about her later.

"Thank you, cadets. How are you today?"

Caroline's many-times removed cousin was about to speak when the boy next to her—*Currano, I'll have to remember that*—coughed out, "Fine, Ma'am. A little tired, but ready for action."

Caroline wasn't sure what he meant by the statement, until she noticed the squadron patch on his and Tepes' shoulders. Both were Alpha Squadron, which meant they'd probably been pulling extra simulator time not only for their exams, but to represent *Indomitable* in the upcoming Fleet competency exercises.

"Good. We can use the help. I'm tired of losing out to...to *Valiant*."

Caroline almost choked herself on the word, but her momentary lapse of composure was covered up by the arrival of a steward with her meal. She bit the tip off a fresh bulb of coffee, and the first sip filled her mouth with the dark, chocolaty flavor of station-grown beans.

Definitely not fleet-standard. I wonder who's been doing some unauthorized trading?

Caroline motioned to the steward to bring two more bulbs, then tried a different conversational gambit on young Tepes.

"And how is your mother doing, cadet?"

Tepes beamed, and started in on all the latest gossip from back home. Caroline was only half-listening, focused in part on the rich aroma of her contraband coffee, but also on the other conversations around them.

While she wasn't a Simak like Horace, Caroline's ability to follow multiple conversation threads at the same time was a valuable skill she'd cultivated while rising through the ranks. Taking another sip, she let the beating heart of the ship envelop and surround her until she found what she was looking for.

"-king bullshit, is what it is. Why am I to blame for some Earther's fuckup? I should-"

"-eard he's going to be spaced as soon as we get back to Earth. Good riddance, I-"

"-ptain Hardass can schedule all the patrols he wants, but good luck getting anybody to fly them. Am I right?"

Caroline closed her eyes and took a deep breath, steeling herself for what she had to do next. She felt a small pang of guilt for the extra attention Tepes was about to draw, but it couldn't be helped.

She'll need to toughen up sooner or later, might as well be now.

"And that's when she told the man, 'I can't believe you think I'd pay that much. Who do you think you're dealing with?' And I said-"

Caroline's hand came down hard on the table, rattling her tray and cutting off young Tepes' story mid-sentence.

"That's enough!"

Tepes and Currano's jaws both dropped open as she stood up, then closed with an audible snap as she winked an eye and gestured to the still-hot bulbs of coffee on the table.

Turning to address the compartment, she put on her Command face and imagined herself made entirely from deep-core iron.

"Some of you are apparently under the impression that this ship is run by committee. It is not."

Dozens of eyes locked on to Caroline, following her every move as she stepped to the middle of the compartment. She stopped walking one table away from the officer who'd made the mutinous remark, but didn't address her directly.

Yet. She can hear me well enough from here, and she's not the only one who needs a correction today.

"If you have a problem with ship's scheduling, you come to me. If you have a problem fulfilling your oaths, you talk to God, then you come apologize to me. And if you—where do you think you're going, mister!"

Caroline fixed her full attention on a pilot who'd stood up from his table with his back to her, tray in hand, and headed for the door before the ice in her words froze his feet to the deck.

"Sit down, Lieutenant. We're not done here, not by a long shot."

The entire mess watched as the pilot turned, twitching a starter mustache and with the beginnings of a snarl on his face. He took a full six seconds to sit down again, straddling the bench as he dropped his tray contemptuously on the table.

This quiet insubordination was just the excuse Caroline was looking for to work off some of her frustration, and she was in his face in a heartbeat.

"Do you have something you want to say, Mr. Farley? How about you, Chao? Or you, Ms. McDermott?" The other pilots at Farley's table shook their heads, but Farley met her gaze with steel in his eyes.

"No, Ma'am. Nothing to say...to you." His hesitation was probably unnoticed by most of the compartment, but Caroline heard his pause for what it was: a direct challenge to her authority, and by extension the Captain's.

"Good. Have a seat then. You're not going anywhere for a while." Caroline ripped Farley's flight wings off his jumpsuit with enough force to snap them in half, and his half-sneer melted into full panic. She dropped the pieces on the bench between his legs, then turned to address the rest of the compartment. This time, she stared directly at the woman who'd first drawn her attention, and enjoyed seeing her previous courage of anonymity drain away before Caroline's righteous ire.

"How about the rest of you? Got any more complaints to share? Perhaps you'd like an extra blanket before bedtime. Some warm milk and a lullaby?"

Caroline slowly surveyed the crew for any more signs of disobedience. The assembled officers wore expressions of surprise and shock, but none had enough spine to confront her in public.

Lowborns and cowards, the lot of them. Tepes and her boy Currano are worth more than the rest of them put together.

"Lunch is over. Anyone wishing to continue this conversation should meet me on C-deck, Forward 3 in twenty for a reminder of how the real Fleet works. Dismissed!"

To his credit, Farley didn't get up from his seat and follow his friends. Caroline's glare kept him pinned until the mess was empty, though she almost cracked a smile at Tepes' whispered 'thankyou' as she and the smell of that delicious coffee passed behind her on their way out.

When they were alone, Caroline cocked an eyebrow at Farley, who, despite his earlier denial, clearly had more to say.

"Well, let's have it."

"Ma'am, with respect, what are we doing out here? When I came on shift yesterday we set up the strangest sensor web I've ever deployed, then a couple hours later we abandon it and are heading home, only to turn around and head back to Earth a few hours after that. The day before, I'm flying back-to-back, full-shift drone patrols in the literal middle of nowhere, running black-box sweeps for God knows what that I don't even get to see before they disappear into the central core forever.

"I think, Ma'am, I...I think we're all due some answers."

Caroline understood the man's frustration, and if the orders had come from anybody besides Horace, she'd probably have made her own move by now. But if Horace Kołodziejski said Aloysius Martin was a traitor, he was, and that's all there was to it.

But this isn't about frustration. It's about the chain of command, and more importantly, it's about manners.

And while I sympathize with your plight, someone has to be the first example.

Farley was about to say something else when she grabbed the side of his head and slammed it into the table, then shoved his face into what was left of his sandwich and rehydrated potatoes. For good measure, she kicked his left leg back so that he fell between the table and the bench, with only her grip for support.

Caroline leaned in close, her voice pitched so low she barely heard it herself over the sound of blood rushing through her head. The smell of his lunch mixed in with coppery blood and some kind of beard oil filled her nostrils, and a she was fairly sure he'd also soiled himself.

"No, you're not. You follow your fucking orders, and you show some fucking respect. If you ever want to fly again, you'll clean yourself up and file for a transfer. Pick your ship, I don't care which one, but you'll never suit up under my command again. Am I clear?"

Farley was trying to get his hands on the table, straining against her superior strength. But Caroline had been doing this since before he was born, and there was no way he was getting free unless she allowed it.

"Am. I. Clear?"

She pressed harder with each word, then bent him back painfully over the bench to hear his response. He gasped and nodded against her grip, which was all she needed to hear. She turned her back on his whimpering, brushing bits of his lunch off her hands as she left the mess hall.

"Don't let me see you again, Mr. Farley. Ever."

Caroline's entire body felt alive. It had been years since she indulged herself like this, and her internal clock told her she had around ten minutes to get ready for the rest of today's disciplinary exercises.

More than enough time.

ANDREISON

MARYA WALKED BETWEEN HER ESCORTS, wondering what voices were whispering in their ears. The occasional "turn here" was all the conversation she'd gotten from either of them, and it was very clear that she wasn't heading back to her quarters as Commander Phillips had instructed.

The gennie transmission was a big deal, but I should either be filling out reports or cooling my heels in the brig. Something else is going on here, but for the life of me I can't figure out what.

To the untrained eye, one corridor aboard a dreadnaught looked the same as any other. But Marya had memorized the ship's plans before coming aboard, and her eyes were more accurate than ones made of mere flesh. Even in the dim lighting, underneath the magnetic grating all around her she could see pipes and conduits carrying power, air, and other necessities throughout the ship—every one labeled and tagged for ease of repair.

We're still on B deck, rounding on a launch bay from the opposite direction. But where is everybody? In the middle of first shift, we should be elbow to elbow with all sorts of people. And what's with the midnight lighting?

There should at least be maintenance drones rolling around in here, even if they've cleared the corridors to hide whatever it is they're trying to do.

The dull thudding of her armored escort's boots as they walked was broken up by voices from beyond the next intersection of hatches. Unlike the circuitous route they'd taken to get here, the area up ahead was fully illuminated, and from the sounds of it very occupied.

Hartley was in the lead, and came to an abrupt halt. Marya pulled up short to avoid smashing into his back, drawing a muttered curse from Starboard behind her.

Anticipating another shove, Marya rolled her shoulders and turned slightly to the left.

Come on, big man. Get it over with already. Because once I'm officially in the brig, I'll have a recorder running on me full time. And I have all sorts of things to talk about…

"Quiet, you two. Company's coming."

What the hell?

It wasn't Hartley's statement that surprised her, but rather the herd of off-duty crew filing through the intersection toward the launch bay under the supervision of another pair of troopers.

Marya counted almost sixty people wearing a mix of duty uniforms and casual dress, all with deployment bags over their shoulders. Edging closer, not only could she make out some of their conversations, but a bit of reflected light spilled over her and her escort.

"-strangest thing. An announcement woke me up, told me to get my gear together. And just like that, I'm on leave-"

"-going to ask. Another shift like my last three, and I'd have put in for a transfer myself-"

"-ander wouldn't say. Just that I'd been approved for emergency leave, and the transport was leaving ASAP."

"Sub-Lieutenant Andreison, you too?"

Marya looked around the trooper's shoulder and saw a young steward in galley coveralls take a step toward them from the general flow of people. She remembered his face from the officer's mess, but couldn't quite place his name. When one of her guards stepped forward to cut him off, she slid around the trooper through the hatch and into the intersection, then put on her best smile.

"Yep. Damnedest thing, isn't it? Don't even know what to pack for!"

Starboard made a grab for her shoulder, but she took another quick step forward and planted herself next to a catch ring, with the talkative steward in front of her and the rest of the crew flowing around them.

"My orders say they'll send the rest of my kit to Lagrange 6, so I just threw essentials in my bag like they said. You'll have to hurry if you want to catch the shuttle, though. We're boosting in fifteen minutes!"

Fascinating. And me without my slippers. Oh well, everything I really care about on this boat is either on my finger or stuffed in my boot.

"No problem, I'll see you aboard!"

This time the Starboard did grab her—her tunic, at least—but she'd anchored herself well enough that he had to take a step across the hatchway to get a better grip. The steward took an involuntary step back, then was swept along by the flow of bodies moving down the corridor.

There was enough loose fabric in the shoulders of Marya's mess tunic for her to shrug free as Starboard readjusted his hold, and she used the space he'd formed in the traffic pattern to spin around, releasing the catch ring with her left hand as she did.

The movement brought her within reach of his flailing left hand, which fastened tight on her right shoulder. He pulled her out of the intersection and back into the darkened corridor, growling at her in a low voice. But in his haste, he forgot to secure her right arm, and she slammed it into the controls for the corridor's emergency doors, sealing herself and her escorts off from the passing crowd.

"That's enough of that, convict. You're not going anywhere."

Her eyes adjusted immediately to the near-absolute darkness, and beneath their mirrored visors she assumed the troopers' suits gave them similar visual assistance. And although she couldn't see his face, his tone through the speakers indicated his mood clearly enough.

Marya kept her face neutral, not wanting to betray any of her half-formed plans. She was clearly in all kinds of trouble right now, but still had her pride. She spared a glance over his shoulder at Hartley, who'd turned his head to look back the way they came for any more surprises.

Keeping her voice just low enough to carry to the two men, Marya chose her next words specifically to make them lose their tempers.

"It's *Lieutenant*, trooper, and you don't know shit about shit. I may have been relieved of duty, but not my rank. So keep your opinions tucked up your ass where they belong, unless you want to have an entirely different kind of conversation."

Instead of pulling away from Starboard's predictable backhand, she ducked under it, grabbing for his belt and the controls that regulated the armor's systems. She gave them two quick spins, and her opponent went completely rigid. She stood up, placed both hands against his chest, and pushed with all her strength.

He toppled onto Hartley, who instinctively brought his arms up to catch the falling man. Both went down, and to Marya's delight they fell far enough back into the shadowed corridor to be invisible from the intersection should someone think to open the doors after she was gone. She grabbed an induction pistol off Starboard's chestplate and placed the muzzle directly in Hartley's visor.

"Sorry boys, looks like you're not going to be keeping me out of trouble after all. But by all means, try something. At this point I've got nothing to lose."

Starboard's armor was completely shut down, but the external speakers on Hartley's still worked fine.

"You think you're going to get away with this, you stupid bitch? There isn't anywhere in the system we can't get at you. You're fin—"

The rest of the trooper's diatribe cut off as Marya shut down his armor too. She could still hear muffled protests from inside their helmets, but beyond a few centimeters she couldn't hear them at all.

And no one else will, either. Nighty-night, boys.

Counting down the time until the shuttle launched in her head, she worked the second trooper's induction pistol loose, and tucked them both into the leg pouches of her flight suit. She opened the hatch halfway and stepped through warily, then closed and dogged it behind her, consigning her erstwhile captors to darkness for the foreseeable future.

It took some running to catch up with the crowd moving into to the transport shuttle, but once she did, it was easy to worm her way into the middle of the pack and walk past the troopers waving people up the ramp.

Don'tlookdon'tlookeverything'sfinenothingtoseehere...

Marya was halfway across the shuttle's cargo deck when the warning lamps started flashing, and she let out the breath she'd been holding. The sound of her sigh was nothing compared the rumbling of the ramp as it closed behind her. She chanced a look back, and was relieved to see that the troopers had not joined them for the trip to L6.

No chaperones, eh? Maybe the thought police didn't send the memo fast enough. Looks like me and the rest of these misfits will have an uneventful trip.

That is, assuming they don't blast us out of space the moment we clear the ship.

Standard shuttles weren't designed to carry a fifth of the ship's compliment at once, and the crowd milling around in the crew compartment was busy stowing their gear and negotiating the best seats for conversation.

While she hadn't heard the orders that brought them here, Marya knew a few things about their situation the rest of the crew did not, and her most pressing concern right now was survival, not comfort.

Marya double-timed it up to the cockpit, shrugging out of her mess tunic as she went and tucking it under her arm in a slightly less than regulation fold.

I'll worry about how it looks later. For now, I need to make sure I live long enough to wear it again.

If that's really what I want...

Marya stopped just before the cockpit hatch, struck by the absurdity of her own thoughts. It was less than a dozen hours since she'd decoded an extra-solar transmission that could well presage a full-scale gennie invasion, and in that time she'd managed to piss off half the battlegroup, disable two armed guards and escape house arrest, and was now about to completely abandon her post and fly off to parts unknown on a shuttle packed to the gills with the most unlikely leave party in Fleet history. The only thing in the universe she was sure of was how much she wanted to chuck her uniform in the recycler and get back to Deb and the girls.

Guess that's your answer, love. I'll clean up this mess, and come home as soon as I can.

Marya leaned her head against the hatch and closed her eyes. The deep thrum of wing thrusters powering to life moved through the shuttle and through her, and she let it carry her away for a few seconds. Marya's second, third, and fourth thoughts were of how much she'd miss being a part of things that mattered once this was all over and done.

Fleet had been her life for almost fifteen years, and her reasons for joining the Academy, for returning to service after prison, and for sticking it out planetside in one shit assignment after another were still valid.

I don't think I'm cut out to be little people. But I'm willing to try if it means I don't have to deal with the stares, the whispers, or being angry all the time.

Marya opened her eyes, straightened herself up, and keyed open the hatch. She breathed another sigh of relief when her access code was accepted, and the hatch opened onto the very welcome sights of a harried pilot running through preflight as best he could with only two hands, and an empty second seat to his right.

Okay, Marya. Time to be charming and indispensable.

"Need a hand, Lieutenant? I've never quite got the hang of being a passenger on one of these tubs, and another minute listening to scuttlebutt's going to drive me completely crazy."

The pilot swiveled his head, took in her flight suit and wings, then waved her forward.

"God, yes. This whole trip is a mess, and I feel the same way. Don't even have a return vector for this one, just a destination."

Marya stepped forward, offered her free hand, and took in the other officer. He was young, with a round, solid face and none of the worry lines she imagined she'd earned today. The pilot's grip was strong, but relaxed, and unlike most men in the Fleet he let go almost immediately.

"Parker."

"Andreison."

"Thanks for this, I wasn't looking forward to my first solo flight since the Academy."

Marya smiled as she bucked in and studied the board. Parker had completed most of the preflight checklist already, and they were already cleared for launch.

"Well, to be perfectly honest it's been a while for me too. At least with something this big. But I think between the two of us we can handle it, yah?"

"Yeah. Let's do it."

Marya pulled up the external cams and noted the flashing green lights indicating the bay was clear and depressurized. She ran through the remaining co-pilot steps from memory—pulling up holos to prep the transport's internal gravity, detach the docking clamps, and signaling...

Oh no. You're not going to catch me that easy. Not when I'm so close to making it out undetected.

"The ship is yours, Mr. Parker. Take us out."

"Roger that, sub-lieutenant."

Marya swiped the comm window across the board to Parker's station, and he tapped it for the final clearance they needed to make their exit.

"Ships, this is CL-7, requesting final clearance for launch."

"Confirmed, CL-7. You are cleared for departure."

Marya leaned forward slightly, willing the bay doors to open. It was the one thing she couldn't control from the board in front of her, and when they opened Marya did her best not to cheer. Instead, she flashed the lights in the crew compartment to warn her passengers of impending weightlessness, and then cut the transport loose from *City of Lights'* gravity with maneuvering thrusters.

Parker took it from there, smoothly accelerating out of the launch bay and into open space. Once they were clear, Marya flashed the compartment lights again, and activated internal comms.

"This is the flight deck. We are clear of *City of Lights*, and boosting for L6 station. Restoring quarter-grav in…five minutes, so we're asking you to wait just a bit longer to break out your flasks."

Marya caught Parker's head turn and surprised expression out of the corner of her eye, and smiled.

"What? They were told to pack essentials. We've got most of a ship-day between us and L6, and I'll wager there's going to be one hell of a party back there as soon as we let them start pouring."

Parker's laughter was infectious, and it was nice to feel something other than fear for a change. But a shared smile didn't keep Marya from pulling up a display of *City of Lights'* energy weapons envelope, or stop her from praying that the next five minutes would be uneventful ones.

And after that, I've got thirty hours and half the solar system to figure out what to do with the rest of my life.

ANNAHKO

CAROLINE STRETCHED in silence in front of the gathering crowd, counting the officers as they filed in and trying to hide her disappointment. Her bare feet scratched along the 15 cm mat that covered most of CF-3's decking, and the whisper of her gi as she moved was like the rustling of leaves in an arboretum.

No matter. This will end the same for all of them no matter how they're dressed.

CF-3 was one of *Indomitable*'s gymnasiums, and Caroline had selected it precisely because it was the closest one to officer country. Basic weapons like staves, clubs, and wooden swords were secured to the compartment's walls, and the ceiling was studded with various armatures, each programmed with a variety of training protocols.

More than half the mess had shown up, but very few were wearing workout clothes; in fact, most of them were wearing the same duty uniforms and tunics in which she'd last seen them. There was very little muttering amongst the crew, and more than a few nervous looks. By now, word of what happened to Farley should have spread throughout the ship, which would make what happened next all the more poignant.

When Caroline was sure no-one else was coming, she stood up and bowed to the assembled crowd. No one returned the gesture, which meant that the remainder of her lesson for today was likely to fall on deaf ears.

Taking a deep breath, she again summoned up the spirit of the Iron Princess, and began what was in effect her first speech as Captain.

"Earlier today I heard some pretty tough talk from a bunch of wet-behind-the-ears junior officers. It seems that this ship has forgotten who our true enemies are, and instead want to fight for the comforts of a posh billet on the Home Fleet's most advanced warship.

"That would be a mistake. Our enemy is stronger than we are, more numerous, and possibly in possession of advanced weaponry we can only imagine. Fighting amongst ourselves is the worst mistake we can make, yet from what I hear scoring a point here and there is all that matters.

"Also wrong. Line up around the mat, and let's begin."

The compartment went silent, and for a moment Caroline thought she was going to have to single out someone at random to deliver her message. Then came a murmuring from the back of the crowd as someone pushed their way forward.

Well, I'll be. Bob Calas. Didn't expect you at this party, but you'll do as well as anyone.

Calas was the one member of Horace's inner circle to whom Caroline had taken an instant dislike. He was a passable officer, and a genius tech wiz. But as a man—or a friend—he had very few redeeming qualities, and Horace's favor was the only stake he had in the grand game all High Dome children learned to play at an early age.

At present, Calas' smirk was what Caroline hated most about him, though she did appreciate that he'd at least dressed for the occasion in a loose-fitting gi and soft cloth slippers. He stepped up onto the mat and gave a perfect bow, which Caroline returned. He was smiling as he straightened—a thin, cruel, rodent-like line that did his face no favors.

Caroline turned her back on her erstwhile challenger and stepped down off the mat. Using her left foot, she touched a control panel on the floor and activated the training sequence she'd programmed into the compartment before the first of her "students" arrived. The crowd gave a collective groan as local gravity shot up from Mars normal to 1.2Gs. Stepping back up onto the mat felt like running up a hill at full speed.

"Our enemies live on far-off worlds, none of which are like our home. Their twisted genes give them all sorts of advantages over we mere mortals, and there's just two things that will save us in the end. The courage of our convictions, and the loyalty we give to one another.

"Without either, we are lost. Mr. Calas, are you ready?"

Calas bowed a second time, and protocol demanded Caroline respond in kind. But she didn't take her eyes off him for even a second, and was ready when he began his attack with a couple quick steps and a textbook jump-kick.

Most fighters favored their right leg and kicked with their left, so when Calas did the opposite Caroline was wary of a feint. She spun to her right, narrowly avoiding three quick punches as he sailed past. As soon as she had a solid base, she executed a somersault that ended with her foot smashing into his cheek, knocking him down hard.

Calas slapped the mat as he landed, and he was still smiling as he rolled away and back up into a ready stance. The higher gravity didn't seem to bother him much, so at least one member of her crew was up-to-date on their mandated 1G workouts.

The pair circled cautiously, but Caroline realized quickly that her divided focus was a disadvantage. Caroline was trying to send a message; whatever his motivations, Calas had come for a fight.

To be honest, I've been spoiling for one too. So let's give them a show, shall we?

Caroline broke rotation first, stepping inside and spinning right to send a punch rocketing at Calas's head. He ducked under her fist and tried to initiate a grapple, but he had spent too much time looking at her hands and not enough tracking the rest of her body. Caroline hadn't expected her punch to land; she'd used it to start a full-body spin which ended with another devastating kick to his midsection.

Calas went down hard a second time, and Caroline took a deep breath to deliver another barb.

"Mr. Calas, if you wanted a nap, you could have stayed in your quarters. On this ship, you give your best or you don't show up at all!"

Calas came up to a half crouch, cradling his left side and looking up at her with an expression she was sure she didn't like.

"Yes, Ma'am!" Calas exploded out of his stance, aiming a monster punch at her solar plexus. Any other fighter would have their diaphragm paralyzed for a few seconds if the punch landed squarely, but Caroline saw it coming and shifted just enough that his fist merely bruised her left breast.

The boosted gravity dropped them both to the mat, and Calas scrambled on top of Caroline, trying to pin her arms. She twisted left to break his hold, then used her right leg to hook his left and reverse their positions.

Both fighters were breathing hard, and Caroline was surprised to find herself smiling just as broadly as Calas. Her blood was singing with the thrill of the fight, and from her new position she realized she wasn't the only one aroused by their contact.

She'd never considered Calas as a temporary partner, dismissing him as yet another toady trying to garner political capital in Horace's orbit. But finding someone who could challenge her on this level was extremely rare, and she couldn't deny the way it made her feel.

She pushed away from Calas, rolling backward and readying herself for another charge. But instead of anticipating his next attack, her mind summoned up the last night she and Horace had spent together, almost a full T-year gone.

Horace was a willing and enthusiastic lover, but it was Caroline who drove most of their sexual encounters. Part of it was her expanded experience, but the truth was that she preferred to be in charge of all aspects of her life, and he was more than willing to follow her lead.

But then the memory turned sour, as the virile, smiling man she'd loved for so long morphed into the gaunt shadow he'd become. She recoiled from the mental image, and came back to herself just in time to see Calas's fist flying at her face.

Caroline caught his arm in both hands, rolling onto her back and kicking hard into his midsection. Thinking her an easy target, Calas was completely unprepared for her counterattack and went flying into the compartment's wall.

He slammed into it back first, and then slid down the bulkhead into a sitting position. He gasped out a tortured laugh, then groaned as he adjusted his legs.

Caroline blushed, and hated herself for it. She'd allowed the situation to get out of hand, and at the same time relished in the uncertainly of their encounter. She and Calas would never be compatible, but their fight was even more satisfying than her brief domination of Farley in the mess hall and she had no idea how to deal with her unexplained, and unwanted, arousal.

Who is this man, that he can upset my life even more than it already is?

Suddenly mindful of the people watching them, Caroline looked away from Calas's laughter to the crowd of onlookers.

"The enemy won't hold back like Mr. Calas, and neither should you. We are in a war for survival, and there's only one acceptable outcome. One strategy. Loyalty, Honor, and Devotion will carry us through, and you must be prepared to sacrifice everything to beat the gennies.

"So I'll ask you one time, and one time only. Are you ready to fight, or are you content to be a footnote in the history of the human race!"

Two dozen voices answered her impassioned declaration, and Caroline relaxed slightly. She wouldn't need to do this again for a while, but Horace's secrets had planted a dark seed in the crew's souls, and it would take her a while to dig it out.

She helped Calas to his feet, careful not to pull him too close. But she couldn't deny there was something happening between them, and one way or the other she'd have to address the issue.

"Hit the showers, Bob. We'll talk about this later." They were far enough from the other officers that only Calas heard her whisper, and his toothy smile gave her a clear indication of how he thought that conversation would go. He walked away with careful steps and head held high, and Caroline had the distinct impression that despite the beating he'd endured, he considered himself the winner of their match.

Maybe he is, depending on what game we're actually playing. But I'm the one who'll come out on top in the end.

Caroline's eyes widened as she registered her inner double entendre and wiped her face with the sleeve of her gi to hide another blush. A second with her eyes closed was all she needed to regain her composure, and then she was the Iron Princess once more, resolute and inviolate.

"All right, who's next?"

17 JULY, 2640 OER

JANTINE

"ALL DONE WITH YOUR PEP-TALKS, BOSS?" MALIK'S WHISPER WAS BARELY in the audible range, but Jantine could hear the smile he normally kept hidden. He was busy strapping himself in to the cargo harness, eyes never straying from his computer. The rest of the team was making the same preparation for insertion, aligning themselves along the outer edge of the "raft" of crates the Omegas had assembled. Assuming Malik could get them to the surface intact, the harnesses should keep everyone secure as they descended.

"Why? Feeling the need to unburden yourself?"

The "pep-talks" had taken most of the two hours she'd allocated, the bulk of which was confirming all post-landing activities with JonB. Jantine could see him now in animated conversation with Doria, and by extension the Omegas, on the same topic.

Wearing encounter suits with the faceplates open, the pair of civvies almost looked like combat mods. But there was something in their eyes, a softness that betrayed their genetic programming.

They're not ready to kill. Not as long as we're here to do it for them.

"I'm good, Boss. Ten minutes, give or take. The readings are a bit different now, but I don't know if that's the end of the hyperspace corridor or something else. If we ever make a return trip, I'll let you know."

"I'll keep that in mind. How long until you kill the lights?"

Malik's response was slow in coming, a personality trait to which she'd never quite grown accustomed. He wasn't a slow thinker, he just liked to be thorough. And he had a habit of translating his very accurate responses back into plain speech to put people at ease. Jantine had no real preference, but understood that others did.

"I can probably manage the power load fine with them on. It's the grav that uses most of the reserves. And we won't start tapping those until we jettison the hyperdrive module."

Jantine considered several scenarios before speaking again. If it truly didn't matter, the civvies would probably appreciate not being in the dark. They'd made the adjustment to living in constant illumination well enough, and it was their idea to stop using the simulated sky projections. Jantine definitely approved of that change—no matter what the weather was supposed to be like at their destination, seeing clouds move with no accompanying breeze just seemed wrong.

"And the other environmental systems?"

"Same general idea. We shouldn't have to use them long enough to make a difference. We'll either be able to land or not."

Something was bothering Jantine about insertion, more so than her earlier doubts. She felt she should be doing something right now, even something small, to increase their chances of survival. In the end it all depended on Malik's ability to land a falling building using nothing but readouts and fast reflexes, but Jantine was responsible for keeping everyone alive, and the team had made sure she knew they had complete faith in her ability to do so.

"Kill them in five, and the other systems too. Save every erg you can. Patch me into the handhelds."

Jantine surprised herself with her confidence, but only a little. This is what she was bred for, and after so long with nothing to do she was now in her element.

Her handheld beeped twice, and checking it she saw eight ready icons waiting for her words. While the Omegas could read just fine, they preferred to communicate through Doria rather than transcriptions.

Okay, here we go.

"In five minutes, we're going to shut down all environmental systems in preparation for insertion. Get your helmets on and breathers calibrated, and then power down all nonessential equipment. I want no stray signals. We will be weapons-hot in five minutes starting…now."

Jantine nodded approval at the countdown that appeared on her handheld, but then frowned at the comm request from JonB. Surrendering to the inevitable, she keyed in a privacy code and answered it. She barely had time to register his face on the screen before he started speaking.

"Is this really necessary, JTN-B34256-O? I'm reading full capacity on all power reserves, and we're well within safety margins."

"It's 'Jantine,' JonB. Or 'Commander' if you must, but yes, these are my orders. This is still a combat mission, and I don't think I have to remind you of the stakes here."

Jantine could almost see JonB's brain working inside his head. After her almost-rebuke, his lips were pressed tightly together and his eyes had narrowed. He was running options in his head, trying to figure out why she would want the extra power.

There was a very thin line between advice and insubordination, and JonB had higher intelligence scores than she did, if less practical experience. Everything he'd said so far was correct, and she was impressed that he'd been monitoring the situation so closely. But the decision was hers to make, and he had to accept that.

I'm really hoping one of the sleepers can replace him.

"I understand…Jantine. I'll message you once I confirm everyone's breathers and suits are properly calibrated."

The connection terminated abruptly, and Jantine felt her own lips pressing together. The next few minutes were crucial to the survival of the Colonies, and if it came down to it, she had to make their sacrifice matter. One by one her team signaled their readiness-well within the deadline she'd set. Doria sent a text-only message along with her confirmation, and reading it sent another chill down Jantine's spine.

They understand, and are ready.

How much, or how little, the Omegas really grasped about what was happening was something only Doria could tell her. But Jantine suspected it was the former, and it probably wouldn't take much longer for the rest of the mods to come to the same conclusion they had.

All, or nothing.

"Boss?"

"Do it. Scenario Five Alpha is a go."

"Acknowledged."

On schedule, Malik disabled the environmental systems. Her encounter suit responded instantly, adding a small puff of air in her helmet every time her chest moved and keeping it the same temperature as her skin.

Jantine didn't think she'd miss the subsonic hum of the container's air exchangers, but without it she felt a little bit naked. With her faceplate sealed, she could only hear the sounds of her own body, and it was a bit unnerving. Nothing would change in the module for a few hours; there was plenty of shielding, and it was a completely enclosed system. But without that constant vibration stimulating the edges of her perception, the mission was now more real than ever, and she tried not to think about the fifty thousand or so things that could go wrong in the next few minutes.

She especially avoided thinking about the destruct charges Malik had just re-enabled.

From her position, Jantine had a clear view of Malik's screen, and the sight of his faceplate illuminated by its glow was a comfort. Just before insertion, he closed his eyes, counting down the seconds until the sequence he'd programmed jettisoned the hyperdrive module and brought them hurtling back into normal space.

Five…four…three…two…

MALIK

MALIK SLAMMED INTO HIS RESTRAINTS AS HIS SCREEN WENT WILD. HE had no more than a second to decide whether his weapon or the computer was more important to hold on to, and given the team's location it wasn't a hard choice at all. His right hand shot out and barely reached the case's handle before it went spinning away. Pulling it closer, he kept his eyes on the readouts as the container tumbled.

The sudden return of gravity to his world was a completely unexpected development, and until he could confirm what had gone wrong with the insertion, his priorities were still to get a lock on the planet and get the containers free of the cargo slug.

Their exit from hyperspace should have been no more dramatic than a few new data points appearing on his screen. But now they were spinning wildly through space, and the mass readings indicated that fragments of whatever they'd impacted were tumbling along with them.

And also that they were definitely not alone in this supposedly empty area of space.

"Boss…not…done…with…bad…news."

"What…happened?"

Jantine's words were as strained as his own, and at least one other member of the team was screaming. Through the chaos, he thought it might be one of the sibs, but there was no telling which one.

"Hit...something.   Above...ecliptic...not...natural.   Have   to... retask...scans."

"Do you...have...planet?"

Malik got his other hand to one of his restraints and released it, dragging the strap across the case to provide a bit more stability. Up and down were still relative and uncertain terms, but at least now the screen was level with his eyes, and he could enter some commands. A few seconds of hurried tapping gave him answers, but not the ones Jantine wanted.

"No. Ships. Lots. Big...ones."

Half a dozen, in fact. But he couldn't spare the syllables to explain fully.

"Want...grav?"

Whatever Jantine was going to say was lost when another impact shook the container. In addition to an expanded debris field from the ship they'd hit, a handful of new contacts appeared on his screen, and none of them the planet he was looking for. But these new arrivals were moving in familiar ways, enough so that he didn't need to wait for the computer to tell him what they were.

"Missiles!"

On the screen, the missiles were converging on a single point, thankfully one on the other side of the cargo slug. So far, the enemy was treating their improvised spacecraft as nothing but an unexplained rock in space, and the targeting made sense. They were trying to break it up before it could do any more damage to their fleet, but Malik could see that their plan wouldn't work.

On target, but definitely too late to do them any good. We're not finished hitting spaceships yet...

Malik stabbed a finger at the broadcast key on his handheld, and was rewarded with a humming inside his faceplate as the suit comms went live.

"Brace...yourselves!"

He could see Jantine from his position atop the crates, and knew generally where the rest of the mods were fastened. When the missiles hit, the subroutine he was running on their suit telemetries gave him a much clearer picture of the team's status. And an unfortunately smaller head count.

Harren and Doria are flatlining...

Malik's grunt of recognition was all he allowed himself to voice before bending his head and starting a new set of burn calculations. There were bigger things to worry about right now. If the civvies were dead, so be it. Unless he could stabilize their flight, they'd have plenty of company soon enough.

Doria, I...

The missiles' impact didn't do much more than blast off a few hundred tons of rock, but as an unexpected benefit the explosions killed most of the slug's angular momentum. Jantine must have realized this as well, and was already unfastening her harness.

"Grav! And find me that planet."

Malik programmed one-quarter gravity, but didn't activate any other environmental systems. All he really needed to do was establish a separate frame of reference for the container and buy them a little more time. Once it came online, he felt a great weight lift from his shoulders, but didn't raise his head from the screen.

Jantine would see to the others—that's what she was here for. Now that he could use both hands, Malik began searching for any trajectory that didn't include a very large spaceship directly in their path.

And when he found one—as with the missiles—it was too late to matter. Using as calm a voice as he could muster, Malik addressed the rest of the team over the open channel.

"Anyone who's not still harnessed should find something to hold onto. We're about to make contact with the enemy."

There wasn't much point in telling Jantine they were about to collide with a Redstone-class dreadnaught, or that they'd already plowed through three of its tenders. All any of them could do now was hold on and hope for a quick death.

As he watched the range to target decrease, his thoughts weren't of the mission, or Doria, or even the people aboard the enemy ship that would die along with him. Instead, he imagined the surface of the planet he'd finally located, and how nice it might have been to stand on it.

Despite the artificial gravity field, Malik was thrown hard against the restraints by the impact, and this time they were insufficient to the task. He rocketed off the raft of crates toward one of the unseen walls of the cargo container. As he flew through the thinning air, he tightened his grip on the portable unit and drew it close to his chest. If he couldn't save his own life, at least he could protect the only chance the rest of the team had for survival.

All right, JonB. Let's see how smart you really are. Maybe you can figure out why an attack fleet is trying to stay hidden this close to—

RAMIREZ

1240 SHIP TIME, **SDF** *VALIANT*

DAMN. Here we go again.

Sub-lieutenant Alonso Ramirez stared at the fire control board in disbelief. For the third time this shift, *Valiant* was mobilizing to deal with a hyperspace emergence he strongly suspected was not real—the same emergence, in fact, they'd detected twice already. The pods hadn't launched yet, and he suspected the officers manning them were thinking the same thing he was.

Protocol demanded that he prep the tenders for sensor pod retrieval, and lock down Comms Division again while he prepared firing solutions based on the lack of data the pods would be reporting.

Unless, of course, I can convince the Martinette *to cancel the whole affair.*

"Lt. Harlan, the pods are spooling up to chase another of those sensor ghosts. Can I have them stand down, and just mark it as a glitch?"

Alonso's voice carried over the team channel, though only he and his superior officer were currently suited up. Even though it wasn't regulation, Harlan insisted that officers in the situation room be fully armed and armored at all times. Her response was predictable, and immediate.

"Prep the retrieval, Mr. Ramirez. Looks like we'll be on station a little while longer. I'll be right there. Call in the rest of the team, I want us at full strength if something happens."

"Yes Ma'am."

Alonso sent the messages, resigning himself to another few hours of sweating in his armor. Since graduating from the Academy and joining Mira Harlan's fire control team, he'd learned to do almost every part of his job while wearing it, but he knew she wouldn't be the one logging the after-action reports, long after this shift was over.

Despite his rank, Alonso was still the junior member of the team, and he'd earned his spot by following orders and being the best there was at what he did. The other five members were online within two minutes, linking together in an independent communications network capable of deploying to any part of the ship in a crisis. On both his visor display and the main board he saw them double-timing it to their damage control stations.

He pulled up the battlegroup's sensor net, marking the location of each ship and initiating a tight beam connection with all of them. The pods were getting final confirmation from Command deck when the alarm sounded again.

"Ma'am, second emergence, at…my God…"

Alonso's voice trailed off as a big blob of something replaced the battleship *Harrow* on his displays, and all communication from that vessel ended.

"I see it. Launch a Geyser spread and move us to full alert. Alonso…Alonso!"

SDF *Cessnock* vanished from his plot, and a gauntlet slammed the board in front of him. He registered the missiles Harlan launched, then saw *Gadwell* come apart as she launched another spread.

"C-Comet?" was all he could get out, but even as he said it he knew it was the wrong answer. For one, it was far too small, and moving way too fast.

And six Geysers with full warheads can destroy just about anything…

"Damnit, Ramirez, get your head in the game! Travers, Zager, get in here."

Harlan triggered the alert, and a klaxon call accompanied by a blue flashing light filled the compartment. Alonso watched the scene as if he was falling away from it, his hands still poised above the board, unable to look away from the inevitable end of the unknown contact's trajectory.

Mira Harlan's voice sounded three times in his helmet; once over the suit's comms, once over his external pickups, and finally over *Valiant*'s shipwide emergency channel.

"All hands, brace for impact. This is not a drill, I repeat, brace for impact. Unknown contact bearing two one seven mark…"

Alonso was thrown from his chair as the lights went out, and saw himself hit the floor through the suit cams of Harlan, Travers, and Zager. Saw himself bounce back up, in fact, spinning slightly as the suit's gyros adjusted to the lack of gravity and his emergency beacon kicked on.

"Well, shit. All right, people. Time to get to work. Ramirez, are you still with us?"

Harlan's voice was now just on the team's private comm network, a short-range redundancy of a redundancy he hadn't seen much use for when she'd ordered him to install it. The fact that she'd switched over to it without warning, and her uncharacteristic profanity, snapped him back to full attention.

"Yes, ma'am. Sorry, ma'am. I—"

"Don't be sorry, Ramirez. Be better. Now grab your kit, and let's get moving."

Alonso almost nodded in response, but six months of drills under Harlan's no-nonsense tutelage had removed most of his planetside habits. Instead, he righted himself using maneuvering jets, and his boots attached to the deck with a satisfying SSSSHUNK.

The suit gyros, however, were still trying to correct his position.

We're tumbling. Things just went from bad to worse.

If Lt. Harlan was having the same problems with her suit, her voice betrayed none of it.

"What do we know, people?"

Trooper Charles Jackson's status window flashed in Alonso's visor just before he spoke, and his feed expanded to fill the bottom half of the virtual display. Jackson had activated his emergency chest beacon as well, and was looking at an opened section of corridor plating.

"As near as I can figure, something is physically interrupting the power conduits on another deck. These here"—he tapped a section labeled *A42-Command*-"should be on an independent circuit straight from the reactors. But I'm not even reading a maintenance charge, which means power's been cut off—or redirected somehow. I've never seen anything like it."

"Okay, that gives us something, at least. Anyone else?" Harlan's response was as no-nonsense as the woman herself. The only thing Alonso had to offer was what he what remembered from the plot just before impact, and since it made no sense, he kept it to himself.

For now, anyway. I just wish I'd sent the pods like I should have, as soon as we saw the emergence.

"Right. So Mr. Ramirez is too unsure to say it out loud, but my gut's saying that we just got hit by something big, possibly a rogue comet. You all know about the sensor ghosts we've been chasing all morning, well this is most likely the reality."

"Not a comet."

"What's that, Ramirez?"

It took Alonso a moment to realize he'd spoken the thought aloud, but the whole team was waiting for an answer to Lt. Harlan's question.

Okay, crazy theory time, I guess.

"The mass is all wrong for a comet, and it was moving way too fast. It blew through *Harrow* and *Cessnock* like they weren't even there, and it hit us hard enough to knock out power and cut us off from the rest of the battlegroup.

"But it didn't destroy us, and a comet would have burst apart if we were large enough to stop its progress. So what does that leave? The geysers we launched didn't even slow it down. If it's a ship, why did it ram the battlegroup? If it's a planetoid or comet, why would it be this far above the ecliptic?"

Usually, at least one member of Lt. Harlan's team would attempt a response, and if the silence continued too long Harlan herself would hazard a guess. But Ramirez had touched upon the central question of their lives of late, the one thing none of them was willing to ask out loud for the last month.

Why is a fully armed battlegroup hiding out just beyond cislunar space, burning a decade's worth of reaction mass to stay way above the ecliptic and with the Earth between us and the Moon?

"All right, those are good questions. Let's go get some answers. Everyone but Jackson, grab all the portable generators you can and make your way to the command center. Rig temporary relief stations at every hatch along the way, and close them up when you're done.

"Charles, your priority is to find a way to contact the other damage control teams and get them working on the power situation. If you run into anyone else, send them along to Command as fast as you can. Are we all clear?"

A chorus of "ayes" answered Harlan's orders, and Alonso moved to comply. The fire control center had three portable generators, with another dozen in the storage lockers outside. Between himself, Lt. Harlan, and Troopers Travers and Zager, they could secure a path all the way to the command center, with plenty of supplies left over. The team's other five members would be doing so from other directions, taking back the ship one corridor at a time.

Taking it back? Where did that come from?

Alonso couldn't answer his own question, so he put it aside as he grabbed a double handful of generators, attached them to his suit's harness, and moved out into the corridor to join the others. But at the same time, he also couldn't shake the feeling that there was something larger going on with all this, some other alternative he couldn't see.

I guess it's like Lt. Harlan always says. Focus on the task at hand. Once one thing is working right, start on the next one, until the rest of the universe falls into place.

"Shake a leg, Mr. Ramirez. Ship's not going to repair itself."

Travers' teasing words could have come from anywhere within range of their mini-network, but by the light of his chest beacon Alonso could see him crouching over a section of removed plating fifty meters ahead as Lieutenant Harlan and Zager stepped through a hatch into the next section of corridor.

Alonso grabbed a transit ring, then propelled himself towards Travers, arriving just as a halo of light appeared around the hatch's frame. Once he killed his momentum on the other side, Alonso pulled a grease pencil from a belt pouch and wrote instructions on the hatch itself for any member of the crew who managed to find the relief station after they left.

<CH-2>FT-1>COMMAND>

Travers gave him an armored thumbs' up, and clambered through the hatch after him. The portable comms, maps, and first aid supplies they left behind could mean the difference between life and death for an injured crew member, but unless Jackson and the other teams could restore power, *Valiant* was dead in space and he people aboard her not far behind.

Our only hope of rescue is someone outside the hull—Hell, outside the battlegroup, most likely—figuring out not only where we are, but why we're here in the first place.

And if they can hurry up and tell me, I'd really appreciate it.

Alonso and Travers leapfrogged Harlan and Zager twice on their journey to the command center, dropping off supplies and messages as they went. By the time all four officers were gathered on the other side of the out hatch, the rest of the team was still a few stops away rigging safety lines between the final aid stations.

Harlan motioned to the hatch, and Alonso knelt down in front of it and locked his boots in place. Protocol demanded that the hatch be sealed during any unscheduled emergence, and without power the junior command crew inside—if they were still alive—were probably at a loss for how to open it themselves.

Troopers Carstairs and Maddox arrived, hooking the end of a safety line through the nearest catch ring. As soon as they were done, Alonso struck the hatch four times with his right gauntlet, his left pressed against the metal to feel any answering vibration. He knocked again, and to his great relief received three knocks in response.

Alive. Pressurized. Ready.

"I have three knocks, ma'am. Are we clear to proceed?"

"Open it up, Mr. Ramirez. Barclay, Harris, hold station where you are, and funnel any stragglers up to us."

"Yes ma'am."

Alonso drew a manual release lever from his kit, and slotted it into the hatch's emergency access panel. Maddox lined up beside him, positioning a chem lamp over his head.

Okay, here we go.

MARTIN

"DAMNIT, WHERE'S THAT EMERGENCY POWER?"

Captain Aloysius Martin was not happy. First, something came out of nowhere and smashed through his battle group. Then he'd lost his grip on the railing. And then just when he'd oriented himself for a secured position along a bulkhead, one of the wet-nose middies panicked and bounced him back out into open air.

If I find out which one it was, I'm going to enjoy showing the kid just how much dirt can hide on a deck, even when you're centimeters away with a tiny wire brush.

Floating blind through his command center, there was nothing he could do until one of the dozen or so screaming people in the same situation either guided him to a wall or followed his damned orders.

And I'm getting a little tired of waiting for answers.

"Sir, I don't know..."

"Captain, I can't..."

"I'm not sure, but..."

Aloysius felt something solid against his back, and used the hand he'd kept on his belt controls since he started tumbling to activate his boot magnets. The *SSSSHUNK* as they made a connection with whatever surface he'd found was the best thing he'd heard in the last five minutes, and it finally gave him something to work with.

Taking in a deep breath, he puckered his lips and gave a shrill, four-tone whistle. The ear-splitting noise had the desired effect, and he let the silence linger for a moment before speaking.

"Listen up! The next person who tells me what they don't know or can't do had better not let me recognize their voice. We have a problem. I want solutions, not excuses. So who's willing to start?"

There was a long moment of silence as his subordinates pondered the rest of their careers. Aloysius was about to speak again when he heard four knocks against some surface across the compartment. Three seconds later, they repeated, standard damage control procedure aboard starships.

There's someone out there!

Aloysius was about to order a response when someone in the same area found enough leverage to give an answering three knocks.

Alive. Pressurized. Ready. Looks like one of you kids was paying attention in class after all.

Aloysius closed his eyes and waited for the command center's access door to cycle. Whoever was out there likely had a portable power unit and came up here to get some idea of what happened. He'd have the answers he needed soon enough.

Aloysius heard the door squeal in protest as his rescuers cranked the manual release. There was a soft sound of escaping air, and through his lids he registered a soft glow.

Looks like I get to live at least a few minutes longer after all.

Opening his eyes onto the green light of a chemical hand lamp, Aloysius smiled at the realization that he'd come to rest inverted from ship normal. The hatch was cranked halfway, just enough for a half dozen crew in hardsuits to come in, but not so far that it couldn't be closed in a hurry if necessary.

The team leader's suit had what Aloysius thought was a red blaze across the shoulders, but in the chem light it could easily enough have been blue. What mattered most were the two circles on either side of their collar, and the professional way the officer was taking stock of the ruined command center.

And very close after it on the list has to be the induction pistol fixed to that chestplate. Whoever you are, you're not taking any chances, are you?

After slapping a tether box to the bulkhead, the lieutenant stepped aside and let the rest of the team go to work. A clear contralto came from the suit's external speaker, and even though no-one could see his face, Aloysius smiled as he recognized who'd come to find him.

"Who's in command?"

Mira Harlan had been with Aloysius for almost five T-years, and was a strong candidate for the captains list the next time there was an opening. If anyone could shed light on their current situation, it was she.

But she's not one of us. Not yet, anyway. There's still a lot that she doesn't know. And there's too much at stake to throw it all away on someone we haven't fully vetted.

Harlan's damage team spread out from the tether box, grabbing and stabilizing crew members as they went. One floated up to the center's nominal ceiling, and anchored themselves much as Aloysius had. Whoever it was planted an emergency lamp, and seconds later the compartment was full of light.

"Sir, at 1245 ship time, an unidentified object approximately 250 meters in length and massing almost 100 kilotons made a hyperspace transition at close range with the *Harrow*, and proceeded to destroy not only that vessel but the tenders *Cessnock* and *Gadwell*. I pumped six Geysers with full warheads into the bogey, and didn't even slow it down."

"Are you sure about that, Harlan?"

"Yes sir. At first we thought it was a rogue comet, but the composition was all wrong, and they don't generally make hyper emergences. The object collided with us forty seconds later, and then we lost comms and external sensors."

Aloysius took in this information while he looked around the command center. Charred panels warred with floating clouds of blood for his attention. His ship was dead, and several of his officers along with it. Commander Williams he knew about; Aloysius was standing next to him when his panel exploded. But the additional losses of Lieutenants Mackie and Charles effectively gutted his senior staff.

Aloysius waved Harlan over, then walked himself down the wall. It felt like running through ankle-deep mud, but at least he wasn't floating wild anymore. Harlan crossed the compartment by launching herself at the ceiling, then caroming down in a perfect shot to a space next to him. Her boots attached to the decking right about the same time Aloysius was upright relative to everyone else, and he had to admire her skill.

Showing off for the boss, Harlan? Or are you like me, and just don't like wasting time?

Aloysius motioned to Harlan's helmet, and the blank glass faceplate nodded. She raised gauntleted hands to her neck and released the helmet's seals, allowing him to see inside and have a more private conversation. The face inside was a match to her voice; sharp and uncompromising. Aloysius held her gaze for a few seconds while he deliberated. Finding something in her eyes he liked, he made his decision.

"Okay, Harlan, you've got my full attention right now. Tell me what happened to my ship."

MALIK

SOMETHING'S WRONG. I CAN'T MOVE MY-

Knives of pain stabbed through Malik's chest, and he decided to stop trying to speak. His eyes refused to focus, and he couldn't quite make out the voices speaking nearby. But they were somewhat familiar, so it stood to reason that at least two other members of the team survived the impact.

Broken arm, broken ribs. Cranial damage, possible infarction. Vision seems to be getting better, I can see some...

"...pupillary response. He's definitely trying to communicate, but there's no telling how much damage there really is. I'd need to unpack some of the..."

"...of the...tion. There's no telling how long we've got until we...pany."

Doria? Jantine? I think I hurt myself. You have...to...

"I said, can he be moved? We can't stay here."

Jantine's voice was getting stronger, but Malik still couldn't see her face, or much of anything else. All he could really make out was a blue-white flashing from somewhere off to his left, but he didn't want to risk more pain by turning to see what it was.

"No. Neither of us are in any shape to go anywhere. But I think I can reach him, with just a little more time. Malik, can you hear me?"

"Na. Na!" Malik's tongue wouldn't move he way he wanted, but from what he could tell Doria understood him. Then JonB's voice came from Malik's left, complaining as usual.

"What do you mean, you think you can reach him? Commander—Jantine, we need to start the descent process. He's got most of it programmed in, but I need your disarm codes. They're almost through, but I can do this!"

JonB, no. We're done. You have to, you have to…

Malik tried to move his arm again but couldn't. When Doria spoke again, her words seemed to strip away some of his pain.

"Relax, Malik. I'm here with you. Just picture in your mind what you want me to tell them, and I'll do the rest."

Picturing his computer closing on JonB's hands, Malik tried to focus on what she was telling him. Doria said she couldn't read minds earlier, but he could hear her voice a lot clearer than he could Jantine's or JonB's—almost as if it was coming from inside his own head. He felt her hand on his cheek, and more of his pain slipped away.

"NnnnNuooo."

"That was a no," said Doria, "in case you hadn't figured it out, JonB. He says not to proceed with his calculations."

"But it's plain as day! It's all right here."

"He says it won't work."

I do? Yes, no. No! That trajectory isn't for us. Tell Jantine to find another way down. Tell her, Redstone dreadnaught. Tell her…

Malik felt a pinching pain in his right shoulder, then a spreading warmth. Doria's hand moved from his cheek to the back of his neck, and something like feathers was moving around inside his skull. He had the impression of something else, something very sad nearby. Two *somethings* in fact, but Malik filed them away as problems to deal with later.

Redstone. Tell her!

Before Doria could relay his message, Jantine spoke.

"JonB, can you tell me anything about where we are? What's around us?"

"There's a big planet down there that we can get to, that's all I need to know. Mass readings match what we have on file for..."

Malik felt something slide into place in his mind, and he heard Doria's voice stronger than ever.

"I'm not exactly sure what it's called, but Malik wants you to know that we hit a ship. And that we need to find another way down to the planet."

"That's ridiculous! How are we supposed to complete the mission if we don't—"

"JonB," Jantine interrupted, "tell me right now if you think you can use those equations to pilot both containers. And remember that Doria's not the only one around here who's good at figuring things out."

Malik felt something new, a vibration of some kind coming from behind him. His back was against a hard surface, and since Doria was unwilling to move him it was likely one of the container's walls. What had JonB said?

"They're almost through..."

JonB wasn't saying anything now, and Malik tried to smile. He'd done it; he'd saved the sleepers. Jantine would take care of the rest— that's what she was here for.

There wasn't any more pain, but Malik still couldn't make his mouth move properly. Then the hand on his neck shifted, and he felt something brush against his right ear.

Doria's voice was soft, warm, and this time on the outside of his head.

"We don't have a lot of time, Malik. Is there anything else you want her to know? I'll be here to help you. Just tell me what to do."

Doria, I...

"It's okay. Jantine and JonB know how badly I'm hurt, but the others don't. The stims are handling most of the pain, and I can stay with you until it's done. Tell me what she needs to know. Just stay focused, and I'll be your voice for now."

Malik felt the paired sadness move inside him, and the strength of it was nearly overwhelming. But at the same time, it gave him some comfort, and the longer he was in contact with it, the less it hurt. Although he couldn't say how, he recognized the presence of the Omegas in his mind alongside whatever it was Doria was doing to him. He pictured their faces as best he could, and when he asked his question, he was sure they heard it as well

I never knew. Is it...are they like this all the time?

It felt to Malik as if the words were plucked out of his mind as soon as he thought them. When Doria's whispered response came a few seconds later, he had the distinct impression that she was smiling.

"All the time," she said. "Don't be sad. And that goes for the two of you as well. This is a natural part of life. This would have happened eventually in any event; you two will live longer than any of us."

Malik tried to find words of his own to share with the Omegas, but as soon as he decided on the right ones, he felt them flow away and knew the mods understood.

Okay, here's what we have to do.

DORIA

DORIA FELT HER BROKEN RIBS GRINDING INSIDE HER CHEST. THE PRESSURE bandage Harren applied before the second impact was likely doing more harm than good, but at least he'd dealt with the bones that had pierced the skin and slowed her bleeding down.

For now. There was no way to confirm the diagnosis without alarming the rest of the mods, but she could feel the cuts inside her body. Every movement let a little more blood flow, and there was nothing she could do to stop it.

Though she was still crouched over Malik, she could feel waves of anticipation pouring off Jantine and JonB standing behind her. Fighting to keep her voice calm, she relayed what Malik had seen on his screen in the seconds before the impact.

"It's hard to be sure, but he thinks there's probably just a few tender ships left out there. The slug was on a trajectory to hit the larger vessel. He keeps showing me something, a small rock of some kind. It's a...oh, I understand now. A red stone. Does that mean anything to you, Commander?"

Jantine gave an uncharacteristic gasp.

"A Redstone dreadnaught. Intelligence says the enemy has about a dozen of them, and they never travel alone."

Malik's thoughts signaled agreement, then he summoned up a

series of images that took Doria a few seconds to process.

"If I understand him correctly, he says if you move fast, you may be able to commandeer a scout ship, possibly a shuttle. But you have to leave us here. It's…it's the only way."

Doria lowered herself to the deck and turned to put her back against the wall next to Malik. In the flickering light of the computer screen, JonB's face matched his emotions: concerned, impatient, and more than a little frightened. But even though Jantine wasn't handling the situation well herself, she was in command, and needed the others to know it.

Like Malik said, it's what she's here to do.

"Can you handle this, Doria? Or should JonB stay with you?" Jantine's voice said she was back in control, even though Doria could sense doubt creeping in around the edges.

JonB's confusion deepened, then his expression hardened as he realized what was about to happen. Doria felt a touch of regret that he'd never truly opened up to her, but given who he was and why he was on the mission, there really wasn't a lot she could do for him until the colony was established.

And now…

"I can…we can do it. Malik's got an excellent visual memory, and my hands are still functional. It's not the kind of detail work I'm used to, but I'll adapt. And if you'll bring the computer a little closer, I should be able to make things a little easier for you in the short term."

Doria gestured to the computer, and JonB slid it closer to her hands. The screen was cracked, but still functional, and by guiding Malik's memories she brought the lights up enough for the mods to see each other clearly, instead of by dim emergency beacons.

It seemed like a lot longer than thirty minutes since she'd seen Jantine's face, but it seemed different now. It wasn't just the low light; her demeanor had definitely changed. It wasn't the uniform either; even with the faceplates open, the encounter suits gave everybody a little more confidence. This was something different, more funda-mental. Reaching out to her mind, Doria felt none of the uncertainty

Jantine had struggled with just a few hours before. She was every bit the commander now, and Doria tried to share some of it with Malik.

She'll be okay. They all will.

Jantine leaned closer. Her eyes conveyed her concern for Malik and Doria, but more for her second-in-command than for the Gamma. Doria shared as much of it as she could with Malik. His response was both immediate, and heartbreaking.

"It's okay, Jantine. He wants you to. Has for some time."

Jantine closed her eyes, and bent down to press her lips to his mouth. Malik couldn't move in response, but he didn't have to. This was about feelings, and feelings were what Doria did best.

The Omegas were already moving along the wall, orienting them-selves by the heat generated by what must be cutting torches on the other side. They weren't big on goodbyes, another thing she liked about working with them.

The rest of the team was lined up behind the Deltas, waiting for the attack to begin. Katra wasn't in very good shape either, but the Omegas were helping her place the breaching charges, and Doria knew they'd be fine too. It wasn't going to be an easy adjustment, but they'd been at this a while.

Besides, Jarl wouldn't let anything happen to Katra. Not while he was alive.

When Jantine finished, she moved over to Doria's side and handed her several grenades from a pouch on her harness. Even though it hurt, Doria pushed them away, and smiled. She answered for both herself and Malik.

"We're covered. And something tells me that you're going to need those a lot more than I will."

Jantine smiled, and stood up. Without another word, she walked over to the rest of the team and crouched into a firing position. She snapped her helmet's faceplate closed, and the rest of the team did the same.

Doria leaned a little closer to Malik and whispered to him.

"Malik, Do you want me to watch her for you?"

Malik surprised her with an image of a handheld, with text

scrolling across the screen. It took her a second to figure out what he was trying to do, but when she did she gave his hand a small squeeze and read his message.

No, it's all right. We have to finish the launch sequence. She'll buy us enough time to get the sleepers down safely, and once I confirm the team's launch, we can let go.

"Malik, I..."

What was it you said? It's going to be all right. We can do this.

"No. That's not it."

Before she could tell him, the breaching charges went off. Jantine and the Deltas sent a three-second burst of hell through the resulting hole, then stopped firing long enough for Jarl and Katra to go to work.

Doria couldn't hear any screaming from the other side of the wall, but the Omegas could see just fine. Through their eyes she watched the thermal blurs of her fellow Gammas tear through the much cooler forms of the enemy. The hallway was clear five seconds later.

The Omegas waited until Carlton and JonB were through, and then paused to look back at her and Malik. Then she felt them enter her mind, sharing their lives with her and showing Doria her part in them.

Doria had spent her life interpreting the emotions of others. The joy she felt when communicating like this was almost as good as the drugs Carlton had given her, but this time the Omegas weren't holding back. Doria finally experienced the full impact of feelings that they always held back from other mods. Doria let it fill up the corners of her mind, taking away her pain and giving her a few more minutes of clarity to work with.

She didn't bother to send her thanks through the link—none were necessary. She'd already said her goodbyes, and they were carrying away a part of her with them to share with their next Gamma.

Instead, Doria turned her thoughts back to Malik, and the job they still had to complete.

"Malik, you should show me how to set a timer on the destruct charges. I don't think I've got that much time left..."

RAMIREZ

1300 SHIP TIME, **SDF** *VALIANT*

ALONSO HANDED off a terrified middie to Maddox and waved away a cloud of smoke as he passed. Fire aboard a spaceship, even one as advanced as *Valiant*, was the second worst emergency imaginable. The fact that the smoke was drifting slowly don the corridor, joining a thin stream hovering just beneath the top grating, meant that the first might well be a reality too.

That's not good. If anything, there should be negative pressure inside the command center. We've got a breach somewhere.

Alonso angled his hand lamp around the compartment, trying to find the source. There was debris everywhere, floating alongside dead bodies and crew members who clearly had not been keeping up with their null-g exercises. The lamp wasn't strong enough to cover the entire compartment at once, but from the motion of the objects inside and the steady stream of smoke spilling into the corridor, Alonso was certain the compartment was sound.

Some good news at least. Now we all we have to do is deal with that smoke, figure out why it's there, and pray for survivors wherever the hull is breached.

We're so screwed.

Standing with one foot on either side of the out hatch, Alonso began keying in a message to Barclay and Harris at the aid station. But a flailing tech specialist slammed into his right arm. Her eyes wide with fear, and her face and tunic were splashed with dark stains Alonso strongly suspected were blood.

Alonso abandoned his message and moved her outside to perform a quick visual inspection. Finding no obvious source of injury, he led her to the catch ring, and tried to summon up his best bedside manner.

"It's going to be all right, ma'am. When you're ready, follow the safety line down the corridor to the aid station. We're going to take care of you."

She nodded dumbly, tossing small globules of blood into the air. They hung in place for a moment, then floated up toward the ribbon of smoke undulating down the middle of the corridor.

I'd almost forgotten we're tumbling. Damn, we need power and propulsion restored ASAP.

And to figure out where that breach is.

Wary of another airborne assault, he activated his suit comm and spoke into the team channel as calmly as he could, trying to keep his very real fear from alarming the rest of the team.

"I'm fairly certain we've got a breach on this deck. Harris, you should be seeing a smoke ribbon in a few seconds, find out where it's going and plug it up."

"Roger that."

Harris' voice was followed quickly by Mira Harlan's no-nonsense tones over their private network.

"Ramirez, we've got more casualties. I need you here with me now."

"Yes ma'am."

Alonso waited while two more members of first shift filed out the hatch, and by the time he got through Zager had installed an emergency lamp overhead, and Alonso saw exactly what she meant. Two of the floating bodies were definitely dead, and he saw Harlan and the captain standing over a third, half-buried under an exploded workstation. Harlan's faceplate was open, and the hard line of her jaw meant bad news all around.

Alonso waved a hand to catch Harlan's attention, gesturing first toward himself, then at the body under the workstation. She shook her head, then waved him over to help Zager with the other casualties.

Between the two of them, they were able to wrestle the floating corpses through the hatch and secure them in the corridor. Alonso was helping the last of command crew through to the safety line when Zager shot straight past them and on down the corridor, using the catch rings to bank around the corner with the fluid grace of an experienced spacer.

At least someone knows what they're doing around here.

Alonso clomped inside and clipped himself to the support rail He was about to move over to Lt. Harlan and the captain, when something slammed hard into the hatch behind him. Turning to look, Alonso saw a vac-suited crewman with an engineer's kit and an open helmet holding on to the hatch with both hands. The man took a quick look around the ruined command center before his eyes focused on Alonso—or rather, his rank pips.

"Sir...we got hit! There's something stuck in us, and it's cutting off power through the ship. We can't...well, I don't know if..."

Stuck in us...that would do it, but what manner of object could affect so many systems at once?

Alonso was about to press the excited crewman for details when the captain's booming voice sounded behind him.

"Stuck? Tell me what you saw, son."

The crewman flexed, then launched himself past Alonso a bit more forcefully than was required for so short a distance. Alonso tracked him right into Harlan's arms, who stopped his progress and left him floating near a support railing. The engineer clumsily hooked a tether from his work harness to the rail, then started talking to the captain too low for Alonso to hear.

MARTIN

ALOYSIUS TRIED NOT to roll his eyes, focusing instead on the first part of the breathless crewman's report. At his side, he saw Harlan also keenly intent on what the man was saying. Aloysius was a heartbeat faster with his question though, and Harlan wisely waited her turn.

She's got definite promise.

"Stuck? Tell me what you saw, son. That's all I can ask."

"Sir, Ma'am, the chief told me to get up here right away, said you'd definitely want to know about it. It's a ship, sir. They must have rammed us, but we've got no way of knowing who or how big."

The engineer's near whisper was annoying, but after a second of his story Aloysius was glad of it. He recognized the man as a junior engineer on Master Chief Henderson's watch. The name escaped him, but there were over two hundred people on *Valiant*, and most of them were new.

"Were" being the word of the day. As far as I know, I've got a little over a dozen people still alive on this ship, and all of them are in this compartment.

But a ship? How…no, who the hell found us?

"How do you know it's a ship, Mr. Carson? And where exactly did you come from?"

Harlan lowered her voice as well, matching the flustered crewman and forcing Aloysius to clomp a half step closer to hear them both. Harlan's damage control team was herding the injured out, but Aloysius didn't want the speculation to get too out of hand. The fact that they were still alive meant something, and he needed level heads around him to figure out what it was.

The engineer was able to handle the captain's scrutiny for the most part, but the ice in Harlan's voice left him momentarily speechless. To her credit, she didn't immediately dismiss the man's report as not fitting her facts, but like any trained tactical officer she wanted specifics, and not everyone thought in those terms during a crisis.

Plus, she knew his name.

Carson swallowed nervously, and his mouth worked a couple times before more words came out.

"Ma'am, we were rotating tertiary power modules on the maneuvering jets up in the hullspace when all hell broke loose. We couldn't hear anything, of course, but we sure as hell felt it. Since we were already into the lines, we ran a trace back until we found the breach.

"There was too much damage to see exactly what it was, and in that compartment we could only see a cross section of it. But it was definitely metal. And curved. It's a hull of some kind, or I'll eat my stripes. The breaching systems sealed up around it good and tight, but once we got back inside we found more of it on other decks. I can't tell you much more, other than it's not radioactive, and it's not one of ours."

Harlan's face twisted in a scowl, but Aloysius didn't think she was upset at Carson's story. He suspected she was working up a new explanation, and just couldn't get all the facts to line up.

"Harlan?"

The lieutenant cocked her head slightly, flicking her eyes to the captain before squaring her expression and turning her full attention on the engineer.

"Sir, I'm—Carson, how many decks did you check out before the

Chief Henderson sent you up here?"

"Three, Ma'am. We found some other debris as well, some space rock and such, but it was the same kind of metal. Definitely a ship of some kind."

When the engineer finished speaking, Harlan stared past him at the destroyed command center. The silence went on a bit long for his liking, so Aloysius prompted her with a question.

"What are you thinking, Lieutenant? "

Harlan blinked twice, and turned her head to look at the captain.

"Sir, I'm thinking that I very much want to know more about this supposed hull."

Aloysius nodded, and was about to send her to find out when Carson interrupted him.

"But Ma'am, it's..."

Harlan cut him off with an upraised gauntlet, and fixed him with a withering gaze.

"Carson, I'm sure the chief needs you right now more than we do up here. Tell him I want emergency power for this deck on standby, and to back away from whatever it is you found for now."

The engineer swallowed, then nodded.

"Yes, Ma'am."

Carson looked at the two officers as if expecting some further commands, but after a few long seconds realized that neither Harlan nor the captain were going to talk with him around. With more skill than he'd shown on arrival, he maneuvered himself so he was facing the out hatch, unhooked, and launched himself back into the ship.

Aloysius took a step forward and grabbed the rail, almost chuckling to himself at how close it had been while he was floating in the dark. The feel of it in his hands was reassuring, and helped to quell the roiling sensation in his gut. His eyes scanned the ruined command center.

What happened to my ship? And why now, when I'm so close...

"What is it, Harlan?"

"Sir, the bogey was moving too fast for a positive ident, but I can definitely tell you it wasn't a ship. No power signature, no outgassing after the Geysers hit. A salvo like that would have cracked a courier vessel wide open, and a hostile would have fired back instead of ramming us. My gut tells me it's a mined-out planetoid, but the mass is all wrong."

"Explain."

"There are rocks that size all around the system, but for the most part they're in stable orbits and fitted with claim transponders. We cleaned the roamers up a few centuries ago, and the rest belong to the mining companies. If something like that was flying around loose, we'd know about it long before it hit one of our ships, and it definitely wouldn't be this far above the ecliptic."

Aloysius nodded, acknowledging the unspoken question many of his officers had carefully avoided asking him over the past few days.

"I think it was a mass weapon, but I'm still clueless as to where it could have come from, or who would have fired it. I...we should scramble as many security teams as we can to midships. We have to assume a hostile incursion at this point, and I want to—"

Aloysius held up a hand to cut off Harlan's statement, and then moved it down to his belt controls and released his boots. He then motioned for the lieutenant to follow him as he shoved down the rail.

A few quick pushes and a hard grab brought him to his destination. Several members of Harlan's team were working to free a body from under a mass of wrecked equipment, but Aloysius waved them away. Activating his boots again, he knelt and searched at Bill Williams's neck for something. He heard Harlan touch down behind him, then her involuntary gasp as he pulled back his hand with a bloody circuit key in his grip.

"Lieutenant, I need for you to designate one of these crewmen as your replacement. As of..." Aloysius tried to establish a timeline in his head based on what Harlan had said, but one of the men nearby realized what he was doing and supplied him with an answer.

"1306, sir."

"1306 ship time, you are now the *Valiant's* executive officer, with the acting rank of Lieutenant Commander. Do you acknowledge this order?"

"Sir, yes sir. Mr. Ramirez, the squad is yours. Get me comms and power, then a shipwide status report."

"Aye Aye, Ma'am."

"Get to it, Alonso. We're dead and blind right now, and I'd like to fix both ASAP."

Aloysius made as good an attempt as he could at cleaning the blood from the command key before handing it to Harlan. She was a good officer, just not part of his inner circle. He already knew she could handle herself in a crisis, but nothing about her politics.

Well, only one way to find out.

"Harlan, you're right. We need a lot more intel before our next move, but there are a couple other things to do first. Get teams down there like you said, and have one meet us at my quarters. I want to get into my hardsuit as soon as possible, and we can talk on the way."

Harlan looked the captain in the eye for a few seconds, then nodded. She put the key into one of the small pouches and pockets affixed up and down her left arm, then resealed her helmet. Her hardsuit's speakers squawked back to life, and everyone in the command center stopped to listen.

"Alright, people, you heard the old man. Ramirez is in charge up here until we get back. Find me every trooper still mobile and scramble the best of the best to the captain's quarters. Get everyone else amidships weapons hot, and I want to hear someone's voice on channel three whispering in my ear before too much longer. Let's do it!"

As the repair crews acknowledged her orders, Aloysius oriented himself on the out hatch. But before he could float over to it, a squad of security troopers appeared just on the other side in with full defense gear, including laser cutters. He turned to Harlan, who shrugged.

"Well, that's one less thing to worry about. You men are with me and Lt. Commander Harlan now. Let's go."

A chorus of 'sir' came back at him, and Aloysius moved past the troopers into the corridor. Once out, he saw that someone—most likely Harlan's people—had slapped emergency beacons all the way down the corridor on their way up.

Aloysius started for his quarters with a practiced leap, sailing down the corridor ahead of the security escort with Harlan just a few meters behind. At the first junction, he held his release just long enough for her to draw a little closer, and once they were floating free again he spoke in a voice he was sure her suit mics could pick up.

"I don't have time to properly read you in on what you have to know, so for now just smile and keep following my orders."

Without hesitation, Harlan popped her faceplate again and answered in the same tones.

"Sir, I'm with you. We all are."

Aloysius smiled, but did not look back at her.

Of course you are, Harlan. That's what we told you to say back in training. It's certainly what they told me, and look how well that's turned out for us.

"Good, I appreciate it. Believe it or not, we have something more important to do right now than process damage reports, or even investigating whatever it was that hit us. There's a prisoner aboard who is vital to our survival. We are going to collect that prisoner now, and then move her to a secured shuttle."

Harlan slapped her chest to activate the suit's emergency lighting as they approached the end of the corridor. They were moving into areas she and her people hadn't secured yet, and Aloysius wondered to himself why he hadn't brought her into the fold before now.

Harlan did something with her left hand, and her boot jets flipped her heels-over-head. She landed on the bulkhead with her boots already magnetized near the emergency release and started working the hatch open. Aloysius stopped himself by grabbing a transit ring while several troopers performed maneuvers similar to Harlan's. Once the hatch was open enough to get gauntleted fingers into the gap, they added their suit-assisted strength to her purely mechanical efforts.

When the gap was wide enough, she swung herself inside, brandishing a weapon he hadn't seen her draw. Once Aloysius was through himself, he activated his own boots and attached them to the wall on the other side. He studied the faces of the men and women filing through the hatch, meeting the gaze of a sergeant who stopped on the other side of the hatch next to him.

"Dog it, and seal it tight. We're not coming back this way."

"Yes, sir." The trooper waited until Aloysius was through, then got to work. As Aloysius launched himself down the passageway he heard the sounds of an emergency hand welder in action.

Good man, he thought. *No questions.*

Aloysius waited until he came up beside Harlan before continuing his explanation. "In case you were wondering why we we're out here in the middle of nowhere in the first place, it's because no sane person is supposed to be looking in this direction. It's cost us twice as much fuel as it should have and most of my political capital to get us within striking distance of the planet below, and it's just our bad luck that someone else seems to have had the same idea."

"Sir?" He didn't have to see her face to know what expression she was wearing. It wasn't fear, it was the hard stare of an officer committed to a course of action she didn't fully understand

"We're at war, Ms. Harlan, whether the people down there know it or not. And I've gone too far down this road to let a broken ship and some lunatic firing mass drivers defeat me. We're going to secure our prisoner and regroup while I figure out how much firepower we've got left."

"Yes, sir. I was going to ask if there's anything I should know about the prisoner."

As Aloysius sailed through the still air of his dying ship with an armed force at his back, he felt almost as young as the officer he'd just recruited into his shadowy, interplanetary rebellion. She was asking the right questions, and that said a lot about who she really was. But as he'd said, the road to here was neither short nor straight, and there was no going back now.

"How much do you know about the Transgenic virus, Harlan? Because whatever you were told in school, I'm pretty sure we've found a cure."

KOŁODZIEJSKI

1320 SHIP TIME, SDF *INDOMITABLE*

HORACE WAS glad for the extra support of his chair, even though it meant suffering through the non-stop noise of the command center. Dr. Watson's latest death cocktail had his senses on overdrive, and he was still getting used to the blood substitute's effects on his body.

Closing his eyes, he tried to shut out the beeps and clicks of first and second shifts working their consoles, as well as the sounds of their breathing, the smell of their sweat, and a dozen other things he'd never noticed before these new drugs hijacked his brain.

It's like I'm wearing a costume made of my own skin. And even though it's smaller than it used to be, it still seems too big.

Indomitable had been back on station for over twelve hours now, and they were still no closer to finding Captain Martin and *Valiant*. All Horace's hopes now rested on finding his former friend and the gennie test subject he'd stolen, but no amount of wishing would summon them up for examination.

Where have you gone, Aloysius? Leaving the system gives you no advantage, and a battlegroup is impossible to hide in a populated system for this long. How many of your people know what you're doing?

How many know why?

There was a certain irony in the thought, given Kołodziejski's own circle of conspirators. But at least he knew his crews, could count on their loyalties. Martin was on the run from everyone, and the Earther was too new to the game to have amassed any significant powerbase in Fleet.

Unless, of course, he's borrowing someone else's...

An insistent beeping rose above the general susurrations of the pit, and Kołodziejski cracked open an eye to identify it. A red ship icon was flashing over Lt. Calas's station in time to the noise, and the profile was one he knew well.

Got you!

Calas' announcement was a heartbeat behind Kołodziejski's own recognition of the missing dreadnaught, and the Captain had to smile at the joy in his subordinate's voice.

"Sir, We've got a hit! A distress beacon from SDF *Valiant*, they're... my God, they're essentially right on top of us! Burning God only knows how much reactor mass to stay way up above the ecliptic and out of the normal space lanes, but close enough to...damn, now it's gone."

"Gone, Mr. Calas?"

Calas's hands flew through his holodisplays, and trajectories, coordinates, and fuel consumption data flashed through them faster than most of the people in the pit could follow. In truth, the rapid-fire images were driving a spike of pain into Kołodziejski's brain, but the story they told was of *Valiant's* last trip around the sun, how hard Aloysius Martin had tried to keep it out of sight, and how long it would take *Indomitable* to get there.

Very clever, Aloysius. But someone on your ship screwed up, and now you'll see what it's like to truly have me as a enemy.

"Yes, sir. From the location data encoded in the beacon, it was active for nine seconds, and we were in position to hear it for five of them. I can have the battlegroup there in...twenty-five minutes."

Kołodziejski didn't need to check Calas' math. Both men were Simaks, and their brains processed information much faster than other humans. It was a necessary adaptation to life on Mars during the early days of colonization, but a natural one, rather than a forced change brought on by the T-virus.

And you want to cure me of this too, Doctor Watson? I don't think so.

First shift held its collective breath, and every eye turned to their captain. Kołodziejski took a moment to savor their loyalty, then set them to their tasks.

"Plot an intercept course, Mr. Calas. Maximum acceleration. Instruct the rest of our ships to follow as best they can, but I want us to be the first ship there. Ms. Monahan?"

"Sir!"

"Analyze that signal for me, if you would."

First shift's communications chief would normally have reported the distress beacon herself, but Alexandra Monahan was manning Auxiliary Control while Calas conducted the search for *Valiant*. Not that it mattered much—control surfaces on a Redstone dreadnaught were interchangeable, and Kołodziejski had made sure that everyone on his command crew knew the ship at least as well as he did himself.

Calas swiped *Valiant's* icon over to Monahan, and started relaying coordinates to the rest of *Indomitable's* battlegroup. There was a brief shudder as the dreadnaught shifted course and left the other seven ships behind, accelerating at a rate far faster than any of them could hope to match.

Two quick steps brought Kołodziejski to her shoulder, and by the time he got there Monahan had surrounded *Valiant* with as much data as *Indomitable* could process from the abbreviated transmission, including the probable positions of the rest of Aloysius Martin's battlegroup.

Excellent. One more order I don't have to give, and another example of why first shift has the highest efficiency ratings on the ship.

And a reminder of why I conduct most of my important work on third...

"Thoughts, lieutenant?"

Monahan's lips pressed together in an almost frown.

"I'm not sure, sir. Distress beacons don't just shut down. As long as there's power, even from solar batteries, it should keep broadcasting. Maybe it's the odd alignment, but I've tracked signals from out past the Kuiper Belt in the past, and they were active long after the crew aboard had died."

Monahan didn't know it, but she'd just touched off her captain's nightmare scenario: something happening to the one chance he had for a cure.

If Lt. Monahan's projection was accurate, most of *Valiant*'s battlegroup was connected by tight beam links when the beacon activated. But only *Valiant* had enough power to reach the FTL comm network from their position, and the battlegroup was seemingly intact.

But why send a distress signal if no-one's listening? What am I missing here? Unless…

"Lieutenant, this looks like a deployed sensor web, but shouldn't there be more points of data?"

Monahan rotated the display, furrowing her brow as she searched for whatever she'd missed. As she did, Kołodziejski gave her a small nod of approval, but kept his eyes on the plot as she spoke in case something else jumped out at him.

"There should be pods, sir, but none are deployed. There's no other reason to have this configuration."

Almost, Alexandra. Almost. But then again, I have more data than you do on exactly who it is we're looking for. Keep at it, though. You're almost there.

"Pull up the transponders for the battlegroup, Ms. Monahan. And work out a minimum power scanning solution for our intercept. If there are any other signals out there, I want you to be the first person to find them."

Signals…why does that make me feel uncomfortable?

Something wasn't tracking right for Horace, and he wasn't going to find the answers hovering over Monahan's shoulder. He moved back to the command chair, and pulled up his own displays.

Thanks to Watson's drugs, Kołodziejski could feel the steady thrum of *Indomitable*'s system drives as she accelerated to a higher solar orbit, and the virtual representation of her on the plot as she twisted through cislunar space filled him with pride.

I don't know if it's worth dying for, but this is the best feeling I've had in a long time.

A notification popped up at the edge of the plot, Lieutenant Monahan's face hovering over three names and an apology.

<HARROW>GADWELL>CESSNOCK>SRY>

Kołodziejski pulled up her new projection, letting it spin into place over his left hand. Monahan was no Simak, but she'd ended up at the right answer anyway. A battleship and two of *Valiant*'s missile tenders were absent from the sensor net, and the cone of null data where they should have been pointed straight at their mother ship.

"Mr. Calas. What's the maximum deceleration you can give me at the intercept?"

Kołodziejski intentionally omitted the word "safe" from his request, and the answer he got was in line with what he expected.

"A fourteen-G shunt should give us plus-one relative on intercept, with enough v to maneuver if necessary. Assuming, of course, we don't break apart in the process."

"Do it."

"Aye, captain. Revised time to intercept…ten minutes."

Sorry people. But I'll risk a lot more than this ship and everyone on it to get that gennie back. And since this maneuver may actually kill me, I don't have time to feel bad about it either.

Kołodziejski returned his focus to the holo of *Valiant* and her remaining ships, registering Calas's voice on the shipwide channel and a switch to emergency lighting with only passing attention. Nothing about Martin's positioning made any sense, other than the obvious lack of scrutiny it afforded him.

Why hide this close to Earth and Luna and not do anything about it? And what could possibly have happened to three of your ships so suddenly it didn't even register on your…

Earth. Of course.

Kołodziejski brushed away *Indomitable* and moved *Valiant* up and to the right as high as he could reach from his chair. He then added the Earth to the projection, causing both dreadnaughts and their assorted support ships to shrink into tiny red dots. Bringing his hands together, he reduced all three bodies even further, then added a fourth—the approximate position of *City of Lights* almost thirty-seven hours prior to the distress beacon.

This makes even less sense than the signal your Earther found, Markus, but what we don't know about hyperspace could fill every data core ever made, and we've seen time distortions like this before.

So, nine seconds of beacon, and an unknown amount of time before it was triggered. Hawking *and* Tyson *were holding station one hundred thousand kilometers away, so that puts* Harrow *here, and emergence...*

Kołodziejski input the final coordinates, then let the bogey's course propagate across the solar system. He accepted a bite guard from one of the orderlies now circulating through the command center, but waved away a tranq shot, or any pills from the dispenser.

Can't chance losing consciousness. Not now. Not without knowing what's out there.

The orderly shrugged, then moved on to repeat the process with Lieutenants Calas and Monahan. Kołodziejski activated the chair's deceleration cushion, then pulled the restraints across his chest as tight as he could tolerate.

Even with the considerable processing power of *Indomitable*'s dedicated command core, the plot took two minutes to complete, which Kołodziejski marked against the countdown to deceleration Calas had displayed in every compartment of the ship.

Five more minutes. Five minutes until I know for sure. And God help us all if I'm right.

Since Earth's gravity was depressingly constant, for an emergence wave to bend around the planet and cast a hyperspace shadow in the vicinity of *City of Lights* a day before it actually arrived whatever it was that had come out in the middle of *Valiant's* formation had to have been traveling at a significant fraction of the speed of light. Regulations held SDF vessels to no more than twenty gravities when transiting a hyperspace corridor, fifteen less than the maximum thrust *Indomitable* was boosting right now.

And we're far and away the fastest ship in Fleet. Only a madman would come out of hyperspace at that velocity, on a course that would send it rocketing out of the system into interstellar space.

A madman, or a gennie.

"Mr. Calas. Weapons hot."

"Aye, sir. Charging energy lances and point defense cannons, Geyser crews on standby. Four minutes to intercept."

"Ms. Monahan. Drop an FTL buoy with all your analysis, and prep a message for our battlegroup. Protocol Alpha. I repeat, Protocol Alpha."

A tad ironic, given what we were chasing when this all started, but I have no choice now but to order us to full alert.

"Ladies and gentlemen, we are now at war."

Three minutes to intercept…

MARTIN

1324 SHIP TIME, SDF *VALIANT*

"WHAT EXACTLY AM I looking at here, sir?"

Harlan's confusion was understandable. Aloysius had his own doubts about the sleeper tank installed in the Environmental Systems bay, but as the person who'd put it there and arranged for an independent power supply and round-the-clock guards, he had at least some of the answers she was looking for.

Harlan was using a private suit channel for the question, so he responded in kind. So far, neither had received any signals from the main comms, but Harlan's damage control teams were the best in the fleet and it was only a matter of time before they'd need to have their stories straight.

"That, Commander, is humanity's future. It's what the gennies call an Alpha, one of their leaders."

Aloysius didn't offer more information, letting Harlan draw her own conclusions as to why it was aboard *Valiant*.

The techs were fitting the bulky unit with a grav harness, but Aloysius's eyes went as always to the doll-like face of the being in deepsleep inside. Whatever dreams he and his co-conspirators had of taking back their destiny rested inside that perfect head, and had done so for longer than he'd been alive.

"It's one of the first ones, actually. We found it in a crashed gennie transport on a frozen planet I'm not cleared to tell you about. But it had been there for some time, so long in fact that the Alphas in the Colonies now are much, much different biologically."

This time he'd aroused her curiosity, and Harlan turned her suited head to look at him directly. Aloysius saw the reflection of his own helmet in her visor, and found the metaphor apt.

Go ahead then, ask it. It's what I'd do in your position.

"With respect, sir, how is this thing supposed to help us?"

Aloysius jetted forward, motioning for Harlan to follow. His hardsuit was the same model as hers, minus all the pouches and extra weapons. And although the extra time he spent reclaiming it and a few personal effects from his quarters might still bite him in the ass, it was worth it to be fully mobile again. He used a gauntlet jet to stop himself, then placed the same hand on the sleeper unit.

"The gennie bloodlines, or mods, as they call themselves, stabilized about two centuries ago. Every one of them comes out of the womb perfectly designed for their role in Colonial society, and then they spend a dozen or so years in a crèche downloading all the education they need to fulfill it.

"This one though..." Aloysius's voice trailed off as he thought about the magnitude of what he was saying, "this one isn't done yet. Its genes are still in flux, being acted on by a version of the Transgenic virus we haven't seen in centuries. When we found it, well, it changed everything."

Harlan's shoulders shifted slightly, and Aloysius wished he could see her face.

Do I really have to right to involve her in this? So far she's just following my orders, but soon there'll be a line she can't uncross.

Aloysius nodded to a vac-suited tech, who released the clamps securing the sleeper unit to *Valiant*'s environmental systems and power grid. The damage to his ship hadn't propagated this far, and the unit's independent power supply was still operational. Watching the techs work, Aloysius was glad Harlan had come looking for him first—he doubted the guards he'd posted would have deterred her for very long if she'd chosen to restore the ship's air and heat instead.

Aloysius switched over to an area broadcast and spoke to the crew. His real crew, the ones he'd selected for loyalty over the past few months. That group also now included Harlan and part of the security team that followed them from the command center.

One other benefit of stopping off at his quarters was a quick consultation of their personnel files—all but three of them were on Bill William's expanded list. He'd had Harlan send those he wasn't sure about to the squads forming up around the intruder object, one to each deck, to deliver his orders.

Stand fast. Observe.

"All right people, let's move out. We're making for transfer bay six, the captain's shuttle. No delays, we'll apologize for any bruised shins or feelings later."

Aloysius watched the security team move into place both ahead and behind the now-mobile piece of history, as well as taking up positions behind himself and Harlan. Like Harlan, they had a lot of gear affixed to their hardsuits, and Aloysius was sure it was all meant for causing damage. Harlan's kit was a combination of extra ammunition and a variety of tools the captain didn't recognize, but he was sure she had quite a few nasty surprises hidden away as well.

Ammunition. Should have brought some more of my own, but I'm hoping it won't come to that. If I can't get the job done with only one pistol...

As soon as it was clear of the bay doors, he nodded to Harlan, who jetted up to kill the portable lighting unit. She detached one of the boxlike compartments on her back and stowed the light away, returning everything to its proper place in a fluid movement.

Harlan twisted through the air as she came back down to land beside him, and the two officers started floating after the rest of the team. Several troopers were waiting on the other side of the hatch; after they dogged it behind them, it would be as if they were never there.

"Still with me, Mira? This can't be an easy thing to learn about, especially today."

Harlan floated silently alongside him for a few meters before speaking.

"Yes, sir. No problems here. I'm assuming you'll give me the full story on who 'we' are before I get shot for treason, but I'm with you."

"I appreciate that, Harlan. More than you know. And it's not treason we're facing, but extinction. We have been, ever since the first gennie mutants expressed. But that one"—Aloysius waved ahead —"it's still cooking. Still mostly human, and with the technology we have now we can properly analyze the changes it's going though and reverse the process."

"Reverse, sir? Are you saying…that we…"

Aloysius had a very real sense that Harlan was about to dig in her metaphorical heels, and spun himself to face her directly.

"No, Lord no. You have to believe me, Harlan, we're not talking about vivisection, or weaponization. We, our people, are looking for a vaccine at best. I don't want to eliminate the gennies, I just want to save the human race! Those of us who are still human, still able to call ourselves that."

This time Harlan did stop, jetting to a halt. Aloysius did the same, bringing up his internal visor lights and making his faceplate clear so she could see his expression. Almost instantly, Harlan did the same, and for the first time since she'd joined him in the command center he could see real doubt in her eyes. She reached out and grabbed his shoulder, locking herself into the same plane of reference. Though they were drifting slightly, they were now doing it together, and he thought that was just fine.

Here it is, Aloysius. Decision time. She's already made up her mind, but she needs to hear the words.

"You said we were at war, sir. I need to know right now with whom, and for how long."

Aloysius leaned forward to touch his helmet to Harlan's. Once he was sure she he had her complete attention, he made a show of moving his eyes down to the left. Aloysius narrowed his focus on the holographic icon that turned off the private channel they'd been using, and waited.

Harlan's eyes tightened, searching his face for some clue as to his intentions. Through their joined faceplates he could hear her breathing, then heard it stop as she made the same mental connection. Without turning her head, she scanned the edge of her peripheral vision for the security troopers that were still behind them in the passageway. When they made no overtly hostile move, she dropped her focus to the lower left of her own display, and killed her comms.

"Go." Her voice was muffled after passing through two faceplates, but its tone was colder than interstellar space.

"Harlan, the reason we're out here, out of contact with the fleet and burning hard to stay far enough above the ecliptic that no one will even think to look for us is because there are people who want to do the exact same thing you were just about to accuse me of. There is a faction in the System Defense Force that's not content with keeping the most important human being in the universe on ice, and from this moment on you have to assume that anyone you know could be the enemy."

Aloysius watched the realization set in, how carefully her eyes stayed fixed on his, how fast the breaths started coming when she finally remembered to breathe. He remembered the cold line of sweat at the back of his neck when Admiral Worthy pulled him aside during a hyperspace hull survey just after he'd been given command of *Valiant*, when he realized the man he'd idolized for half his life was prepared to shove him off into interdimensional space if he gave the wrong answer.

The same moment Aloysius realized his superior officer was contemplating genocide, and that he was willing to do anything in his power to stop him.

"I didn't find the Alpha, Harlan. I stole it. Then I stole this whole battlegroup, and parked it out here until I could be sure of who I could trust. You can hate me for what I'm planning, you can hate my methods, but you have to believe me when I say that I'm one of the good guys here."

"How?"

Aloysius was taken aback by the simple question. There were so many things she could have asked, so many different ways he could have answered why. But Harlan didn't want justification. She didn't want an explanation. She wanted a reason to trust him, and to believe.

He had an answer. Of course he had an answer. But it pained him to even think about it, and explaining it was even worse.

"Because gennies always travel in pairs, and the fleet has already tried to kill one of them. Tried, and succeeded. If we can't protect that little gennie girl in there, I think they're going to use the virus to kill us all..."

KOŁODZIEJSKI

"…AND…NOW! 0.8 relative, all systems nominal. Beginning my scan."

Bob Calas's voice gave no sign of the crushing deceleration *Indomitable* had just completed, and the rest of Kołodziejski's weary command crew took this as their cue, unhooking themselves from acceleration harnesses and getting back to work. Horace was too weak to do anything but spit out his bite guard, and second later, all he could think about was the twisted, tumbling wreckage of *Valiant* on the main holo display.

What have you done to me now, Aloysius?

Nothing about the scene made any sense. What should have been a functioning battlegroup was instead a miniature asteroid field, with ships and stones tumbling through space in no particular direction. *Valiant* herself was floating dead, with a massive rock buried in her midsection, pressed into the ship like some sort of geologic parasite.

"Analysis."

The word almost caught in his throat, but Calas and Monahan were each ready with an answer. In their rush to comply, they started talking at the same time, adding even more beats to the tom-toms banging in his head.

"Sir, as suspected, I have no transponder hits from *Harrow*, *Gadwell*, or *Cessnock*. The extent of *Valiant*'s damage is as yet unknown, but I-"

"I have a ping, captain. The package is secure, but on the move. I have comm requests from *Hawking* and *Tyson*, collecting their logs now."

"Activate Alpha protocol, Mr. Calas. Ms. Monahan, please continue."

Alexandra had stopped talking when she realized Kołodziejski was paying more attention to Bob, but her hesitation now definitely drew his full focus.

"Ms. Monahan, is there a problem?"

Another few precious seconds ticked by before her answer. Kołodziejski tried to lean forward and read her displays himself, but the harness dug into his shoulders, and everything went white for a second.

"...pods, sir. About half as many as there should be, and they're not using the normal frequencies. Trying to decipher their encryption now, sir."

Pods...wha...where am I...

Kołodziejski felt a hand on his shoulder, and the harness fell away. A blur to his left resolved into Caroline's face, pinpoint rainbows swimming around her concerned expression as she dipped her head to whisper in his ear with more emotion than he expected.

"Don't worry, Horace, I'm right here. I've got you."

Kołodziejski matched her gaze as she pulled away, hoping his weakness had not embarrassed her. And even though he drew strength from their brief contact, he worried again that any association with him in his current state would ruin her forever. But once again, Caroline had given him what he needed, and it was enough to bring him back to himself.

"Get us in there, Mr. Calas. I want you and Commander Annahko aboard *Valiant* ASAP. Ms. Monahan, I'm sending you an override sequence. As soon as you crack that pod network, I want you to lock it down. Nobody talks to anybody but us from now on."

On another ship, with another crew, Kołodziejski would have asked for confirmation before moving on to the next problem. Instead, he tapped in the command codes for *Valiant*'s battlegroup, and turned to watch Caroline organizing strike teams for herself and Bob to board the damaged vessel.

"-n't care if you're worried about the intercept. Get the shuttles prepped and ready to fly in five, or I'll be down there myself in six to do it for you!"

"Captain, I have secured group communications. Should we begin retrieval?"

Monahan had a valid question. Whatever data the pods had collected would go a long way to explaining what had happened, but bringing unvetted Earthers aboard *Indomitable* was too great a risk.

"No. We need to know more. Analyze the logs from *Hawking* and *Tyson*, and continue monitoring their systems. I don't want any more surprises today."

"Yes, sir."

"Mr. Calas?"

"Almost ready, sir. With all this debris, it's difficult to chart a clear path. Also, I think whatever hit *Valiant* is messing with our scans. I'm not reading anything from it, and precious little else from the surrounding sections. But I can get our teams within a few hundred meters of the package, and that should be enough."

There was nothing Kołodziejski could say to stress the importance of recovering the gennie test subject to Calas that he didn't already know, and it seemed trite to wish him good luck. Instead, he just nodded his approval, and then waved him on his way. Caroline locked down her station and followed after Bob, but came back to his side as Kołodziejski motioned her over.

In as hushed a tone as he could manage, he said, "Let Bob take point on this one. You're too important to the ship, and to me, to lose. But if you have to make a choice, get his cargo off first. He knows the score."

Annahko narrowed her eyes, and Kołodziejski wasn't sure if it was because of his sentiment, or that he was keeping yet another secret from her. But she still took his hand, squeezing it gently before passing behind his chair and out the hatch.

Savoring the pain, he bit his lip and studied Lt. Monahan's revised plot. Her initial analysis of the beacon data was good, but with the full sensor web to work with she'd constructed a remarkably detailed model of events, complete with time codes.

The emergence of the unknown object now lodged in *Valiant* was marked by a massive burst of radiation that completely scrambled the battlegroup's collected sensors for three seconds. In that time, the object plowed through the *Harrow* and began tumbling through the rest of the battlegroup. Two full spreads of Geysers met it after *Cessnock* and *Gadwell* were destroyed, and the combined impacts had no effect other than redirecting the object directly towards *Valiant*.

On impact, there was another radiation discharge, and then pieces of the *Harrow* started impacting the remaining ships of the battlegroup. Their captains wisely pulled back out of the engagement area, reporting minor damage and isolated power failures.

"Captain," said Monahan, "I've redirected *Valiant*'s externals through the pod network, and now have control of their core. What's left of it, anyway. It looks like someone's been deliberately taking nodes offline on the fore decks, and everything behind that rock is still dark except for the engines. She's not going anywhere now, but could if she had to, I think."

"Good work, Monahan. Plug Mr. Calas into what you have, and keep digging. Focus on security feeds, if you can get them. I need to know who's alive on that ship, where they are, and what they're doing."

"Yes, sir. I'm on it. Any message for *Valiant*'s battlegroup?"

Kołodziejski had indeed considered what he might say to the traitors who had followed Captain Aloysius Martin into hiding, but decided to wait until the rest of his own ships arrived. Not only would a show of force make his point better than any speech, but if Bob and Caroline could reclaim both the gennie and the stolen research data before they arrived, it was one less thing he'd have to explain to the Reclamation council about why he'd been looking for *Valiant* in the first place.

After all, dead men tell no tales, and history is certainly rewritten by the victors.

"Keep a channel ready, lieutenant. I've got something in mind for when the time is right."

RAMIREZ

A SMALL CHEER went up in the command center as the lights came on, followed by a shout of alarm as a workstation shorted out in a shower of sparks.

Damn, missed one.

Alonso made a mental note to amend the damage control protocols. In hindsight, draining any residual charges from the holo-emitters before restoring power was an excellent idea, but since a complete systems failure like this was unheard of aboard a Redstone dreadnaught, it wasn't something he or the rest of the team thought to check before getting the compartment back on line.

So many things about today are completely fucked, what's one more fire to put out?

Other than the sparking console, *Valiant*'s command-and-control center was now theoretically functional, a minor miracle given how little time and how few materials he'd had to work with. In addition to power and life support, Alonso's team had restored grav, and cleared out most of the wrecked equipment. But the comms were still down, and *Valiant* was still tumbling, cut off from the universe around them. The damage reports they did have were arriving from around the ship via runners and the fire control team's private network, and none of them were good.

I'd need a dozen teams and a space station to get this ship fully operational, and we still haven't found that breach.

After getting checked out at the aid station, about half the middies from second shift returned to help with the repairs, and Alonso was glad to have the extra hands for a while. Despite their relative inexperience, they'd all earned a place aboard *Valiant*, and a few of them were skilled enough to assist the fire teams as they attempted to rewire the ship's systems, one deck at a time.

But even with half a dozen people in the command center, it was eerily quiet. The constant stream of information that should be flowing in from around the ship wasn't, and Alonso had no idea of how to get it back.

Lucky for me, I don't have to do it alone.

Sealing his helmet so he could access the team's network only made the aural isolation worse. It did cut him off from the smell of the command center though, for which he was happy. It would take a while for the scrubbers to clear away the haze of smoke and blood and worse he'd been breathing in for the last half hour.

Keying up the network, Alonso saw that four of the eight team members out searching were in communications range. Travers was the farthest out—if you didn't could the blank spot in his display representing Mira Harlan—so Alonso directed his comments toward him.

"Travers, I need to get air moving back this direction. Any progress on plugging our mystery leak?"

"Negative, Ramirez. And I've lost contact with another repair crew. There's plenty of power for the handheld comms, but there's some kind of intermittent interference all over B-deck. Over."

"Roger that. I'm sending the others out to help you look, there's not much else we can do without comms and sensors. We also haven't heard anything from LCDR Harlan since she took herself out of the team channel. If you see her, tell her I'm still working on getting shipwide back up and running."

"Will do, Alonso. Travers out."

Alonso turned to face Carstairs and Maddox, who were already gathering their gear. With a nod, he sent them on their way, and returned his attention to the damaged station.

Now let's see about getting you back up and running.

Travers was right, there was more than enough broadcast power from the emergency network to run the ship, if they could convince the systems to switch over to it. But like the damaged console, *Valiant* shut down when whatever hit them interrupted the primaries, and was convinced that turning itself back on was a bad idea.

One thing at a time, Alonso. One thing at a time.

Damage Control 101 meant disconnecting the station from *Valiant*'s non-existent power, and replacing all the holo-emitters in the panel before attempting any fancy workarounds. After verifying there was no residual charge in the system, installing new banks took about a minute each, and testing them all another five.

Satisfied with his work, Alonso plugged a cable from his suit into the workstation, and sent a pulse through the emitters. He already knew they were functional, but seeing them in action was the final test.

But instead of the blue test pattern he expected, he got a red, low resolution holo of a small compartment, a blurred face, and a very rumpled jumpsuit. A second later, an equally red light flashed in the image, and the person on the other end of the improbable holo spoke.

"It's about fucking time! What the hell are you people doing up there?"

Alonso recognized the voice of Lt. Lucas Garza instantly—after all, he'd spent most of the morning chasing down hyperspace anomalies with him and his team. But it was crisis time now, and their usual banter would have to wait.

"Lucas, this is Alonso. What's your status, over?"

"My status? My fucking status is that I'm stuck in a fucking sensor pod with a broken arm, a big fucking wall of fucking rock outside my porthole and no fucking contact from you for almost a fucking hour. That's my fucking status, thank you very fucking much!"

I might have deserved that. Then again, I'm technically in command of Valiant *right now, so I need answers more than arguments.*

"Lucas, listen closely, I don't know how much time I have. *Valiant* was struck amidships by some kind of object…"

"No fucking shit!"

"…and power and comms are down everywhere. I only just now got Command up and running, we're cut off from the rest of the battlegroup, and I need to know how you're sending this signal. Over."

Garza sat back in his chair, and was silent for almost a minute. The transmission wasn't good enough for Alonso to make out much of the pod, but there was enough out of place to suggest that Garza's experience during the impact had gone much worse than his own.

"So here's the deal. I boosted the tight beam transmitter, and have been rotating through all the frequencies I can generate every few minutes. Occasionally I hear voices, but until I got you I couldn't make out who's speaking or what they're saying.

"The pod is intact, but the hatch won't open, and I honestly don't think there's anything on the other side. I can detect traces of what's left of our sensor web out there, but it's way out of alignment. Oh, and something's draining my batteries, so if you have a clever plan to get me out of here, I'd love to hear it."

Alonso was surprised by the almost clinical detachment with which he took in the news of Lucas' situation. They'd come aboard together when *Valiant* last resupplied at Earth, and in the months since they could hardly be described as friends. But there was no time to make up for that now—*Valiant* was dying, despite the best efforts of her crew.

And some of us aren't going to see her through to the end.

"Lucas, we're not much better up here. Blind and deaf, really. I can try to get a crew out to you, but I think you're right about the hatch. Reports of the object have it occupying several decks, and we still don't know what it is."

"Well that's just fucking great, isn't it?"

"Lucas, I…"

"Listen, don't sugarcoat this. My O2 is fine, but I'm down to 60% power. I blew out half my board trying to reconfigure near-space sensors into an emergency beacon, and the fact that someone's actually listening to tight beam is the only good news I've had in a while. But it sounds like you don't know what's happening either."

Tight beam. A pod's tight beam transmitter is locked on the ship's main array while deployed, and requires a constant verification loop to operate. Something that wasn't possible until I brought the console back up, and initiated the same kind of loop using the test signal.

"Alonso? You still with me man?"

"Yeah, sorry. I might have an idea about that, but I'll need to disconnect for a few minutes. Hang tight, Lucas. Command out."

Alonso disconnected the cable, and the blurry holo faded from view. If he was right, re-initiating contact would be easy, as long as Lucas kept pumping his dwindling reserves into the tight beam transmitter. But Alonso's orders from LCDR Harlan were clear: comms, power, and a shipwide status report.

And I don't think Lucas will like my plan for that any more than I do.

Alonso re-opened the workstation, then removed the transceiver connecting it to *Valiant*'s data network. With the working theory that none of the ship's thousands of hard-wired systems would function with an unknown mass draining power and interrupting signals, trying to repair any of them was a waste of time. Not only was it a distraction he didn't need, but exactly the kind of problem he was on the ship to solve.

Garza just gave me the missing piece of the puzzle, and now I know what the picture really is.

He then disconnected the console completely from ship's power, then dragged the backup generator into the command center and connected it directly to the workstation. Taking an emergency transmitter from his kit, he keyed it to the fire control team's private network, and then wired it into the workstation.

Ok, let's see what blows up next.

In his helmet display, Alonso pulled up the team channel, and was relieved to see Carstairs and Maddox still within range. The rest of his team's indicators were dark, but no-one was due to check in for another ten minutes.

"Team, I need your help with something. Where are you?"

"B-41," replied Maddox. She'd made good time since leaving Command, and was now most of the way towards the Object. "I've hooked up with a maintenance crew, and we're going to check out the impact zone."

"Good plan. But first backtrack to the last generator you dropped, I need you to trigger its beacon. Carstairs, how about you?"

"Just dropped one in DF-8. Any particular frequency?"

"Ours. Send me a ping when it's done, I think I know what's causing our power problems."

"Roger that."

"Give me sixty seconds, Mr. Ramirez. I'll get it done," said Maddox, and the tech's indicator winked out. Carstairs did the same a second later, leaving Alonso alone again with his thoughts.

We've got backups for everything on this ship, except ourselves. And despite the repairs we've made so far, we're only a step or so up the ladder from Lucas in his pod, waiting around for someone to come save us from whatever the hell killed our ship.

Well, I'm tired of waiting.

Right on schedule, Carstairs and Maddox pinged the network. Alonso read two signals from each of their locations, as well as two from his own. One for each tech, and one from each of the generators.

Alonso brought the workstation up to 50% power, and initiated a confirmation loop. A few seconds later, a perfect image of Lucas Garza and his sensor pod appeared in front of him, and another point appeared on the network.

"Lucas, I need you to launch your pod."

Garza was silent for a few seconds, then straightened up in his chair.

"With respect, I don't think that's a good idea, Mr. Ramirez. Over."

Alonso didn't either, but it was the only plan he could come up with that had any chance of success.

"You're only in contact with us now because your pod thinks you're already free of the ship. And if I'm right, the longer you stay where you are, the more power you're going to lose. I need you to get clear of *Valiant*, and then initiate contact with as many of the other pods as you can. Make all the noise you need to, but get them talking."

Garza used his left arm to activate a wired readout on a very charred console, then nodded.

"All right, I think I see what you're trying to do, Alonso, but without airlock pressure I'm going to have to use my emergency reserve. Why not call in the rest of the battlegroup?"

Alonso had been wondering that himself over the last half hour, and gave Garza the only explanation he'd come up with.

"Because I'm not sure they're around anymore. At least three of them were destroyed by that rock next to you when it popped out of hyperspace, and we haven't heard a peep out of them since. The rest of them either bugged out, or are just as screwed as we are right now.

"If you're right about the sensor web being active, they'll find you when you start broadcasting. But our priority right now is establishing communication with our own people. Stay on this channel, and get as many other pods active as you can. Copy?"

Something halfway between a frown and a smile settled on Lucas' face, and Alonso knew he understood the rest of the plan as well. He slowly fastened his harness with his good arm, careful not to jostle the broken one any more than necessary.

"Roger that, Command. Keep a light on for me. Garza out."

Without the data core, Alonso couldn't confirm a successful launch. But the holographic image of Garza being tossed around in his harness as the pod's emergency thrusters blasted him away from *Valiant* told him all he needed to know.

I've never ordered someone to their death before, and I sure as hell hope I'm wrong about the rest of the battlegroup. Because there's no way we're getting those pods in using backup generators and fancy tricks.

JANTINE

Jantine felt the launch vibrations shake the corridor, but didn't have time to reflect on what it meant for her and her team. Her attention was wholly focused down the sights of her pulser at the enemy.

That's it, just a little closer...

She could make out eight figures limned in soft green light floating in a staggered formation down the center of the corridor, each carrying some kind of bulky weapon twice the size of the one in her hands.

She fired a shot high over their heads, almost pitying them for their lack of mobility. The hardsuited opponents drew up fast with hasty course corrections, but were essentially helpless in the seconds before they could redirect themselves with boot or hand jets into secure firing positions. Just like the first group, they were no more threatening than target drones.

Jarl and Katra waited until the last enemy was past them to disengage their active camouflage, then opened fire with hand weapons. In less than three seconds all eight humans were dead, and Katra was bounding down the corridor back the way they came.

You people have to have grav generators, otherwise this area of your ship wouldn't have a "floor." Why do you keep wasting your tactical advantages by coming in weightless?

Malik would have an answer, he always did. Jantine tried to bury her sadness, but his loss was too raw to process right now.

How am I going to do this without you?

Jantine took a moment to steady her breathing, and then removed her faceplate. The cold air of the corridor was like a slap in the face, and an urgent reminder that they needed to get off this ship as soon as possible.

"Wrap it up, JonB. It's time to go."

Jantine's whisper was barely audible, especially compared to the sounds of combat from just moments ago. JonB shot her a worried look then turned his attention back to the pile of technology laid out in front of him.

JonB started tapping on his handheld, while at the same time intently studying Jantine's portable terminal. He'd had to power both down while the mods set the ambush and now was catching up on what was happening outside the ship.

When he didn't acknowledge her order, she waved Artemus ahead and then chanced a look at the rest of her team. Even in the soft light of the terminal, she could see that Carlton was in bad shape. One of the Omegas had a hand on his shaking shoulder in a gesture strongly reminiscent of Doria. Jantine understood—she wasn't doing much better, but wishing wouldn't bring her friends back.

JonB was another matter. He seemed more annoyed than upset that three members of the team were either dead or permanently incapacitated. The scientist wasn't on the mission to make friends— none of them were. But he hadn't gone out of his way to do so either, even with her. If anything, he'd kept the other mods at a distance intentionally, as if predicting this exact situation.

"JonB. We need to move."

"Another minute, Commander. Please. I need to confirm the container's course. The debris field out there is huge, and any number of things can go wrong."

Jantine understood what JonB was saying, but she didn't have to like it. Malik was good at what he did, and even using Doria's hands she trusted him to get the sleepers out of danger. But no one could have predicted the presence of enemy spacecraft at their insertion point, and there could be even more surprises coming their way.

"Take two, and then we're leaving even if Crassus has to carry you."

JonB returned to his energetic tapping. Jantine couldn't pretend to understand the calculations necessary to track the container—she wasn't born that way. Her responsibility now was to get the team down to the planet and recover the sleepers. She needed the scientist, now more than ever. But she also needed to know her orders would be carried out.

Malik is—was—so much better at this.

The thought triggered a fresh wave of grief and self-doubt. Jantine needed to start thinking of Malik in the past tense, and let go of the memory of her second-in-command propped up against the wall with a massive head wound. The knowledge that Doria was dying alongside him didn't make it any better.

I need to be doing something. Moving, killing enemies, anything. Waiting around here is just making this worse.

Harren's death was unfortunate, but what bothered Jantine was that her reaction to it was so clinical. Carlton was barely upright after the loss of his sib, and she'd simply written Harren off when she saw the body. It was more that their specialties weren't immediately useful to her, so Jantine regarded the support Betas differently than she did JonB.

If they ever did get down to the planet, Carlton would be far more valuable than just another pair of arms. Jantine's job right now was to make sure that happened. And to do it, the team had to get moving.

Crassus waved a free arm to catch her attention. The Delta was a bit cramped in the corridor, but at least he and Artemus could still stand upright. The Omegas had it much worse, almost doubled over when not moving. The enemy ship seemed to be designed for a fairly narrow range of human being, and no one they'd seen so far was out of the ordinary.

Jantine gave Crassus her full attention.

"Commander Jantine. Scout Katra reports the corridor is clear for two hundred meters then opens into an intersection. Scout Jarl has secured a cache of enemy equipment and awaits further orders. He believes we can use scattercomms undetected but worries about the atmospheric integrity of this vessel."

Jantine nodded. The thought had crossed her mind as well. The air here was too cold for comfortable living, though she'd encountered worse during training. Even the most undisciplined commander made environmental systems a priority in an emergency.

"Thank you, Crassus. Is there anything else?"

Jantine had worked with Deltas before and knew they tended to prioritize information. She couldn't think of anything else Artemus might have relayed from further down the corridor, but she wanted to make sure.

"No, Commander Jantine. Do you require me to discipline Scientist JonB?"

JonB blanched at this but did not say anything in response. Jantine didn't hide her smile.

"That will not be necessary, Crassus. Everyone here knows what we have to do."

"Yes, Commander Jantine. I have taken personal responsibility for Support Technician Carlton and the Builders. No harm will come to them while I live."

The Builders. Such an elegant name for the Omegas, even when spoken so formally. Crassus, you are a poet at heart.

If JonB was bothered by his omission from the Delta's vow of protection, he didn't show it. It was simple mathematics—the Deltas had divided responsibility for the civvies, and he wasn't on Crassus's list. Artemus would have him covered, even from his position up the corridor next to Jarl.

Jantine looked over her command and judged it ready for travel. Katra and Jarl would find them a path; Artemus and Crassus would make sure they got there. Her job was to give the orders, especially the unpleasant ones. So far her choices had gotten three of her people killed, but the rest still needed her.

"Time's up. Let's go."

JonB closed the computer's case and handed it off to Carlton. The civvie Beta stood and tapped out something on his handheld then held it up to the Omegas. One of them looked at it, and then picked up several of the bulky packs the first wave of enemies had been carrying.

When Jantine gave him a questioning look, JonB sidled over and tipped his head toward her.

"The laser cutters may be useful. Just about everything else they've got is garbage, but they burned almost all the way through the container's hull in a lot less time than it would have taken us."

Jantine thought about the other tactical advantages her mods had over the enemy. The team's grav generators were the biggest ones, and the suit technology they'd seen so far was laughable. The enemy's vac-suits were twice the thickness of even a civvie encounter suit, and offered much less protection. The armored suits were better, but even more bulky. And unlike the recoilless pulsers used by the combat mods, the enemy's induction slug throwers seemed ill-suited to fighting in a weightless environment.

It's a wonder you people ever made it out into space. You're like children playing with knives.

Now that she had time to think about it, Jantine's curiosity was aroused. It also helped that for once, JonB actually seemed to be helping her, rather than complaining.

"What else can you tell me about them? While we hop."

JonB fell in beside her as she started moving. Crassus dropped back to shield his charges, and Jantine knew he'd make sure they kept up.

Jantine pushed off, keeping her strides small so as to not overrun Jarl and Artemus. At the preferred quarter-grav the team was using, she could easily cover a dozen meters with each jump. Katra's report said there was an intersection ahead. The Gammas would have to scout both directions before they could move on, so there was no need to hurry.

"I think Jarl's right about the scattercomms. The first group wasn't carrying any personal transmitters, but in the damage control packs they had a relay unit of some kind that I think keys into the power system. The cargo slug's impact must have taken out their primary infrastructure. Essentially, everyone we encounter will be operating independently, and I don't believe they've got a lot of surprises for us."

Jantine had only glanced at the packs in question, but what JonB was saying made sense. The first group had been carrying far more gear than was necessary to breach their container. They must have been a repair crew, and she felt a momentary twinge of guilt at killing noncombatants. But from what she knew about the Redstone-class dreadnaughts, there should be a lot more—and a lot better resistance arrayed against them.

It's as if someone decided to crew a ship with untrained recruits, rather than combat veterans. The techs certainly knew what they were doing, but that patrol was a joke.

Jantine saw Jarl and Artemus shoulder several of the downed enemy troopers and carry them forward. It was a reasonable precaution, and she wagered that JonB was as interested as she was in examining their gear.

By the time the two Betas reached the intersection, Katra and Jarl were already gone. Artemus was standing guard over the enemy corpses, bodies Jarl had selected based on the amount of damage they'd suffered.

The first corpse was nearly intact save for the shattered faceplate. A pair of pulser shots had destroyed the second's chest, most likely killing it instantly. Or, more accurately, her. JonB wasted no time in wrestling off the helmet of the dead human's hardsuit.

The woman's features were fascinating. She might have been in her late teens, with an unlined face and hair that ended neatly at the base of her neck. Jantine studied the contours of the dead woman's face, searching for something, anything relatable to her own life. In the green glow, it was surprisingly asymmetric, instead of the designed and proportioned faces she was used to.

Jantine resisted the urge to raise a hand to her own face and feel her cheekbones and orbital ridges; her mental picture was as accurate as any mirror could be. Instead, she knelt and moved the woman's head further into the light.

The appearance of the dead trooper was unnerving, a fact that bothered Jantine in and of itself. Not three meters behind her were mods whose faces were much more removed from the human baseline. But this woman was…almost familiar. There was no one thing wrong with her features; it was just that none of them were "right."

Jantine let the body fall, and scanned both sides of the passageway for some sign of the Gammas. When none came, she closed her eyes and listened instead. She could hear JonB tinkering with the helmet, and filed the sound away in order to narrow her focus.

In similar fashion, she catalogued the sounds of the bundles the Omegas carried moving against one another, Crassus's careful footsteps, and even Carlton's compulsive fidgeting. Finally, she focused on the sound of her own heart beating, letting it drop below her normal resting rate of forty beats per minute until she could feel it pulsing throughout her entire body. With each heartbeat, she considered another of the facts before her.

We have met no solid resistance.

Our opponents are inexperienced.

This ship is either dead or dying.

This area of space should be empty.

Malik said ships, *plural.*

Our opponents are inexperienced.

We are not alone.

"JonB. I need blood samples from both these bodies. Artemus, Crassus, get the Gammas back, at least to comm range. Carlton, I want a full, functioning suit of this armor and some of their weapons for analysis. I don't care how many pieces either is in, just as long as they work."

Jantine was about to include instructions for the Omegas, but she had a sense they were already busy with something. Turning around, she saw they were moving their heads back and forth, as if trying to zero in on something with their exceptional auditory range.

Jantine watched the pair for another few seconds. It didn't seem right to stare at them, but Doria's smiling face wasn't there as a buffer anymore. The Omegas didn't seem concerned by the noises JonB and Carlton were making while they dealt with the bodies, or by the sound of the Deltas' feet skipping down the corridor. It was if the thing they were searching for was just beyond their ability to sense, and that thought was a sobering one.

Whatever it is, they'll let me know about it when it's relevant. Until then, I've got a job to do.

Undisguised footsteps from both sides brought her back into focus. Katra and Artemus were together, but the Gamma's eyes and shaking head were just as effective a report as any words would be.

From the other direction, Crassus came back alone, with something small and dark held in a lower hand. He raised it to his head once he was sure she could see him, then extended a long forefinger and trailed it along his jaw.

Scattercomms were standard issue for combat ops. The organic circuitry was easily applied along the underside of the jaw and melded quickly into the skin, with one end resting just under the chin and the other tucked into the left ear.

Though the devices were powered by piezoelectric charges from the skin of the wearer and nearly undetectable while active, it was impossible to have a truly secure conversation while using them. The main advantage of scattercomms were instant group conversations over a medium distance, when helmet channels or handhelds were impractical.

Jantine ran a finger down her jaw to activate her unit, then pumped her mouth twice without speaking to open a channel. She heard three clicks in her left ear, one for herself and each mod already in the loop. Crassus set whatever he was carrying on the decking, and then moved back down the corridor to act as a relay. When he was almost at the edge of her visual range, she heard four clicks. She swallowed, and began talking from the back of her throat in a whisper that barely escaped her lips.

"Jarl. Go."

"Encountered another repair group, boss. No weapons or cutters, but this one had emergency lights, a power relay, some handheld comms, and a map."

Jantine's heart beat faster at the news, but she kept her voice calm.

"Is that what Crassus brought back?" She nudged JonB with her foot, making the comm motion with her left hand and gestured at the object with her pulser in her right. He signaled understanding and moved forward to collect it. Five clicks sounded in her ear, and Jarl spoke again.

"No. Comm unit. It's unlocked, but don't..."

A high-pitched squeal rang out from the black object in JonB's hand, and Jantine dropped into a firing crouch. Over her sights she watched the civvie fumble with the device for several seconds until he managed to reverse whatever he'd done to make it react like that.

"... turn it on while using active scatter. There's a feedback loop."

Jantine frowned slightly, marking up yet another reason not to use the supposedly untraceable comms.

"Were you detected?" She heard four clicks, and saw JonB hunch his shoulders somewhat. His lopsided smile was all the apology she needed, and as she and the other combat mods lowered their weapons, he relaxed his posture and went to work on the captured device.

"No. They had no time to send a signal. Map shows a mainte-nance entrance ten meters from here, but I have no visual confirma-tion. Found what looks like a transit bay, but it's the long way around and one level up."

Jarl didn't waste any breath on the fate of the repair team, and Jantine didn't bother to ask. If he was being observed, Jarl was too good to risk comm chatter, especially after discovering the feedback loop.

"Hold position. We're coming to you. Next comm in sixty seconds."

Jantine used her left hand to swipe her jawline, killing the connection. As she stood up, she held the same hand out to Carlton and the Omegas, then gestured down the passageway in Jarl's general direction. JonB started back to the group as Carlton finished packing away the hardsuit's components.

Out of her armor, the dead woman looked even younger than she had from the neck up. She had well-muscled arms, but she still had a softness that indicated she'd only been engaging in intensive exercise for a short time. She lacked the physical definition of Jantine and the Gammas, but then again, most humans did.

This last thought cemented what Jantine found so troubling about the bodies, and made JonB's blood samples mostly irrelevant.

It's as if she's virus-free. But that's not supposed to be possible.

JonB reached her just as Carlton finished, and he packed up his gear in seconds, leaving the portable enemy comm out on the deck. Jantine looked at it, weighing whether or not destroying it was the right call.

"Can you make that thing work?"

"Yes. It has an internal power cell, but the default setting is to function on broadcast power. It's just bad luck that it thinks the scattercomms are part of that system. As long as I can bypass the protocol, it should be fine. And I found a volume control; we should be able to listen in at a rational level."

"All right. Don't experiment without telling me first. I don't want any more surprises."

"Of course, Commander. But..." JonB looked nervously at the other mods while he shouldered his pack.

"JonB, you and I have to trust each other for this to work. If there's a concern, it comes straight to me now. And if I'm not around, to Jarl. Understand?"

Jantine watched the Omegas and Carlton move ahead to join

Crassus, while Artemus took a position that allowed the Delta to still see JonB. Katra was guarding their rear, and if she took any offense at Jantine's statement, she gave no sign. Technically, Jarl was next in command, even though Katra was older and more experienced. But the same lack of imagination that made her sims predictable also kept Katra out of the command structure. She was a creature of instinct, not intuition.

A distinction probably lost on JonB. But this mission doesn't require that we all like each other.

"Yes, Commander. I was wondering why you wanted the blood samples? You already know the answer..."

Jantine held up her hand to stop him, then gestured down the corridor. JonB was a bit slow in following her meaning, and instead of repeating the gesture, she grabbed his shoulder and gently shoved him after the rest of the team. The scientist stumbled briefly, but he still had a Beta's grace and was able to keep up with her long strides as she started skipping down the corridor.

Jantine didn't bother looking at him when she spoke. There'd be time enough to whip him into shape once they got through the current crisis and onto the next one.

"Look around us, JonB. These people, this ship. They're not advancing, not as fast as they should be. If this is the best they have to offer, our mission is pointless."

Before he could answer, Jantine activated her scattercomm, trusting that JonB had disabled the enemy device as he'd said. She received five clicks in response.

"All clear."

"No change, boss." Jarl's whisper was controlled, and Jantine imagined he was under active camouflage again.

"Rear secure." Katra's check-in was expected, and Jantine knew the other listeners were the Deltas, spaced out to function as signal relays. Part of her had hoped that JonB would follow protocols for once and join in, but the Beta was silent at her side.

"Out."

Jantine shut down the scattercomm, thinking a bit more on how to deal with JonB. Her original plan to replace him once the sleepers were activated seemed somewhat petty now that they'd taken casualties. He might ask too many questions, but that was his job. An analyst had to have as much information as possible, otherwise he couldn't formulate effective plans.

In many ways, he was the polar opposite of Katra, and that comparison as much as anything else told Jantine what she had to do. It was incumbent on her to get better at answering JonB's questions, not the other way around. The Alphas' plan included them working together for a long time, and he hadn't been selected at random. Further, if she felt Katra's planning skills were deficient, it was Jantine's duty as her commander to improve them.

The corridor ahead grew lighter, and as she felt the ship's gravity field take hold, Jantine slowed her steps and powered down her personal generator. Both JonB and Katra were long-term projects; getting her team off this vessel intact was a more immediate one.

The scene she came upon was textbook perfect. Jarl had taken out a team of six techs and then arranged the bodies among the bulky repair gear so cleverly that a casual observer would think the area abandoned. There was no sign of the Gamma himself, but Jantine knew he was there all the same.

Carlton moved up to the assembled gear, examining each pack briefly for useful items under Crassus's watchful eyes. The Delta stood over him with pulsers in all of his hands, covering the corridor in front of them. Artemus took up a similar stance facing the other direction, while Katra skipped past everyone to scout further ahead.

The Omegas were swiveling their heads around again, and Jantine was starting to worry. Something was bothering them. Doria had said they would get by fine without her, but Jantine suspected her absence was affecting them a lot more than they let on.

"Show me the map."

To his credit, JonB did not scream when Jarl appeared seemingly out of nowhere between them. But he was visibly shaken, and Jantine lost a battle with her smile.

Jarl held up a thin sheet of flimsy, translucent material in both hands. With a small flourish, he unfolded it along an invisible seam, and a holographic representation of a Redstone dreadnaught appeared in the air above it. JonB's eyes widened, and Jantine had to admit she was impressed as well.

Finally, some sign of advanced technology. But why are the techs so well equipped, and the combat operatives so inexperienced? Who are these people?

Jarl clearly had been experimenting with the map, because he moved to the side of the corridor and placed the clear sheet against a bulkhead at chest height. It stayed in place, allowing Jarl to place his hands into the image then spread his arms. The holographic ship expanded, and both JonB and Jantine leaned forward to examine the details. The civvie was first to speak, but since he and Jantine had the same question it didn't really matter.

"So where are we now?"

Jarl's fingers were spread wide. He twisted his wrists, and the ship rotated, revealing a line of green dots making its way through the ship.

"They've restored power along this route. I can't simulate the cargo slug, but we're logically closer to the hull than the center of the vessel. So, this end must be us."

JonB caught Jarl's eye, and raised his own hands to manipulate the image. The Gamma stepped back to stand at Jantine's side. JonB was focusing on the edges of the image rather than the details of the ship, poking at some unfamiliar icons with an intent expression.

Jarl kept his eyes moving, taking in not only what the scientist was doing but also the actions of the rest of the team.

"Commander. These people. I..." Jarl's voice was unsteady for the first time in Jantine's memory.

"I know, Jarl. Something about this ship is very wrong, and we need to leave it as soon as possible. Once we're away, we can take time to worry about who and what we had to kill. You said there was a maintenance access hatch?"

"There is, but I don't think it's an option for us. They're not going to..."

When he didn't resume speaking, Jantine turned her head to look at Jarl, who was wearing an uncharacteristic expression of surprise. It took her a moment to understand what had affected him so, then realized the rest of the team had gone silent as well.

Most of them, anyway. The Omegas had stopped their slow head motions and were moving toward JonB and the holographic projection. One of them placed a broad hand on his shoulder, gently pushing him aside

What are they doing? This isn't like them at all.

The Omegas took up seated positions on either side of the projection and expanded it even further. Unlike the rest of the mods, they still wore their jumpsuits, and the orange skin of their arms and faces was exposed. Jantine, JonB and Jarl moved into the center of the assembled repair gear, marveling at the speed and grace of the Omega's hands.

Fingers that could crush rock danced through the holographic ship, spinning it almost too quickly to see. Jantine recognized some of the icons JonB was studying only seconds before as they enlarged and contracted, seemingly at random. The ship was taking on more definition, additional lines of light forming as they worked.

More green paths spread through the ship, and a large solid section of red appeared. Jantine felt a wave of deep sadness wash over her as a blue dot appeared inside the red and then expanded into a solid line. She watched the team's path move down several corridors to their present position, and then resolve into nine softly pulsing glows.

It took Jantine a moment to realize they'd stopped working, and that the image also showed two glowing dots back at their starting point, and one in approximately the area Jarl had identified as a landing bay.

Then she noticed that both Omegas were staring at something. Or rather, someone. Following their eyes, she saw Carlton standing alone, with his handheld in one hand and the oversized pack he was using to carry captured enemy gear in the other.

"What? What is it? What do you want?"

Carlton's voice was trembling, and Jantine could hear the pain of their collective losses fully expressed in it. He was on the edge of losing control, and she had no idea how to help him.

She looked back to the Omegas, searching their orange faces for some clue of what to do next. The nearer one stretched out a hand to Carlton, and pointed.

"I don't understand! I'm not a Gamma. I can't...I can't help you!"

Carlton walked forward, but the expression on his face indicated he really didn't want to. Every step he took was punctuated with another denial, and by the time he reached the Omegas he was nearly in tears.

The analytical part of Jantine's mind noted that he left the oversized pack behind but was still wearing his own and carrying his handheld. The Omega reached out to Carlton and gently relieved him of both, placing them on the deck. The Omega then placed his hands on Carlton's shoulders, using four eyes to stare into the Beta's two. Carlton started shaking, and the Omega leaned forward until his broad forehead touched the top of Carlton's helmet. The support tech was sobbing openly now, and he collapsed into the Omega's arms.

"Thank you. Thank you. Thank you."

Hearing the raw emotion Carlton had been holding in since his sib's death made Jantine want to cry herself. Not knowing what else to do, Jantine looked at JonB. The scientist's face was streaked with tears, and he made no move to wipe them away.

Carlton disengaged himself from the Omega and walked back to join the rest of the mods. Jantine kept watching the Omegas, but pulled him back a step to make sure he was okay.

"Carlton, what just happened?"

The one who hadn't comforted Carlton reached for the handheld and began tapping in commands. The other one opened the pack and withdrew the case containing Jantine's portable computer terminal.

"He helped me, I think. Since Harren died, I've been...I was...lost, I guess. He took some of that pain away."

Jantine wasn't entirely satisfied with this explanation, but what the Omegas were doing now needed all of her attention. From Jantine's vantage point, she could just make out the terminal's screen, and saw it was still running JonB's course tracking program. JonB must have seen the same thing, because he powered up his own handheld and gasped.

"They can't—they shouldn't be able to do that!"

Jantine watched the projection as small red objects began appearing around the ship. The image contracted, and then a new green line stretched out from the cargo slug and to the edges of the projection. It contracted again, adding more red objects until they nearly filled the corridor.

Nearly. There were green objects making their way through the debris field as well, and their inexorable progress sent a shiver down her spine.

JonB's next words echoed Jantine's thoughts completely.

"We have to get off this ship!"

Jantine turned and addressed the team. "Pack it up, everyone. We're leaving. I want—"

The Omega's hand on her shoulder was an unexpected interruption. She raised her eyes to the other mod's, preparing herself in case the Omega was going to do to her whatever they'd done to Carlton. Instead, it pointed to the projection. The other Omega spread its hands wide, zooming in on the wounded ship represented at its center. Jantine started a mental clock on how soon the closest of the green icons she'd seen would reach the ship, uncomfortable with both the size of the image and the time she had left.

The dreadnaught's familiar wireframe was back, but the Omega wasn't done yet. The projection focused on the transit bay Jarl had mentioned earlier, then the Omega brought its hands close together. The projection collapsed into a cloud of colored lights then resolved into a video image.

Jantine saw a column of armored figures walking down a wide passageway, escorting some piece of bulky equipment into a large compartment. The Omega squeezed her shoulder for emphasis while pointing with its other hand at the image. Jantine tried not to think about how much pressure the Omega could exert on her if it wanted to, focusing instead on the intense feeling of need that pulsed through as the long finger indicated the equipment.

"I think I understand," Jantine said, "but our priority has to be getting off this ship. If we can secure whatever that is, we will, but..."

The sound of the other Omega's hands slamming together at full speed was like a small explosion, and it nearly stopped Jantine's heart. The projected image disappeared, and the feeling of need changed to a sense of dread.

Jantine desperately wanted to escape, but the Omega's hand on her shoulder held her fast. She was keenly aware that the rest of the mods in the corridor were staring at her, but like them she had no idea how to deal with an angry Omega. The very concept was inconceivable, but there was no mistaking the expressions on their faces.

The Omegas were giving the orders now, and they weren't taking no for an answer.

Doria had told Jantine they didn't think about the same things other mods did, but it was apparent now that they were more than capable of doing so. She'd also told Jantine they had faith in her leadership, and would do whatever she asked of them. But nothing Doria said could have prepared her for this.

Squaring her courage as much as she could, Jantine put her hand on the Omega's wrist and pushed. The hand came off her shoulder, and she backed up a step so she could look at both Omegas at the same time.

"Fine. But you have to tell me why. If we don't get off this ship, all of us are going to die. You understand that, don't you? You have to."

Both Omegas raised their left hands to their jaws, trailing a finger down the line of their broad faces in a gesture that did nothing to soften the hard expressions they wore. Jantine was about to repeat her question when Crassus's low rumble came from the other end of their makeshift encampment.

"Commander Jantine. Scout Katra on the scattercomm. Says it's urgent."

The Omegas made the gesture again, and Jantine realized they were trying to answer her question. She mirrored their action and heard seven clicks in her ear.

I guess I can't blame any of you. I'd want to hear this too.

"Go."

"Boss, I've acquired another enemy comm. You need to turn yours on. Now."

Jantine's eyes darted to JonB, who moved forward holding the small, black box. He pointed to a switch on the face of the comm and gave her a weak smile that did little to mask his fear.

"Should be fine. We're back on their power grid, no feedback."

Jantine nodded, and pressed the switch. An unfamiliar voice sounded from the comm, but the tone of the speaker was one she recognized instantly.

This man is in charge, and is not happy.

"-eat. This is Captain Horace Kołodziejski, of the System Defense Force. I hereby assume command of your battlegroup and order Captain Aloysius Martin be placed under arrest as a traitor. Power down all weapons systems, and prepare to be boarded. Any person or persons attempting to assist Captain Martin will be considered enemy combatants and subject to the Interstellar Compact's rules of war. This is your final warning."

Jantine turned off the device and looked at the Omegas. The one on the left picked up Carlton's handheld and tapped a command. The holographic image sprang into life again, and this time she could see what looked like the nosecone of a shuttle, and the edge of an open cargo ramp.

But more importantly, she saw a large number of weapons in people's hands, half of which were pointed at a tall figure in a hard-suit whose own hands were empty and raised in the air. At its side was a slightly shorter individual holding two hand weapons, constantly shifting targets in what looked to Jantine like a defensive pattern.

Drawing on her memory of the ship's schematic, Jantine made her decision.

"Katra. Look around your present position for a maintenance access panel. There's a flight deck one level up and two hundred meters from my current position with multiple hostiles. Get there and secure the situation."

"Yes, boss."

Six clicks sounded in her ear as Katra deactivated her comm. Jantine turned to Jarl, who was starting to fidget.

"Go. We'll catch up."

Jarl sealed his faceplate and started running. He stopped briefly to rip a panel off the wall, then disappeared inside the revealed maintenance shaft before it hit the deck.

The hole was too small for either Crassus or Artemus to follow him, which was probably why Jarl had dismissed the shaft as a viable path. The Omegas certainly wouldn't fit through the opening, so the rest of the team would have to go the long way around to the flight deck.

It's time.

"The rest of you, get ready for a fight. Make sure you've got your handhelds and packs, but leave any captured gear you're not sure of behind. Crassus, on point. Move out."

The Delta started running down the hall at an impressive pace, weapons ready. JonB stepped forward to retrieve the map panel, and the Omegas watched him with burning eyes. Whatever was going on inside their heads, they were still clearly intent on the projected image, and when it powered off they turned their attention to Jantine.

Jantine matched their glares as best she could, but she didn't have any time to waste on power games. Breaking eye contact, she tightened her grip on the pulser and started running after Crassus. She trusted Artemus and JonB to get the rest of the mods organized— Katra and Jarl needed her more than they did right now, and she wasn't going to lose anyone else today if she could help it.

If the Omegas were no longer under her complete command,

she'd deal with it when the time came. She had to trust that whatever agenda they were following now was in her best interests, and those of the Colonies.

Because if they're not on our side anymore, I have no idea of how to stop them...

MARTIN

1345 SHIP TIME, SDF *VALIANT*

"ALL RIGHT, everyone. Let's not do anything we're going to regret later."

Aloysius tried for his most amiable smile, turning his head from side to side in an attempt to win over any of the security troopers on the flight deck who were wavering. It was hard to look like a trusted commander with your hands in the air, but he'd been a line officer for a lot of years and knew that just about anything was possible if you refused to give up.

Kołodziejski's broadcast couldn't have come at a worse time. Another few minutes, and he and Harlan would have been off the ship and commandeering one of the remaining tenders. They would have been able to disappear into interplanetary space, and the Alpha would have been safe.

Well, as much as it could be, under the circumstances.

The way Harlan kept shifting her targets certainly wasn't helping matters, and he was of two minds about what to do next. He was still processing Horace's words when Harlan snatched his pistol from his belt, and her aggressive posture was making his negotiating position very difficult.

He could surrender, and hope to negotiate some sort of mutually beneficial deal, or he could try and charm his way out of immediate danger and proceed with the original plan. But as long as everyone was pointing weapons at one another, it was only a matter of time until something happened he couldn't talk his way out of.

From the looks of things, about half the troopers on the flight deck and all of the techs were on his side. They'd already stowed the gennie on the shuttle—if he could just get himself and Harlan aboard with a minimum of casualties he might still be able to salvage the situation.

"There's a completely rational explanation for all this. What you just heard is only half the story, and I'd like to think that I've earned enough respect to tell you the rest. Can we just take a few minutes and talk?"

It was hard to get a read on people in hardsuits with blanked faceplates, but Aloysius saw some of the troopers aiming at him shift their feet a little.

It was the newer, younger members of his crew that he needed to win back—men and women who hadn't lived enough to understand how many shades of gray there were in the universe. He'd made a point of sending the more reactionary troopers they'd met elsewhere; if he could appeal to just one of these youngsters, the rest would follow.

"Sir, ma'am, lower your weapons, get down on the deck, and remove your helmets. Captain Kołodziejski's orders are valid, and I am required to enforce them."

The trooper's voice was somewhere between cold confidence and abject terror, and if the rest of the people currently pointing weapons at him felt the same way, Aloysius had more to work with than he'd originally thought.

Smile still in place, Aloysius turned to face the speaker. He was one of three troopers with their slugthrowers raised, and the trio didn't seem at all fazed by either Harlan's steady aim or the pair of their comrades aiming at the back of their heads.

I'd be proud of you all, if I wasn't so damn scared this will end in a bloodbath.

Aloysius kept his eyes fixed on the troopers. It was easier to be brave when no one could see the fear in your eyes, and that fear had to have these troopers asking some hard questions right now.

Okay, time to roll the dice.

"Son, everyone, I'm going to remove my helmet now, all right. No tricks, I just want to talk this thing through."

"Sir."

Harlan's one-word statement was a question, caution, and declaration of support. So far she hadn't technically aided and abetted him, but as soon as the shooting started there would be no going back for her. If this plan had any chance of succeeding he needed at least one other senior officer free to act.

"It's all right, Commander Harlan. I don't have anything to fear from these people. They're following orders, just like I am. We all want the same thing here, to understand what's going on. Here I go, I'm taking my helmet off, nice and easy."

Without the suit mics relaying his voice over both the comms and external speakers, he'd have to pick his words very carefully over the next few minutes. Every second Aloysius wasn't winning back his people, Horace Kołodziejski got that much closer to coming aboard and taking physical control of *Valiant*.

The seals at his neck released, and Aloysius lifted the helmet up and over his head. He hadn't been wearing the suit all that long, but he was shocked by how cold the air in the launch bay felt. The flight deck had its own power and gravity generators, but the air temperature was regulated by the same systems that maintained the rest of the ship.

*If Harlan's people haven't got them online by now, they're probably too far gone to salvage. In that case, it won't matter how much power they can reroute—*Valiant *is dead and so is its crew. We're too far away from any friendly faces out here for hope of rescue.*

Aloysius felt a momentary twinge of guilt—after all, it had been his orders that put *Valiant* and her support ships in this region of space in the first place. He'd picked this position specifically because nothing was supposed to be out here, and no one could have predicted the random appearance of the space rock or ship or whatever it was that had hit them, or that it would cause so much damage to so many systems at once.

"What's your name, son?"

"Maranov, sir. Please, don't move."

Aloysius had been about to step forward, in an attempt to block the man's view of Harlan aiming for the middle of his faceplate.

"It's okay, Maranov. No one wants this to get ugly. I'm putting my helmet down, but I want you to promise me something, all right?"

Come on, son. Think this through.

"I can't do that, sir. Please get on the ground. Ma'am, lower your weapons. Captain Kołodziejski's orders—"

Still holding his helmet in his hands, Aloysius turned his head to catch a glimpse of Harlan's face. Her expression hadn't changed, and he knew that if he couldn't get the situation under control, and fast, there was no way out for anyone.

The boy's right about one thing. People have got to stop pointing slugthrowers at one another.

In a move that must have appeared far braver than he felt, Aloysius turned his back on Maranov and his two flankers. He held the helmet out to Harlan, fixing her with a knowing stare. The woman's dedication to his safety was admirable, but he wondered how much of it was loyalty and how much pure adrenalin.

Stick with me, Mira. We'll live through this if we can just stay calm a little longer.

Harlan made a face like she'd swallowed something vile, but seemed to understand his intent. She slowly placed the induction pistol in her right hand into a holder on her chest plate, then took the empty helmet from her captain. She didn't let go of the other pistol, but at least she wasn't pointing it at anyone.

All right, that's one...

Aloysius made a slow turn, noting the positions of everyone on the flight deck. There were twenty people besides himself and Harlan, most of whom were pointing at least one weapon at someone else. As he turned, he kept his hands at shoulder height, palms down and making gentle patting motions.

Apart from his personal shuttle, this deck held a few smaller vessels under repair, along with the machinery and supplies necessary to work on them. But he and Commander Williams had seen to it that no crews ever got assigned to those ships, and it was about as private a place as one could find inside the hull.

Good. The last thing I need right now is someone I'm not sure of charging in here and shooting people.

"Everyone, please, do what the man said and lower your weapons. No one needs to die here; I just want to talk. Maranov, is it? Any relation to Commodore Maranova? She's good people, and I'd like to think she would want you to listen to what I have to say."

Maranov was silent for a few seconds, and then he lowered his weapon halfway. The gesture caught his comrades by surprise, one of whom spoke up.

"Ivan, what are you doing? We have our orders."

Aloysius recognized the trooper as Randall Jensen, another name on Bill Williams's list of potential recruits.

"He's thinking, Jensen. Like all of you should be doing right now. I'm no traitor, and neither will you be if you lower your weapons. Horace Kołodziejski is mistaken, and I want to hear what he has to say as much as the rest of you. But I can't do that with a weapon in my face."

From Jensen's aggressive tone, Aloysius didn't think he'd stand down without a lot more convincing. But Maranov wanted to talk, and since at the moment the others were taking their cues from him, Aloysius wanted to hear him out.

Stepping in front of Harlan for a second time drew a muttered curse from her, but the longer Aloysius could keep the troopers talking, the better it was for everyone.

"Sir, my great aunt, sir," Maranov said. "She's spoken fondly of you in the past. She was very proud when I was assigned to *Valiant* after graduation."

Aloysius was glad he'd guessed right. Ykaterina was more than good people—she was on the right side of all this.

"As am I, son. As am I. Now, if you can just convince Jensen there and your other friends that the weapons aren't helping, I can try and explain what's going on. You all know I've taken great pains to secure that sleeper unit aboard my shuttle, and the rest of the information you need to see is aboard as well. If we can just go inside and talk..."

"Not gonna happen, sir." Jensen took a firmer grip on his weapon, the exact opposite of what Aloysius wanted. "Now get on the ground, hands on your head. Do it!"

Worse, it was exactly what Harlan was afraid of, and she'd apparently had enough of waiting. Aloysius heard his helmet hit the deck, and he could only assume she'd filled that hand with a weapon immediately.

"Mac, Callen. On me!" Harlan's order blasted out at full volume, and Aloysius flinched away from the sound. He spun to face her directly, but before he could countermand her, the sight of several techs sneaking up behind a security trooper changed everything.

"No, you fools. Don't—"

Aloysius's warning was too late for the unarmed techs. The first stumbled as he ran forward to make a tackle, and the trooper nearest to him whirled and fired his weapon. The tech went down in a heap, and Aloysius knew from the angle of his head he wasn't going to get back up again.

Oh shit.

Something hit Aloysius in the chest, and for a moment he thought he'd been shot as well. But the pressure continued all the way to the deck, and the sight of Harlan kneeling on his chest while firing both her weapons was truly impressive. He marveled at her cool competence, right up to the point where he followed her line of fire and saw Maranov's chest plate disintegrate as grav-accelerated micro-slugs punched through it.

Shock didn't do justice to the captain's state of mind. He'd almost done it, almost talked everybody back from the edge. Now he was trapped in a worst-case scenario, and his newest recruit was the one doing the most damage.

The deep-throated growl of Harlan's induction pistols was nearly deafening, and the accompanying electric tang of ionized air stung his nose. It wasn't until she stopped to insert new ammunition canisters that he could make out her shouted commands.

"-'ve got to fall back! Everyone, get to the shuttle!"

Before Aloysius could stop her, Harlan sent another short volley at Jensen, who ducked behind a maintenance frame just in time for one of Aloysius's faceless allies to come up behind him and put a dozen micro-slugs into his back. The trooper had no time to celebrate, though, as someone else walked a deadly line of fire up her body from waist to armpit. The last few micro-slugs shattered the hardsuit's faceplate, and the look of complete surprise on the young woman's face tore at Aloysius's soul.

What have I done?

The noise over his head dropped in intensity, and Aloysius turned his attention back to Harlan. Her faceplate was blanked, and the mirrored finish made her seem inhuman. He thought he heard something like a grunt come through her external speakers, but he had no idea what the sound meant.

Before he could speculate, Harlan slapped one of her pistols back into its holster and used the now-free hand to grab Aloysius's collar and drag him towards their escape craft.

It took several meters for Aloysius to process that the muzzle of the pistol on her chest was glowing cherry red. When the one in her left hand stopped firing as well, she dropped it and started running, with Aloysius bouncing heavily behind her as she made a dash for cover.

Somebody watching the lanky fire control officer dragging her middle-aged captain along the deck in the middle of a firefight might have found the sight amusing, but as the one being dragged, Aloysius was glad when she let go of his collar and he rolled to a stop behind a workbench. He couldn't make out the rest of the flight deck from where he was, but from the sound of things it was still going at full tilt.

I have to stop this. If they'll only just listen!

Aloysius got to his knees, but he couldn't see over their improvised cover. From the sounds of the rounds slamming into the other side, she'd picked right. But Harlan wasn't firing back at the moment; she was busy repairing her remaining weapon.

First, Harlan ejected the fused barrel of her induction pistol and replaced it with a spare drawn from one of the many hard pouches on the front of her suit. She then snapped a new ammunition canister into place, held the weapon at arm's length, then triggered the acceleration module. He heard the miniature gravity generator whine to life, and the amber light on the side of the pistol switched over to green.

Aloysius played back the frenzied activity of the last two minutes, and realized why she had to fix the weapon in the first place.

One, two, three…was that really her fifth reload?

Quickly doing the math, Aloysius realized that Harlan had just fired at least two thousand micro-slugs at members of her own crew in an attempt to save his miserable hide, and the thought that she was prepared to do so again moved him to action.

"Harlan, Stop. Everybody, stop! You don't understand what's at stayiaaaaagh!"

Hot metal rained down on Aloysius as a section of the bulkhead above them shattered. He couldn't see Harlan's expression behind the mirrored faceplate, but he was pretty sure what it would look like if he did. He was making it increasingly harder for her to save his life, and there was only so long they could hold this position. But the lives of every man and woman in human-controlled space depended on the outcome of this encounter, and despite his desire to stop the killing Harlan might have the right idea after all…

Harlan fired her remaining weapon dry over the maintenance bench, and then slapped in another canister and continued shooting. From his position on the floor, Aloysius could see a distorted version of the flight deck reflected in her faceplate, and the people fighting across it.

Harlan shifted her aim, and the pistol growled as one of the hard-suited figures running across the floor dropped. She moved again, and a trooper positioned at the base of the cargo ramp doubled over.

A fresh round of impacts slammed into the workbench as she ducked back down to reload, and Aloysius wondered how Harlan could tell friend from foe in all this chaos. She wasn't hesitating in her target selection, but neither was she firing indiscriminately. That discretion was somewhat encouraging, and Aloysius decided to take another approach.

"Harlan, that sleeping Alpha is the only priority here! You have to survive and get it to a safe harbor. So forget about us. Leave me here to deal with this, and I promise you'll get away clean."

Harlan wasn't paying attention to him, or if she was, she didn't turn her head in his direction. Her faceplate was angled out over the top of the bench, as if she was looking at something in the firefight. Aloysius chanced a peek of his own around the side of the work-bench to try and figure out what it was.

About six meters away lay a fallen trooper. At first he thought Harlan might be eyeing the weapon lying next to the body, until Aloysius saw a second suited figure moving towards it. Then the trooper's head just disappeared. The body slumped forward, and when it hit the deck a crimson fountain erupted from its neck.

Aloysius stared at the corpse, noticing that the sounds of combat had diminished. He dove back behind cover and turned to look at Harlan. Her faceplate was tracking slowly to their left now, while her hands were busy reloading her pistol underneath the bench.

Harlan hadn't said a word since they'd taken cover. He chanced a whisper in her direction, although it was more for his own sanity than concealment. Anyone with eyes and ears knew where they were, yet no one was coming for them.

"What is it?"

Harlan stopped moving her head, apparently looking at something in the direction of the shuttle. Then she was back under the bench almost too fast to see, and another section of the bulkhead exploded with a small shower of sparks. Aloysius looked up at the two shining craters in the supposedly indestructible surface, and shuddered.

"There's someone out there shooting at both sides. And one of these," she said, hefting her induction pistol, "can't do that." Harlan gestured at the gouged out sections of bulkhead, and the captain nodded his understanding.

It's too late, they're already here. And they don't care about taking me prisoner anymore.

"Whoever it is, they're herding us. I count five groups out there, and all of us are afraid to stick our heads out. We have to get aboard the shuttle as soon as possible, but it's too far. If we go out without cover, I don't think both of us will make it."

Aloysius tried to think of some way to distract the sniper so that Harlan could take him or her out. Other than just stepping out into the open, none came immediately to mind.

"Harlan, how many of our people are still up?"

"I clocked Sergeants Callahan and Sykes holed up against the far wall. I'm really not sure who the ones without heads are at this point, but there are at least six hostiles active, three of whom are more or less dug in at the ramp."

Damn. I guess it's not a hard decision after all.

"Okay, I'll make a dash back the way we came and try to get a weapon off somebody. You get to that shuttle, and get the Alpha away from here. Once you're free, contact—"

"No."

"What?" Harlan's refusal caught him completely by surprise.

"No, sir. Even if I do get off this ship with the Alpha, I haven't got a clue what to do with it. And as we've seen over the last few minutes, I have no idea who I can trust, or even who's in on your little secret."

"On the shuttle, Harlan. It's all there. Your command key will—"

"Negative, sir. We go together, or we blow the damn thing up. But I'm not leaving you behind in either event. You have to make those casualties out there right, and whether I like it or not I'm in this now up to my neck. So it's both of us, or not at all."

A flurry of weapons fire brought their attention back to the flight deck, where two hardsuited figures were running broken lines toward their position. Aloysius was alarmed, but they weren't firing as they ran, and Harlan wasn't aiming at them.

Must be Callahan and Sykes. They've probably come to the same realization Harlan has.

A third trooper popped up from behind a partially disassembled thruster and sent a line of micro-slugs after the sergeants before his chest exploded.

Aloysius ducked back behind the workbench as micro-slugs started bouncing around, but two very different facts made him feel even worse about his situation than he had before. First, one of the sergeants was down, though Harlan's cover fire let the other roll behind the workbench to join them.

But the second thing he'd just learned was more important than congratulating the scrappy sergeant.

I didn't hear a shot when the trooper's chest exploded. What kind of a weapon has that much power, and makes no sound?

Harlan reloaded quickly, and raised her head for another look at the flight deck. If she was struggling with the same question, she gave no sign of it in her voice.

"Callahan. Report."

"There's motion in the corridors, ma'am. If we're going to do something, it needs to be soon."

Callahan ejected his slugthrower's grav accelerator and replaced it with a spare drawn from a pouch on his abdomen. Once it was in place, he repeated the same aiming and activation ritual Harlan had used with her pistol.

When he was satisfied with his weapon, Callahan clenched a fist and let it fall, and Aloysius saw Harlan nod in response. Callahan's faceplate went clear, and Aloysius saw earnest blue eyes crinkle in a smile as the sergeant addressed him.

"Sir, stay behind me. I'll get you aboard in one piece."

Before Aloysius could answer the trooper, the flight deck's speakers sputtered to life again, and his heart sank. Given how quickly his plans had deteriorated after the last shipwide announcement, he was sure time that this one would only add more fuel to the fire.

"This is Lieutenant Ramirez in the command center. Captain Kołodziejski and his men have come aboard through the port cargo bay. I repeat, Captain Kołodziejski's men have breached the port cargo bay. Sir, if you can hear me, we're all with you. Crew of the *Valiant*, resist these invaders to the best of your ability! Don't let them—"

The sharp report of an induction pistol cut off Harlan's former second, and the sounds of a scuffle closed out the transmission. Aloysius closed his eyes, wishing he'd seen Alonso's face at least once before he and Harlan left the command center in his charge.

"Harlan, I—"

Harlan vaulted the workbench with an easy grace and was running at full speed toward the shuttle before Aloysius had a chance to continue his apology. Callahan was right behind her, and Aloysius stumbled to his feet after them, keenly aware that he had neither a helmet nor a weapon.

Callahan's weapon was braced at his shoulder as they moved. The sergeant was sending streams of micro-slugs not at the troopers at the ramp, but seemingly at random angles as he advanced. Aloysius did his best to stay behind him, but as the trio grew closer to the shuttle, he noticed return fire coming from several directions.

"Down, sir." Callahan stopped suddenly, and Aloysius dove for cover. The captain heard the pinging of slugs all around him as Callahan fell to his knees. A second burst spun him around so he was face up, and Aloysius watched the light leave the sergeant's eyes.

Harlan's pistol finally went dry, and this time instead of reloading she threw it ahead of her as she ran. Aloysius scooped up Callahan's weapon and aimed over her head, hoping to add some kind of distraction to her insane charge. But when one of the two troopers left on the ramp was suddenly missing a head, he decided that his poor marksmanship would only complicate matters.

Not knowing what else to do, Aloysius sprinted after her, firing the slugthrower blindly off to his right. Harlan launched herself at the remaining guard, who was staring at the downed and headless corpse of his partner when her outstretched arm took him in the neck. Both of them slammed into the cargo ramp, but Aloysius saw Harlan's arm raise and start slamming a gauntleted fist into the other trooper's faceplate.

Aloysius was almost to the ramp when his weapon ran dry, and he was so focused on Harlan's struggle that he didn't see the figure hurtling from his left side until it was too late. The new opponent's tackle was hard and fast, and Aloysius's head bounced against the edge of the ramp hard enough for him to see stars.

He felt, rather than saw, additional figures piling on top of him. Everything was spinning, and the sounds of fighting slowed until they were a distorted growl. A mirrored faceplate was shouting something at him, but Aloysius couldn't make his mouth work anymore. He was cold, and tired, and his suit weighed a ton.

The faceplate bobbed again, and something grabbed at his suit collar. Aloysius felt himself being dragged up the ramp, accompanied by a hideous slow-motion screeching sound. The faceplate disappeared, and Aloysius felt something hot and wet on his face as everything went red, then black.

As *Valiant* slipped away into darkness, one last thought went through his mind.

That could have gone better.

RAMIREZ

1352 SHIP TIME, SDF *VALIANT*

THE POUNDING on the out hatch was the only sound in the command center besides Alonso's frantic breathing, but like his fear, Carstairs and Maddox weren't going to go away anytime soon. Their last communication through the tac network had made that clear enough, and Alonso had already met and surpassed his daily quota of dread.

Helmet and gauntlets off, he was keying commands into the partially disassembled workstation as fast as he could, praying he'd never have to use any of them against his own crew.

Fucked doesn't even begin to describe this situation—mine, or *Valiant's.*

The arrival of *Indomitable* would normally be a relief to a vessel as badly damaged as *Valiant*, but Captain Kołodziejski's message had had the opposite effect on her crew. Even though many aboard had questions about their mission, the majority of them remained loyal to Captain Martin, and the resulting infighting was almost as damaging as the impact of the Object.

The one bright side to *Indomitable*'s arrival was the override sequence they'd used to unify all of *Valiant*'s systems under a single command. With it, Alonso now had access to most of the ship's systems, even some without any direct connections between them.

In addition to the dozen holos showing him armed insurrection around the ship, he had an amazing view of the debris field surrounding *Valiant* and the planetoid lodged in it. The remaining vessels of *Valiant*'s battlegroup had been ordered to withdraw, and a troop shuttle from *Indomitable* was on the way.

Because nothing says "let's be friends" like a shuttle full of armed hostiles.

In another circumstance, on another ship, Alonso might have opened the door and surrendered. But since whoever re-enabled *Valiant*'s communications network was downloading data from it as fast as they could, ignoring his hails, and preventing him from contacting the rest of the battlegroup, he had a low opinion of their good intentions.

Especially since the pod network shows firing solutions on both us, and the rest of the battlegroup.

The pounding stopped, and one of the many holos floating over Alonso's workstation showed his teammates give up on brute-forcing the hatch he'd jammed, and unpack a cutting torch just as a couple more troopers came up the corridor behind them. Carstairs dragged the cutter back to the hatch, and Alonso waited until he gave it another tug to kill the gravity.

Carstairs yanked himself off his feet, smashing his faceplate on the corner of the unit. He bounced once off the deck plating, then up and over the cutter on his way to the top of the corridor. He was almost there when Alonso turned the grav on again, and was slow getting up after a hard landing on the other side.

Basic protocol, Henry. Always use your boot magnets. And now Janet has to check you out before you can start on the door again.

Alonso had bought himself another few minutes in which to work, but there were no good endings to this standoff. He had nowhere to go, and he wasn't looking forward to shooting either of his teammates—his friends, over a difference of opinion.

The feeds flickered again, as the randomizing algorithm Alonso had implemented switched to another section of the ship. While he hadn't been able to stop his opposite number on *Indomitable* from downloading the comm feeds, Alonso had definitely been able to slow them down. And since the comms were also routing through the deployed sensor pods, he was able to delay each transmission just a little bit longer by storing an encrypted copy in the pods' recorders before it went over to the other dreadnaught.

I just need enough time to find the captain and LCDR Harlan, so we can figure out what to do next.

The feeds flickered again, and this time, one of holos showed a stand-off in a hangar bay full of half-repaired shuttles. It was the state of the ships that caught Alonso's eye at first, but then one of the armored figures removed its helmet and revealed himself as Captain Aloysius Martin.

Alonso dragged the holo out of the feed, locked it in, and keyed in the audio. He knew the activity would flag it over on *Indomitable* in about ten seconds, but he had to know what was going on down there.

"What's your name, son?"

One of the troopers aiming a weapon at the captain took a half step forward, and Alonso used the holo controls to focus on his chestplate. Part of his brain registered the arrival of two more armored figures outside the hatch, but his eyes were fixed on the hashmarks indicating the name and work-group of the trooper the captain was addressing.

Maranov. Shit. And Jensen's behind him. Hardliners, and clearly on Kołodziejski's side.

"Maranov, Sir. Please, don't move."

Bright light from the cutting torch flared on the corridor holo, and in the few seconds it took Alonso to shut down the blaring alert it triggered on his side of the hatch, he missed the Captain's reply. When he returned his attention to the hangar bay, Captain Martin had his back to Maranov and Jensen, and was handing his helmet to the armored figure of Mira Harlan, faceplate open and scowling like she'd just eaten something awful.

Alonso spared a glance at the hatch, the right side of which was glowing cherry red. He had exactly three more cards to play in his hand before he'd be forced to use his induction pistol, and resolved to make each one count.

"Everyone, please, do what the man said and lower your weapons. No one needs to die here, I just want to talk."

You've got that right, Sir. But Captain Kołodziejski and his supporters seem to have other plans.

The cutting torch shut down in the corridor, and Alonso had to hand it to Janet Maddox. Rather than cut all the way through the locking mechanism, she'd elected instead to disable the bypass circuitry and leave the hatch fully functional. Now all she had to do was rig a bypass of her own, and four heavily armed troopers would pour through the open hatch and take him into custody.

Although he didn't expect to fool them with the same trick twice, Alonso attached a safety tether to the workstation and killed the gravity again. All four troopers in the corridor stayed in place, though the loose equipment Alonso had piled in front of the hatch, as well as the safety netting containing it, began to jerk and flow to the rhythm of the still tumbling ship.

Surprised at how calm he was in the face of a potentially violent confrontation, Alonso pulled on his gauntlets, watching the green indicator lights on Maddox's minicomp come on one by one as she worked. He checked his pistol, then the display on his own minicomp wired into the workstation.

"No, you fools. Don't..."

Alonso snapped his head back to the holo just in time to see Mira Harlan throw the captain to the deck, kneel on his chest, and start firing with an induction pistol in each hand. Maranov's chestplate exploded as a twin volley of micro-slugs tore through his armor like it wasn't there, and while watching the almost balletic violence of the ensuing conflict, Alonso almost missed the opening of the hatch.

Precisely as planned, the floating mass of equipment hung in the air for a moment, obscuring the troopers' view of Alonso. He disengaged his boots, and pushed off gently from the deck. Once he was no longer directly connected to the metal grating, he tapped a virtual button on his minicomp, sending a massive electrical charge through the deck, the troopers, and the safety netting.

SDF hardsuits were insulated against static discharges, radiation surges, and most hostile environments. But magnetic boots still obeyed the laws of physics, and all four troopers were held fast to the deck in an unbreakable electromagnetic embrace, just as the safety net responded to the charge by contracting to its minimum dimensions. The floating equipment inside was expelled in the only direction it could travel, straight down the corridor into the misguided members of Fire Team One.

The debris itself wasn't deadly, but Alonso had packed his helmet with explosives, and a second tapped command filled the corridor with smoke and fire. A third sent a pre-recorded transmission on shipwide channel three, piggybacked through every emergency generator, sensor pod, and securecam in the network.

"This is Lieutenant Ramirez in the command center. Captain Kołodziejski and his men are coming aboard through the port cargo bay. I repeat, Captain Kołodziejski's men are now cycling through the port cargo bay. Sir, if you can hear me, we're all with you. Crew of the *Valiant*, resist these invaders to the best of your ability! Don't let them—"

A volley of micro-slugs poured through the hatch, destroying the workstation and cutting off the transmission. Alonso spun on his tether, coming around with his own pistol raised. He fired when he was aligned with the hatch, using the stream of grav-accelerated projectiles to correct his course and send him across the command center.

Either drained of its charge or compromised by return fire, the generator gave out, plunging the compartment into darkness. Enough light from the corridor made it through the netting to reveal an armored form slumped on the floor, but Alonso was unsure of which of his crewmates he'd just killed. In any event, he didn't have time to grieve as the net tore loose and the remaining three troopers rocketed in on maneuvering jets.

When they were halfway across the compartment, Alonso fired his own jets, thrusting perpendicular to their course with one hand on the safety rail. His tether tangled with at least one of the oncoming troopers, pulling Alonso hard to the right and swinging him out into open air.

He released the tether, intending to sail out into the corridor and escape. But he was a fraction of a second too slow, and his improvised trajectory was no match for the armor-enhanced strength of the arm that slammed him to the deck.

He heard the *SSSSHUNK* of magnetic boots connecting to the deck less than a meter from his unprotected head. A large mass settled on his chest, and a second later one of his unseen opponents activated Alonso's belt controls and locked down his suit.

Someone connected a second generator, and the lights came back on. From his position on the deck, Alonso couldn't see much more than the glowing barrel of an induction pistol centimeters away from his face, and a pitted and scratched faceplate to go along with the angry voice of Henry Carstairs.

"Damnit, Alonso, why'd you have to kill Janet? We could all have got out of this alive, even the captain. Now we have to figure out how bad you've fucked us, and whether or not to shoot you in your damn fool head."

Alonso knew exactly what he'd done, or at least he thought he did. His last transmission had contained not only a warning, but a dataworm that should have *Indomitable's* networks tied up for some time. Not only were they now getting all the feeds at once, but the images were displaying on every screen connected to their core, with the audio portion shuffling on a random sequence. Undoing the scrambling would mean breaking the worm's encryption algorithm, which Mira Harlan had assured him was the best available on any world.

And if there's anything I can still trust, it's that when Mira Harlan says her wives are the smartest people she's ever met, she probably knows what she's talking about.

At the same time, the worm was dumping *Indomitable's* logs into the sensor pods; on the off chance that Alonso lived long enough to have a court martial, he'd want some evidence to present in his defense.

"What the hell is that?"

Mindful of the pistol pointed at his head, Alonso fought the urge to snap his head towards the still active holo.

"Shit, look at the size of that thing! It must be—"

"Priorities, people!" Carstairs moved the weapon away from Alonso's temple, which let him turn his head enough to see the other troopers huddled around a flickering holo. He glimpsed a flash of something large and orange over their shoulders before Henry stepped between them and barked an order.

"I want a list of everything Ramirez did when he was alone in here, and I want it now!"

"But, Chief, you've got to see this. It's..."

Alonso couldn't see the holo proper, but he had an excellent view of armored feet shuffling to the side, presumably to let Carstairs see for himself what they were marveling at.

Whatever it was, it shook Carstairs enough to loosen his grip on the induction pistol. It clattered to the floor, and Alonso could barely make out his next words, spoken so softly that Henry might not know he'd voiced them at all.

"But...but that's not possible..."

Then the slowly spinning deck jumped up and punched Alonso in the back of his head. He was pressed "down" into the deck for a few seconds as if *Valiant* was under heavy burn, and then he was floating free in darkness.

Alonso felt something warm spreading through his hair, and tried to raise a hand to see what it was. But his suit was still locked down, and he could do nothing but float helplessly until he either bounced off a wall, or one of his former friends decided he was to blame for this too and took him completely out of the equation.

And things were going so well...

JARL

Jarl heard weapons fire echoing down the maintenance shaft and slowed his advance. He didn't believe anyone was looking for him, but his active camouflage would do nothing to muffle the sounds of his movement if an enemy happened to be standing near his exit point.

The sounds of combat were coming from the other side of a ventilation unit, and as he approached, Jarl saw that Katra had fused a two-meter fan in place with a low-powered pulser blast, and then scored a centimeter-long arrow pointing down into the metal.

Jarl listened at the panel. The sounds of the unseen combat were mainly confused shouts and the growls of the earth weapons—*slugthrowers*— he'd seen earlier. The whine of Katra's pulser was an indicator of her status, and he allowed himself a smile.

Picking her shots. Not under any particular stress. Good.

Jarl applied pressure to the base of the panel. From this angle he could see a free space directly under the vent, about a three-meter drop from the maintenance shaft. Wishing he could see more of the immediate area, he dropped through feet first.

There was a flurry of shots as he hit the deck. Something hit the wall behind him—a lot of somethings. Jarl let his legs go limp and continued his fall until he was lying flat on the decking with his weapon out in front of him. A volley of tiny projectiles ricocheted through the space he'd just vacated and tore through the surrounding crates and equipment.

When he wasn't killed by a follow-up volley, he rolled until his back was against something solid and aimed at a gap between crates about two meters from where he'd landed. Jarl counted out ten seconds, then eased himself to his feet. He was careful to keep himself completely covered by the surrounding crates as he took a few soft steps forward. The helmet's pickups registered another shot from Katra's pulser, but there were no more slug throwers firing in his immediate vicinity.

Jarl readied his fingers on the firing studs and spun around the corner. Instead of a crouching enemy waiting to kill him, he saw two downed combatants, one missing part of its torso and the other apparently dead from several hundred small punctures. The weapon in the first body's hands had a red-hot barrel, from which rose small tendrils of smoke.

Interesting.

Jarl was concerned with the blood covering all the nearby surfaces and its likely effect on his camouflage. Judging passage through the narrow space to be too risky, he looked up at the wall of crates enclosing the free space under the vent. It looked sturdy enough to support his weight, so Jarl slung his weapon across his back, aligning it with his spine and triggering the static charge that stiffened the weapon's strap and fixed it in place.

He pulled his hand weapon from its chest sheath and then leapt for the top of the nearest stack, using his free hand to steady himself once he landed.

Jarl blinked twice as he scanned the area, giving his brain two quick images to analyze for immediate dangers. With his faceplate closed, he couldn't use his own senses to their fullest potential, so he set his subconscious mind to the task instead.

Jarl didn't feel threatened, so he took two long strides across the piled supplies and swung down to the deck on what looked like maintenance scaffolding. Mindful of the weapon on his back, he didn't roll forward when he landed, but to the side to take cover under a landing strut. Keeping his hand weapon out in front of him, he listened for the whine of Katra's pulser to orient himself. The rapid-fire growls of multiple types of slugthrowers told him the approximate locations of the enemies he couldn't see.

The center of activity seemed to be a shuttle located directly opposite his position—apparently the only intact craft in the bay. A large group of suited figures were wrestling on a ramp that angled back into the vessel.

Lining up a shot, he announced his location to Katra with a pulser shot into an exposed enemy back, and ducked behind the landing strut in anticipation of return fire.

Katra's answering shot killed a second enemy, and some of the remaining figures scrambled up the ramp dragging several others.

Two factions. What have we stepped into?

Jarl worked his way under the small vessel's hull to Katra. Her fire was coming from inside a partially disassembled machine on the other side, the function of which was a mystery to Jarl. It looked too large to be a component of the ship above her, and though something about its construction seemed familiar the pile of parts nearby seemed to be of different manufacture altogether.

Jarl pulled a gravity grenade from his harness and thumbed it active. The fist-sized cylinder was a stripped-down version of the personal generator built into his encounter suit, designed to create distractions rather than casualties. They were dangerous to use aboard spaceships, but Jarl wasn't particularly concerned about the enemy's safety. If a few of them got crushed by their own gear as two grav fields worked out their differences, so be it.

Jarl moved to the front of the small craft, listening for hostile activity. Picking a spot near where he'd last heard a slugthrower, Jarl threw the grenade and sprinted back along the hull. As he moved, he replaced the hand weapon in its sheath and released his weapon.

Jarl spun to face the rest of the bay before sitting down, and ducked behind a workbench, and a second later Katra settled into place beside him.

The reunited Gammas deactivated their camouflage and came together in an interlocking, seated embrace. Both kept their weapons at the ready, aligning themselves so that they could see all of the immediate area.

Their faceplates touched, and Jarl noticed Katra's face was slick with sweat. Her pupils were also larger than they should have been given the light level in the bay. It wasn't enough to interfere with her aim, and her arms seemed strong around him. But unless something had happened he didn't know about, the signs of stress were troubling. Before he could say anything, she gave him a tactical overview.

"Eight left, two factions. More coming. Hear the announcement?"

"No."

They were speaking barely above a whisper, trusting their helmets to insulate the sound of their voices. Jarl had seen three actives heading up the ramp with two prisoners; he stopped looking at Katra's face and scanned for one of the others. He hadn't heard any firing since the grenade went off, but that didn't mean they were out of danger.

"*SDF Valiant*. Coup in progress. Boss?"

Jarl processed Katra's summary quickly, knowing she preferred action to planning. His response was equally brief.

"Inbound. Three minutes, no trouble."

Jarl's estimate was based on the route the Omegas outlined before he left the main group, and his belief that Jantine and the Deltas could handle any force outfitted like the enemies they'd encountered so far. But a second, possibly third hostile force aboard the ship complicated matters.

Katra shifted, and Jarl was surprised when some of her weight fell onto him. She didn't change the angle of her arms or lower her weapon, but the sounds of her breathing were…odd.

I don't like this. Something is wrong.

Jarl's mind raced through new tactical situations, working out fire plans requiring only one active. But the longer he dwelled on the subject, the more he had to know what had happened to Katra.

"Status?"

Jarl decided the risk of attack from his left side was negligible and turned to read Katra's expression. Her eyes were still wide, and he wished he could see enough of her neck to time her pulse.

"Three hits, micro-slug ricochets. Collapsed lung, impact fractures in left arm. Suit sealed up, stims. Operational."

Jarl understood her firing solutions better now. Firing prone, all of the pulser's action was channeled into her right side. She was still more than a match for these opponents, but she'd need to get out of her encounter suit sooner rather than later for treatment.

Jarl considered what to say next, counting down the seconds until Jantine, and now more importantly, Crassus and Artemus, would arrive. He could capture the shuttle on his own, but he'd rather have a Delta with him to be sure. And no matter what, they needed more intel on the situation aboard the *Valiant*. If there was a third force of actives heading their way, it was even more imperative that Katra receive proper treatment.

In the end, he decided to take her at her word. She'd never lied to him before, and with the stakes so high, wasn't likely to start now.

"Noted. Flush?"

"Negative. High ground."

Jarl nodded, then leaned back, twisting to the side as he broke their embrace so that both Gammas could disengage without spoiling their aim. Katra sat up straighter, and now that he knew what to look for, he saw that her movements were a little stiffer than normal. If things got worse before the rest of the mods arrived, he trusted her to let him know.

Jarl scanned the area for new firing positions. Whoever had organized the repairs on the *Valiant*'s small vessels had done a good job of leaving the center free of obstructions, but their discipline wasn't absolute. For some reason, the area felt more abandoned than active, and scaffoldings like the ones surrounding the crafts being repaired were everywhere.

Jarl aimed his weapon at several positions that would offer him good sightlines of both the intact shuttle and the bay's main entrance. Katra indicated a third inside one of the partially disassembled vessels, which Jarl realized would also let her cover parts of the corridor outside.

He pumped his clenched fist once, and the Gammas split off. As he ran, Jarl saw a hardsuit moving closer to the shuttle's still-open ramp, and he snapped off a shot in its direction. Katra must have seen the motion as well, because her shot changed the body's direction as it fell.

The enemy must have been about to fire when it died, because its weapon discharged when it hit the deck and sent a stream of micro-slugs toward the shuttle. Jarl couldn't tell if the vessel was damaged as a result, but one of the bodies still lying on the ramp was hit a few times, and the results were impressive. Portions of the hardsuit simply disintegrated, severing one of the legs and sending painted shrapnel bouncing around the immediate area.

Jarl reached the scaffolding he'd selected and swung himself upwards with his left hand. If Katra's count was correct, there was still one hostile at large, and he needed to locate it as soon as possible. Settling into his perch, he realized he could see through the forward window of the shuttle.

Three armed and suited individuals had their backs to him. On any other mission, Jarl would send a volley of pulser fire through the window and be done with it. But they needed the shuttle to make their escape, and it would probably be hard to fly even without unnecessary damage.

Malik would know what to do. He was our tactician. I'm just a weapon with legs.

But that's not how Malik had treated him or the other Gammas. Malik's attitude was far above that of a typical Beta, more tolerant than even Jantine. Jarl and Katra were the only ones left now, and it still felt odd to be outnumbered by Betas in such a small group.

The whine of a pulser brought him back to the present. Jarl shifted as subtly as he could to see what Katra was shooting at, and the sight of two dozen fresh opponents both excited and troubled him. They were clustered at the entrance to the bay, and Jantine was due within seconds.

Katra had waited until the newcomers were all the way inside before firing, and it looked to Jarl like the bodies on the floor had been moving to meet them. Jarl took aim at a faceplate, steadied his hands, and fired.

The shot took one of the enemies high in the throat. While not as spectacular as Katra's precise shooting, it had the same general effect and dropped the enemy instantly. He sighted on his next target, tracking it as the enemies split into several groups and sought cover.

Katra's next shot was as accurate as ever, and Jarl noticed she'd waited ten seconds after his shot before firing. Counting down that same period, Jarl cleared his mind of distractions and surrendered to the moment. His heartbeat slowed down, and when the time came he stopped his breath and made his body perfectly rigid.

Seventy meters away, a helmet exploded in a shower of bloody white fragments. The enemies around it went into a panic, splitting their forces once again. There were now three distinct target groups —four, counting those inside the shuttle. A corner of Jarl's mind registered that only one suited figure was standing in the shuttle's window now, positioned sideways in an attempt to see the deck outside and also keep a weapon trained on two other figures inside.

Prisoners. Nice of the enemy to police themselves.

Jarl shifted his aim to the base of the ramp, counting down the seconds until another head presented itself. As if responding to his needs, two enemies came down the ramp. Jarl waited for a clear shot, then sent a pair of pulser blasts at them.

The first hit one of the suited figures in the shoulder, spinning it to the right. The second destroyed its target's left arm before carving a hole in its chest.

Not a warrior's death. But it serves.

Jarl switched his focus to the entrance, marking the positions and numbers of the two enemy groupings. He selected a target for his next shot, confident he'd guessed Katra's choice as well. He shifted his aim towards the front of the launch bay for a follow up shot, but Katra's target dove aside right before she fired, revealing Jantine and Artemus charging down the corridor.

Katra realized she was firing into her own people just in time, but too late to stop the pulser shot. She did manage to pull it off to the right, causing a shining crater to appear about three meters off the ground. Unfortunately, walls made more sound when struck by a phased plasma pulse than people did, and both enemy groups turned to see what had happened.

Jantine hit the deck instantly, firing her weapon as she dropped. One of the Deltas ran across the opening to draw fire while the other opened up with a weapon in each of its upper hands.

Jarl heard another weapon fire, this time from the base of the shuttle's ramp. He thought it a pointless gesture at first, given the observed range of the enemy's weapons. But then he realized there was another possible target, and saw Katra's uncamouflaged body fall out of her perch.

Jarl was moving almost before he'd fully registered what had happened, pulser on rapid fire and aimed at the base of the ramp as he dropped from the scaffolding. He lost line of sight when he reached the deck, but he was satisfied the shooter was dead.

Another volley of combined pulser and slugthrower fire sounded in the still air, and then he heard nothing else. He reached Katra just in time to see several punctures in the encounter suit sealing over on her upper back.

Jarl put down his weapon and cradled Katra in his arms. She wasn't moving, and when he turned her over he saw her faceplate was broken in several places. Fearing the worst, he popped the seals at her neck and removed her helmet entirely. It came away trailing a line of blood, and Jarl sat back heavily on his legs. He removed his own helmet and watched her bloody face in stunned silence for several seconds, and it was only when he saw her eyelids flutter that he remembered to breathe.

"Pulled...shot. Jantine...okay?"

Jarl's instinct was to brush away the clear fragments of faceplate embedded in her right temple, but he couldn't bring himself to touch her.

Not her. Not now.

Looking at the blood flowing freely down her face reminded him for some reason of what else was touching her skin, and his. He swiped a finger down his jawline, then Katra's, and heard five clicks in his ear just ahead of Jantine's voice.

"Report."

"At least one hostile inside shuttle. One group of reinforcements already arrived. Katra injured, multiple suit punctures."

Jarl heard Katra's voice both from in front of him and in his ear as she gave her own status report.

"Op...Operational."

Jarl helped her to a sitting position, keeping an eye out for more hostiles. She had a pained expression and raised a hand to feel around the area where the faceplate fragments had cut her face. He offered a helping hand, but she waved it away and continued speaking.

"I can...Good to fight, boss."

"If you're sure, it's good enough for me. We should take the... what are you do—"

Four clicks sounded, then three, then two as Jantine's voice cut off mid-sentence. Jarl grabbed for his pulser and vaulted over Katra, rolling into a combat crouch as soon as he could see the bay doors.

"Jarl. Jarl, what's happening?"

At the bay entrance, Crassus was standing in front of Jantine and holding all four arms wide in an attempt to stop the Omegas from entering the bay. Artemus was pulling at one of them, but the Omega shrugged him off with a casual motion that belied the force necessary to send the Delta staggering across the corridor.

"Jarl, report!"

Before he could respond, a volley of slugs hit the scaffolding behind them and filled the air with deadly ricochets. He felt hits in his side and leg, and fire spread inside his chest. He fell to his knees, left hand clutched to his abdomen. The gauntlet came away bloody, revealing three ragged tears in his encounter suit. He watched the smart fabric seal around them, and then a flush of endorphins widened his eyes as the auto-doc's stims kicked in.

So that's what it feels like...

He felt a hand on his shoulder and turned his head to see Katra's face hovering centimeters from his own.

"Jarl, what are our orders?"

Jarl looked into Katra's widened eyes, and he wondered just how much time the two of them had left. The stims were only partially dulling his pain, and he felt something grinding inside his left knee as she helped him into a crouching position.

Neither of them could see Jantine from where they were, but the renewed sounds of pulser fire gave them a fairly accurate idea of her position. Jarl knew more than that, though. He knew the Omegas had been acting erratically since they'd abandoned Doria, and that they were very insistent on getting to this part of the ship.

And since there was only one thing worth having in the compartment, Jarl also knew what Jantine wanted the Gammas to do.

"We take the shuttle."

KOŁODZIEJSKI

1406 SHIPTIME, **SDF** *INDOMITABLE*

"G ET THE FEEDS BACK. Get them back!" Horace's headache was not going away anytime soon, but not knowing what was going on aboard *Valiant* was far worse than the pain.

Watson's blood-replacement treatment is making things worse, not better. I have to have that gennie!

"I'm trying, sir. But it seems like someone's installed an interrupt circuit. Compensating now." Monahan's voice was calm as she worked, but Horace saw sweat on her brow, amid a cascading aura that promised even more pain in a few seconds.

The pit was full of noise and activity, with officers from both first and second shifts manning every station to coordinate not only what was left of *Valiant*'s battlegroup, but also the first of his own ships to arrive. Horace was hovering over Monahan's shoulder, and the constant barrage of sound and light threatened to overwhelm him. But as bits of data floated up from the jumble of noise coming from her console, Horace added them to his ongoing mental diagram.

"-40% power and dropping. We have foreign matter lodged in our starboard hull-"

"-had no warning-"

"-well someone ran power down here, we should at least look-"

This last statement caught his attention, and he narrowed his focus to just that voice, and the one that answered it.

"All right, but we should be careful." Bob Calas' voice was strong enough to pick out in any crowd, even if Horace hadn't been desperate to hear it. A few seconds later, Monahan got the visual feeds back online, and his third-in-command's helmet cam gave him more data to process.

Six of *Valiant*'s crew members lay dead in front of a wall of black stone, cleverly arranged among repair kits and a series of crates so as to be not only hidden from casual inspection, but also secured from floating away in null gravity.

The surreal nature of their placement was alarming in and of itself, but the markings on the crates were much more concerning. They weren't in the Marsscript commonly used aboard Fleet vessels, or even Standard English. Instead, each bore a legend of flowing symbols interspersed with blocky numbers, and if Calas got close enough Horace was sure he'd see smaller patterns of concentric dots surrounding them.

One for each of the outer colonies. So Martin's in league with the fucking gennies after all, and now we've got an even bigger problem to deal with.

Kołodziejski was about to give his crew a warning when another of Calas's team finally discovered what their captain's keen eyes saw instantly.

"What the hell happened here? It's like they were torn apart."

Calas' viewpoint shifted, and Horace heard a sharp intake of breath before he spoke.

"I don't know, but Captain Kołodziejski wants visual confirmation of all *Valiant* personnel. Get their helmets off, and scan the faces. Martinez, you're with me."

Now that the survey team's lights were all pointed in the same direction, Horace could see that the black stone wasn't the only anomaly in the corridor. What he'd taken at first for a natural formation was actually dull black metal, with a door-sized hole cut through it.

Calas sent Martinez through the opening with a gesture, following close behind him with his weapon drawn. Martinez took one step into what appeared to be a large compartment, then fell flat on his face, sending his hand light spinning off into the darkness.

"What the—Lieutenant, there's grav in here! And the floor's different."

Calas's next words weren't for his man inside the anomalous structure, but for Horace himself.

"*Indomitable*, this is Survey One Actual. Be advised we've discovered an entry point to the embedded planetoid, a man-made structure of some kind. Proceeding as per Alpha protocol."

Good, he saw the crates too.

Horace opened his mouth to speak, then thought better and leaned forward to tap out a reply. With so many people crowding the pit, he didn't want to inspire anyone to ask questions he wasn't ready to answer just yet about exactly what, or rather, who, he was looking for.

>>HK ACK>GOOD HUNTING>

Calas sent back an acknowledgment of his own, then stepped through the makeshift door. Horace watched with intent eyes as Calas's perspective shifted about thirty degrees, then settled as he adjusted to the new surface he was standing on. There wasn't much to look at in the blackness, but as Calas's light played down the wall of the chamber, it revealed two thin figures huddled together about twenty meters away.

Both were wearing a form-fitting black garment, almost as dark as the compartment around them. One of was a young girl, who raised a hand against the light, then started coughing. It looked like she was holding something in her other hand, and the second figure slid down from where he'd been cradled against her chest to rest his head in her lap.

"I've got survivors over here! Anderson, get in here with the scanner, and mind the first step. The floor and grav field in here are both angled away from *Valiant*."

Without waiting for a response, Calas moved forward past Martinez. Horace thought he was moving a bit faster than necessary, but was unsure what to do with this new data point.

A few seconds later, Calas was kneeling next to the girl and her companion. Her mouth moved, but a gasping wheeze was the only sound she made. She flashed Calas a bloody smile, and when her left arm moved below Calas' field of vision, Horace had a sudden overwhelming sense of dread.

DORIA

Doria sat in the darkness, watching her life counting down on the handheld. The numbers were comforting, and promised an end to her pain.

Not long now.

Malik was resting comfortably with her right arm curled around him. She felt a tinge of regret that he wouldn't be with her when the time came, but in the end his pain was too great, and she'd had to massage his mind into unconsciousness. Even while asleep, she could still feel his strength, and that's all that mattered

The handheld was the only light in the compartment that had been their home for the last few weeks. Malik had helped her configure it as a switch for the destruct charges before succumbing to his injuries, and as long as she kept her left thumb on the activation panel, they stayed alive.

Doria smiled, amused by how fiercely she clung to each one of the fifty-nine seconds of life she had left. Then a cough shook her, bringing up blood to fill her mouth and nose.

Fifty-five...fifty-four...fifty-three...

Wait. What was that?

At the edge of her vision, the faint green glow she'd grown used to was getting both brighter and whiter. Sharp lines now outlined the hole through which the others had left, and as it grew in intensity, Doria could hear voices.

"What the hell happened here? It's like they were torn apart."

"I don't know, but Captain Kołodziejski wants visual confirmation of all *Valiant* personnel. Get their helmets off, and scan the faces. Martinez, you're with me."

Two spots of light bobbed through the hole, and Doria saw answering spots form on the raft of crates in the center of the container. A human form started in, and then fell to the deck with a small cry

"What the—Lieutenant, there's grav in here! And the floor's different."

Oops. But to be fair, we weren't expecting visitors, were we Malik?

A second form came through, a bit more cautiously than the man picking himself up off the compartment's deck. Doria saw the light it was holding swing around the container. She tried to focus on their faces, but after so long in the dark even their small lights were blinding.

When one of the lights swung over her and Malik slumped against the wall, her right hand came up reflexively to shield her eyes. Malik groaned softly as he slid down into her lap, and the combined movements started her coughing again, this time much louder and wetter.

"I've got survivors! Anderson, get in here with the scanner, and mind the first step. The floor and grav field in here are angled away from *Valiant*."

The speaker moved forward, followed by his two companions. Doria tried to reach out to their minds, but her own pain was almost overwhelming. It was all she could do to keep sitting up straight, and her grip on the handheld.

She tried to speak, but couldn't manage more than a pained wheeze. When the man holding the lamp kneeled down in front of her, she flashed him a bloody smile.

"I don't believe it. Guys, they're just a couple of—"

Doria's smile widened as she lifted her thumb. The countdown stopped at fifteen seconds, but she didn't mind.

It's going to be all right, Malik. It's over n—

KOŁODZIEJSKI

HORACE PRESSED himself back into the command chair, unwilling to acknowledge that one his best friends was about to die. Even though the recording was broadcasting from a hundred kilometers away, Bob's last words were like a micro-slug to the heart.

"I don't believe it. Guys, they're just a couple of—"

A flash of light filled Calas's faceplate, and the feed went dark. Kołodziejski heard a deep rumbling sound on half a dozen other audio channels, and looked up at one of the screens Monahan had dedicated to *Indomitable's* forward sensors. *Valiant's* aft section was now floating free, and what had been a giant mass of black space rock was now a steadily expanding debris field.

All chatter in the pit ended, and Kołodziejski relaxed, slumping deeper into his chair. He'd expected resistance from Captain Martin's crew, but despite the suspicious crates he'd had no expectation of any gennie presence other than his missing text subject.

And one of them just killed a Redstone dreadnaught, with something small enough to fit in the palm of her hand. What the hell have you gotten us into, Aloysius?

"Sir? Sir?"

Still processing what just happened, Kołodziejski acknowledged Monahan with a distracted wave. Something else wasn't right, and he couldn't quite put his finger on it.

"Sir, it's Commander Annahko. She's..."

Caroline. My god, I've lost Caroline too!

"—ting more information. What should I tell her, sir?

I've killed her. I've killed Bob, and now the gennies are going to kill the rest of us. I've...

"Sir, Sir?"

Kołodziejski closed his eyes, trying to summon up the image of Caroline's face. But all he could see was the strange, alien features of the gennie girl who'd killed her, smiling at him with bloody teeth.

"Get...get us out of here, Alexandra. Order all ships to retreat, then blast what's left of *Valiant* out of existence!"

It was perhaps an overreaction, but there was no way Kołodziejski could let Aloysius Martin get away from him now, not after what he'd done.

I hope you burn in whatever Russelites consider to be Hell, you bastard. And if you're not there already, I'll be happy to send you the rest of the way.

"Sir, Commander Annahko is still waiting for orders. What do you want her to do?"

Kołodziejski's eyes snapped open, and he saw Monahan's face hovering far too close. It did block out the riot of holographic information behind her, but he couldn't help but see outlines of the dead gennie around her eyes. He drew himself up until he could sit up fully in the command chair, then broke the silence with a stuttering reply.

"Put—put her through."

Monahan touched something on her handheld, and Kołodziejski flinched. But instead of a blast of searing white light, Caroline's voice came from Monahan's station, and when the junior officer moved away, he saw the face of the woman he could not dare to love.

"Captain, I'm...we're okay. We're fielding distress calls from survey teams, including an active fire situation in one of the transfer bays. I'm not sure which one exactly, but given that it's still going on, it has to be in the forward section. We lost the boarding tube in the explosion, but can still attempt a hard lock with *Valiant* if necessary. Please advise."

Distress calls…gennies…boarding…

Of course!

Despite the pain of Bob Calas's loss, despite the near loss of Caroline, the last piece of the impossible puzzle fell into place, and Kołodziejski felt more like himself than he had any time in the last few months. The next steps were clear, but first he had to protect the future.

"Negative, commander. Pull back to the edge of the debris field, and coordinate our teams aboard *Valiant* as best you can. There's too much of that planetoid still tumbling around out there, and we're having some problems resolving her internal feeds. You'll have to be our eyes and ears for now."

"Understood, sir. Annahko out."

Kołodziejski looked around the command center, selecting the people he knew he could trust absolutely. The list was smaller than it should have been, but still left him with enough hands for what had to happen next.

"Lieutenants Monahan and Henderson, Chief Kirk, please begin a spectral analysis of that black rock. I want to know what it is, what it came from, and how to neutralize it. Everyone else, get to the shuttles, Commander Annahko is going to need some help getting our people off *Valiant*."

Despite his earlier reservations, first and second shifts were still members of the finest crew he'd ever served with. They didn't waste time with questions, just secured their duty stations and filed out of the compartment. As soon as they were gone, Horace used his command key to lock down the command center, and turned to address the other three people in the compartment.

"It goes without saying that I trust you three, and it's time you know why we're out here. Captain Martin and his people are colluding with the gennies, and have stolen a gennie prisoner from a secured Fleet installation. We believe it to be aboard *Valiant*, and locating it is our top priority.

"How many of you saw the last few seconds of Lt. Calas's feed?"

Henderson and Kirk looked nervously at one another, then shook their heads.

"Bring it back up, Alexandra."

Monahan picked up on what he wanted, and enlarged the holo enough so that Kołodziejski could point out the gennie supply crates, and the black uniforms the two dead gennies were wearing.

"Yesterday, we intercepted a gennie transmission, which I believe was a precursor to this cowardly attack. I have no idea what that rock is made of, or even why or how they used it to disable *Valiant*. The one thing I do know is that there is a gennie invasion force aboard that ship, and we need to capture them.

"So here's what I need you to do. Henderson, you and I will start working through every second of footage you can find for individuals wearing these black uniforms. Once we've got a fix on them, we'll relay their location to Commander Annahko and she'll get our people moving in the right direction. Monahan, find me some way though this interference. If someone has been scrambling *Valiant*'s feeds as you suspect, we'll need our own intel to work with."

"And me, sir?" Senior Chief Michael Kirk wasn't a communications officer like the other two, or even an officer at all. He was the ballistics master of first shift, and the best shot in the fleet.

"I need you to maintain our firing solutions on *Valiant*'s battlegroup. The moment any one of those ships makes a move contrary to my evacuation order, I want you to destroy it. Can you handle that, son?"

"Sir, yes Sir!"

"Good. Let's get to it, people."

Kołodziejski settled back in his chair, and pulled up as many feeds as he could see without turning his head, starting from the timecodes closest to the distress call. Henderson was good at his job, but he was no Simak, and would rely too much on the computing core for pattern recognition. Since *Valiant* and *Indomitable* were essentially the same ship, all he had to do was find where the gennies had come aboard, and extrapolate their path to the transfer bays from there.

This would be a lot easier, and a lot less painful, if Bob's feed had captured that corridor designation in his last moments of life. I'll have to watch them all at the same time, and discard the superfluous ones until I've got them in my sights.

Of the transmissions Monahan had already decoded, about half had no usable visual cues. Either the corridors were without power, or were on the wrong side of the ship entirely. It took him almost a minute to find the repair crew cutting into the metal surface, and he paused the feed just before they got all the way through.

Collapsing the hemisphere of light in front of him to a single image was a welcome relief from the pain in his head, and gave him a starting point to work from. Kołodziejski took a few moments to rest his eyes, and savored each one of them.

Alright, you gennie freaks. Let's see how many people you've brought to the party.

"Mr. Henderson, I have them. Ms. Monahan, focus your efforts on transfer bays four through eight, and have Commander Annahko move all available personnel in that direction. I want prisoners, and I want them now."

"Yes, sir."

Henderson moved closer to the command chair, and Kołodziejski expanded the holo so that both men could get a better look. The light of the cutting torch in the image gave him an excellent view of the wall itself, which appeared to be the corner of a standard-issue cargo container. When combined with the dim emergency lights of the repair crew, there was more than enough illumination to see there were only Fleet supplies in the corridor, and no gennie crates.

Interesting.

Kołodziejski made sure to set the playback to normal speed before he started the feed again. Although he wouldn't have any problem processing the information, his head was fuzzy enough from recent events that having Henderson's eyes as a backup was not only convenient, but necessary.

One of the techs in the holo moved to pull the cut section of metal free, but before he could attach the grab handles it exploded out into the corridor, followed quickly by a barrage of energy blasts. Then came two gennies in black, form-fitting suits topped with helmets so thin Kołodziejski wondered if they offered the wearer any protection at all. The pair were moving so fast Kołodziejski had to check the playback settings again, and five seconds later, there were no humans left alive in the corridor.

Then things really got weird.

The next two gennies through the opening were giants, with what appeared to be extra arms coming out of their torsos and long, black weapons in each of their four hands. They bounded past the others into the darkness, followed by three regular-sized gennies.

Then the monsters crawled through the hole, and a cold pit formed in Kołodziejski's stomach. Even though they were crouching, they had to be at least three meters tall, with wide, flat heads and what looked in the dim light to be orange skin. They did not wear sleek black suits like the other gennies, but instead simple coveralls. Each one was pulling a double load of the crates he'd seen earlier, and given their relative size each of the monsters had to have been dragging at least two metric tons behind them, if not more.

Omegas, shit. Which means this isn't just a simple attack, but a full-blown invasion force. Those monsters are far too valuable to risk on anything else, which means…

Which means they might have an Alpha with them too!

Kołodziejski kept watching the feed for more gennies, but none came through the hole. Then one of the monsters turned its mutant head and focused a double set of eyes on the securecam. The recording was at least 45 minutes old, but it felt to Horace like the monster was staring directly at him, even though at the time he was millions of kilometers away.

Then its mouth closed into a tight line, and the transmission wavered and cut out.

"Thoughts, Mr. Henderson?"

"I'm not sure, captain. I've read the intelligence briefings, of course. But to see them in action...how can we stand against that kind of power?"

"With discipline, Randall. Discipline and honor. As long as we don't give in, as long as we keep the goal of a free and pure human race in mind, we'll persevere. Ms Monahan?"

"Almost there, captain. The interference seems to have stopped, but all that rock out there is definitely making things difficult. There. I have them! Transfer bay six. Relaying their position to Commander Annahko now, as well as all the feeds from that area."

"Excellent work, lieutenant. Put them up."

Unlike the dim corridors and low quality helmet footage they'd been studying, transfer bay six was well lit, and had enough secure cams in place for Alexandra to give them a true holographic image, with sound. In fact, it was real enough that when a black-clad figure shot past him into frame, Kołodziejski and Henderson ducked away from it as fast as they could.

The gennies he could see had those long black weapons, and were not shy about using them. In short order, they took out two squads of troopers, one from *Valiant*, and another with *Indomitable* suit markings. The gennies moved in and out of cover with an almost feline grace, ducking away from volleys of micro-slugs like they weren't even there.

The transfer bay was full of machinery and shuttles under repair, with engines, grav generators, and scaffoldings everywhere. Monahan was keeping the image focused on the gennies, but Kołodziejski could still see the effects of their strange weapons on hard-suited troopers, and it wasn't at all encouraging. One blast per kill, and from the way they moved, Kołodziejski surmised they were the same two that had taken out *Valiant*'s repair team. Armed, experienced SDF troopers seemed to pose no greater threat than had the helpless techs, and despite what he'd said to Henderson, Kołodziejski had to admire their skill.

The gennies were taking hits as they raced across the transfer bay, but even though several took the larger one high in the chest, it didn't seem to slow them down at all. Their black suits just melted around any micro-slug punctures, and they kept on moving toward to the aft ramp of the only shuttle in the bay that looked even remotely spaceworthy. The pair obliterated the human guards at the base of the ramp, then charged up into the vessel.

"Caroline, are you seeing this?"

"Affirmative, captain. I have three squads en route, and the first should be getting there right about now."

The deep-throated roar of an induction pistol sounded somewhere in the bay, and Monahan refocused the image on the entrance while keeping the shuttle under observation in a second holo. Kołodziejski saw the orange giants squaring off against a squad of *Indomitable* troopers, or what was left of them, anyway.

In the scant moments since Monahan shifted the image's focus, one of the monsters had taken out one of the incoming troopers by the simple expediency of bringing its massive hands together, with the trooper in the middle.

Kołodziejski could hear the ceramaplate armor crack even over the roar of slugthrowers and induction pistols. Then the monster did something even more barbaric, picking up the trooper and using him or her as a club to batter away the rest.

The other one moved into the corridor, micro-slugs bouncing off its broad chest in a deadly spray of shrapnel. Kołodziejski couldn't see what happened next, but seconds later as monster charged back into the transfer bay its jumpsuit was drenched in blood Horace suspected was not its own.

My God. Is there anything at all we can do to stop them?

JANTINE

JANTINE SENT ANOTHER BURST OF PULSER FIRE TOWARD THE ENEMIES surging through the bay doors, wondering just how many more she'd need to kill before the day was over. She saw Crassus drop behind a scaffold to slot energizers into all of his pulsers, just as Artemus intensified his fire from the other side. The Delta had claimed several enemy weapons from the fallen, and the noise as he emptied them into the oncoming foes was incredible. Jantine also noticed dark blood falling from Artemus's shoulders, fat droplets shaking loose with the recoil of the captured slugthrowers.

How long will it be before we're reduced to throwing rocks? They just keep coming...

If not for the Omegas' bizarre actions they might be aboard the shuttle by now. She had no idea if the Gammas were successful in eliminating any resistance inside the small vessel, only that her force was pinned down and separated.

A warning beep sounded from her own pulser's energizer, and she dropped behind the stacked crates she was using as cover. Whether the containers would offer her any protection at all from the enemy's ridiculously overpowered slugthrowers was somewhat in question, but the skill level of their opponents was finally matching up to her expectations.

With the sounds of battle raging around her, Jantine ejected the spent module. Slotting in a fresh energizer took only a few seconds, but waiting for it to generate a charge took a bit longer. She used the time to do a sight check on her people. JonB was crouched beside her with his eyes closed, mouthing some silent mantra she couldn't make out. Carlton was across the bay next to Crassus, and the Omegas...

The deck pitched wildly to the side, and the crates toppled onto her. The unexpected impact forced the air from her lungs, and all she could do for several seconds was stare at her pulser on the deck, half a meter from her outstretched hand.

"Jantine. Jantine!"

JonB's voice seemed far away. Darkness was closing around her as she fought for air, and she felt rumbling of some kind through the deck. The rumbling became a pounding, and then the weight on her back was gone.

A pair of tree trunk legs was standing in front of her, and Jantine rolled over to take in a painful, gasping breath. One of the Omegas was holding the crate high over her head, then spun around rapidly before releasing it. It sailed away like a rocket, and she felt rather than heard its impact. She raised her head, and saw a jumble of arms and legs struggling feebly beneath the crate as it came to rest in the corridor outside.

Dazed, she couldn't make out what JonB was saying. Something about charges and detonations, but all she really wanted to know was where her weapon was, and how many of the enemy were left.

Another crate went flying, then another. Jantine couldn't help but stare at the casual way the Omegas were thinning the enemy ranks.

Even now, they're beautiful. All that strength finally unleashed, and it's still just the smallest part of themselves.

The Omegas were moving now, and with each step they took they transformed from peaceful architects into orange-skinned engines of death. Powerful arms were swinging, swatting enemies aside like flies. One trooper had enough time and presence of mind to fire a weapon, and Jantine's amazement grew as the slugs bounced harmlessly off an Omega's chest.

JonB was shouting now and trying to pull her up from the floor. Artemus shouldered him aside, using one lower hand to yank her to her feet, and placing her weapon in her hands with the other.

Jantine accepted it mechanically, unable to tear her eyes from the sight of the angry Omegas. Meter-and-a-half arms came together with a trooper in the middle, and she heard the hardsuit cracking from across the bay. The Omega spun again, now using the dead trooper as a club to batter the remaining enemies to the floor.

The fight was over, but the deck shook as both of the Omegas ran toward the shuttle. But for the blood streaking their coveralls, they might be children chasing a ball. She felt JonB shaking her shoulders, and finally heard what he was saying.

"Commander, we have to go! Malik and Doria...the container blew! We can't stay here, can't you feel the air leaving? There's a massive breach somewhere, and everyone still alive on this ship will be coming this way!"

Jantine turned to look at JonB, wondering how he could fail to comprehend the threat posed by Omegas willing to kill. The look of sheer terror in his eyes was sobering, and although everything he was saying was true, it paled in comparison to what might happen without a support Gamma to help the Omegas deal with the emotional ramifications of what they'd just done.

Jantine didn't say anything; she just tightened her grip on her weapon and started walking toward the shuttle. She saw Carlton heading up the ramp, and Crassus was already on station outside.

By the time Jantine, Artemus, and JonB reached the shuttle, a helmet-less Jarl was walking unsteadily down the cargo ramp. His hands were empty, and there were spots of blood on his pale face.

Jantine stopped and waved the others inside. From the base of the ramp, she could see the Omegas and Carlton excitedly shucking their packs and moving to examine the bulky piece of equipment she'd seen earlier. It looked like a sleeper unit, but it was three times the normal size.

Jarl's last step sent him crashing into one of the piston assemblies used to retract the ramp, and Jantine saw his eyes were wide and fixed. His encounter suit was covered in puckered scars, each one giving her another reason to get her team off the Valiant as soon as possible.

"Boss, shu…shuttle secured."

Jantine didn't know what to say. Jarl's normal rough whisper was full of something she'd never heard from him before. Pain, raw and unmasked. All she could do was take his report and try and live with the consequences of what she'd asked him to do.

Putting on her best command face, Jantine nodded up the ramp.

"Katra?"

"She'll live. I won't."

Jantine felt the darkness closing in again. This was Jarl, untouchable, indestructible Jarl. He'd done the impossible once again, but this time would be the last. Images of Malik, Doria, and Harren spun around Jarl's face, and the thought of another of her people—her friends, dying on this mission was almost too much to bear.

I can't do this. It's too big…

"Commander. Boss. You need to leave. Complete the mission."

Her mouth worked silently several times, almost apologizing, almost screaming her building rage. But Jarl's blue eyes were the cool center of a still pond, and if he could still stand after what had happened, so could she.

Jantine pulled a spare energizer and some grenades from her harness and handed them to Jarl. He waved off the energizer, instead pulling his hand weapon from its chest sheath and holding it out to her. She nodded, took the weapon, and tried to think of something, anything she could say to acknowledge his sacrifice. Before she could, Jarl took the grenades, straightened up as best he could and walked down the ramp.

"Jarl, wait." Jantine finally found her voice, even though it sounded strange in her ears. Removing her faceplate, she felt cold air moving past her cheeks.

Dammit JonB, why do you always have to be right?

The Gamma paused, and he stumbled slightly as he turned to

face her. He smiled, then grunted in surprise when she pulled him into a tight embrace. She felt his hands come around her, then shift to tap her twice at the base of the neck and spine. When he whispered in her ear, it was the old Jarl speaking one last time.

"Rookie mistake, boss. Two touches, total paralysis. You'll have to do better."

Jantine buried her face in his neck, determined not to let her emotions overcome her. She needed Doria, needed Malik here to tell her what to do next. But Jarl had said it as well as anyone could, which made it that much harder to let go.

I have to do better.

Jantine closed her eyes and maintained the embrace for another three heartbeats. It was just long enough to start feeling uncomfortable, and she knew she was ready to go. Thinking her thanks to him, she turned without looking and walked up the ramp.

She was halfway up when she heard JonB complaining.

"How am I supposed to know what to do? Look at this place. Is there anything you didn't shoot at?"

Jantine looked around her new command. Close up, she saw that there was a small female form inside the sleeper unit. Carlton and the Omegas were fussing over a bank of monitors on its side, but what drew Jantine's attention were the piled bodies of half a dozen enemy troopers.

As she walked up a twisting internal passage in search of JonB and the others, her feet brushed aside countless micro-slugs. The shuttle's interior was scored with thousands of shining scratches, but no craters like she'd seen on the bulkheads outside. At first there were occasional splashes of blood, but halfway up the ramp the walls were covered in dark red from floor to ceiling. Despite JonB's complaints, Jarl and Katra were too disciplined to fire at targets they couldn't hit, and at least one of them had scored a headshot.

How much of that blood is ours, and how much more will be spilled before we're through?

Following the Beta's voice, she came quickly to a flight deck. The rest of her team was crowded inside, and the Deltas were aiming every hand full of weapons at two enemies in restraints on the floor.

Katra looked even worse off than Jarl had. But despite the dried blood and cuts on her face she was still standing with her pulser clutched tightly in shaking hands, intent on two enemy troopers secured on the floor in front of her.

From the markings on their suits, Jantine recognized the captives from the brief vid image she'd seen earlier: the man who'd had weapons pointed at him, and the woman who had been guarding his back.

JonB stopped talking as Jantine entered, and Crassus took the opportunity to rumble a report.

"They surrendered. The male's the one they're looking for. Says we need them to get off the ship."

Jantine examined the lined face of the man who'd gotten so many people killed. Captain Martin, if Crassus was correct, had a bruised face and wore a dark beard with many patches of white. He was definitely past his prime, but she recognized the haunted look in his eyes as one she imagined in her own.

Without taking her eyes from Martin, she called over her shoulder to JonB: "Prep the shuttle for launch. Artemus, go tell Carlton and the Omegas to dispose of the bodies and get secured."

"Okay, but these controls…it's going to be a bumpy ride, and even if I can get it flying I don't know for how long or how far."

"No excuses. Get it done."

JonB swallowed whatever he was going to say and got to work. His hands flew over the controls, searching for whatever switches were necessary to prep the ship for flight.

"Commander Jantine," said Crassus, "how long will Scout Jarl need to complete his sweep and get aboard?"

Jantine let the question hang in the air, as she turned to regard the second prisoner. Whoever she was, the woman wasn't afraid, and Jantine had to give her credit for that.

"Jarl's not coming."

Katra's cry of rage was exactly the one Jantine wanted to voice, a raw knife-edged scream from the depths of her soul that made everyone in the compartment stop and stare. Before anyone could stop her, Katra stepped forward and drove the butt of her pulser into Martin's head. His neck snapped to the side, and he slumped in his restraints, but Jantine didn't think he was dead.

Yet.

Artemus pulled Katra away, using three hands to restrain the Gamma and the fourth to take away her weapon. Katra struggled against the Delta's strength, but the rage that drove her drained away as the enormity of what had happened settled in.

If the prisoner was bothered by the attack on her captain, she didn't let it show. The woman maintained eye contact with Jantine, narrowing her eyes slightly as if trying to divine some weakness in her captor. Jantine thought she was about to speak when JonB broke the silence.

"Commander, the shuttle's powered. The drive systems seem operational, but I can't initiate a launch sequence. There's just too much damage."

The prisoner smiled, and when she spoke it was with a clear voice of authority.

"You'll need my command key for that. Or Captain Martin's, but I doubt he'll give it to you now."

I suppose it doesn't matter either way. We die here, or out in space, it's all the same. But I have to try, I owe them that.

"I am JTN-B34256-O. You are my prisoner, and any attempt to escape or harm one of my people will result in the deaths of you and your captain. Do you understand this?"

The prisoner laughed, seemingly unimpressed.

"We already tried to escape, and our own people started shooting at us. Considering how that turned out, I've got nothing to lose. Now, I'm assuming you're not going to untie me, so here's what you have to do."

Jantine studied the woman's face as she talked, searching for any signs of falsehood. But her face had none of the cues she normally looked for, and like the darker-skinned young woman she'd examined earlier, it was just too alien for her to get an effective reading.

Doria, Malik, I need you now more than ever. How will I ever know who to trust, now that you're gone?

HARLAN

1419 SHIPTIME, SHUTTLE **EFSC-II**

LIEUTENANT COMMANDER MIRA HARLAN watched as one of the gray-skinned monsters pulled her command key from the hard pouch on her left shoulder. She was still wondering how in the worlds the Colonials had found out about the Alpha, or even knew where to look for it. Captain Martin had managed to keep the sleeping child's existence a secret from everyone aboard, apart from his immediate circle, and yet these children showed up right on cue to reclaim it when everything seemed lost.

They're all so young. Even compared to all the middies aboard Valiant. *Their leader can't be any more than sixteen years old!*

The handsome dark-haired boy they called Janbi accepted the key from the four-armed brute, then searched the board for where it was supposed to fit. Mira almost spoke up again, but the icy daggers stabbing her way from JTN-B34256-O's eyes kept her silent.

Those eyes were the worst part. The Colonial's face was impossibly beautiful—all of them were—but her blue eyes were like nothing Mira had ever seen before. They betrayed no emotion whatsoever, whether she was threatening Mira and the captain or discussing ammunition levels with one of the brutes.

I wonder what kind of gennie she is? She's clearly in command, but what does that mean? There's just so much we don't know about them.

Janbi gave a small shout of celebration, and shoved the key home. Mira felt a familiar vibration through the floor, that of the cargo ramp closing and the outer doors sealing tight. She also saw flashes of light out the shuttle's forward windows, and wondered how many more of her people were dying while she was relatively safe inside.

"Let's go, Janbi. We're wasting time. Is there anything else we need to know?"

"Is there a code for the bay doors?"

JTN-B38726-O inclined her head to Mira, who cleared her throat. So many bodies packed into the pilot's compartment was making the air a bit ripe.

"Input 'Harlan 4-9-3-8-Alpha-7-7' on the green buttons under the small monitor by your left hand. But first you'll want to-"

Janbi's hands moved faster than she thought possible, and the shuttle lurched to life before she could finish her thought. There was another flash of light outside, and JTN-B34256-O stepped over to a side window, looked outside, and tightened her jaw. Something that might have been a emotion flashed across her face, and she moved forward to sit in the copilot's chair without another word.

It was clear was that Janbi had never flown a shuttle. Mira had been about to tell him that he needed to engage the force barrier before opening the launch bay doors, but he didn't give her the time and just released the doors without a second thought. Now everything not secured to the decking was being sucked outside, along with what was left of *Valiant*'s air.

Including us.

Mira felt waves of nausea as the shuttle's grav field dipped in and out of the transfer bay's. Janbi had turned everything on at once, instead of waiting until the shuttle was clear of the bay doors.

As the shuttle raced towards the slowly widening doors, she felt a scream building in her throat, but none of the Colonials seemed concerned with the very real danger facing them. If anything, they seemed a bit bored, as if spaceflight were no more dangerous than sitting around talking in a well-lit room.

Who are you people? Do you have any idea of what can go wrong out here?

Just when she thought the shuttle was going to smash into the slowly opening doors, Janbi spun the ship on its side and they sailed through with centimeters to spare. But instead of making for open space, for some reason he swung around to follow the hull.

One of the equipment crates floating out in front of them got caught between the shuttle and *Valiant*. The shearing sound of metal against metal echoed throughout the cabin, and Mira wondered if it might not have been better to get shot in the head after all than to get killed by a joyriding gennie.

Even the tall gennie with the cuts on her face seemed unconcerned by the wild motions of the shuttle. Her blood-caked blonde hair gave her face a savage beauty, but she looked no more troubled than when she was blasting her way onto the flight deck while her partner took a full volley to the chest.

Mira turned her head and looked at the captain, whose unconscious face seemed younger than his normally stern expression. With the restraints effectively welding them to the bulkhead, the two SDF officers were probably safer than the gennies in the event of a collision. But at the speed Janbi was pushing the shuttle, she wondered if any of them would live long enough for it to matter.

Just my luck. First he flies a rock into my ship, now he's going to fly us into a rock. And for this, I escaped execution for treason?

If siding with Captain Martin over Captain Kołodziejski hadn't already sunk her career, collaborating with the Colonials certainly would. She took some small comfort in having made it this far in the first place, but it was only a matter of time before her luck ran out.

The gray monster standing closest to her seemed to stand a little taller, and Mira stared up into its broad face. It was smiling, and seemed to be looking at something in the passage. From where she was secured Mira couldn't see what it was, until an even more horrifying creature crawled in on hands and knees to stare at her with four beady black eyes set into a round orange face.

Then the nose of the shuttle dipped, and Mira heard the blare of a collision warning just before she was slammed back against the bulkhead and a herd of elephants landed on her chest. Even the orange monster grabbed at the bulkhead for support, and Mira saw its fingers dig furrows into an alloy that could survive a drop from orbit unscathed.

Impossibly, the creature pulled against the g-forces pressing Mira back, until its massive head loomed over her. Its tiny mouth opened, and a cloud of white mist came out of it and settled on her face. Then the whatever it was brought up its other hand until its fingers just brushed against her skin.

There was a fluttering sensation inside Mira's head, and then the pain in her chest went away. An unfamiliar woman's voice spoke to her from no direction in particular, and she felt a sensation of warmth wash over her.

≈*It is going to be all right. We are with you now. Do not worry.*≈

Mira screamed, and the world came crashing down around her. Thousands of images flooded her brain, and she could feel each one digging in and nestling alongside one of her memories. An image of a sunlit park came to mind. She and Debbi McAllister were walking home from school, whispering about the new boy in class and whether or not he was worth talking to. Then the scene twisted around to include the sight of a woman lying in a hospital bed, reaching out broken fingers to a little girl's face.

The universe exploded a second time, and another lifetime of memories came rushing into her. Over and over again she watched other people's lives in reverse, unsure of where Mira Harlan began or ended.

She saw herself meet the Builders for the first time, with Marta's memories fresh in her mind as she left the trauma center. The touch of their thoughts was like kissing a cloud, and she heard music in her soul that made her bones cry. She saw a smiling, dark-skinned boy, and kissed him on the cheek before turning away to hide her tears.

Her heart broke, and she felt the pain and confusion in Harren's mind as the second impact tore him away from her and snapped his neck.

From somewhere far away, she smelled something sharp and acidic, and heard JTN-B34256-O shouting.

"What's wrong with her? What did you do?"

The deck pitched wildly, then all motion in the cabin stopped as the crushing thrust ended, and the lights dimmed to half-strength. The shuttle's grav shut down, but that was the least of Mira's problems.

Her body felt strange, as if it didn't belong to her anymore. Her skin itched all over, and the hurricane inside her head kept spinning. A dozen half-heard voices reminded her of how to make it slow down, if only for a little while. She could feel sweat beading on her forehead, with nowhere to go and no outside force to tell it what to do.

Artemus bent down, and two strong hands released the restraints holding her to the wall. Mira floated up from the floor, guided by the Delta's gentle touch. She felt the Builder's eyes still on her, and turned back to look at it. Its tiny mouth closed, and the memory of a smile appeared in her mind. Then its attention shifted, and a rainbow of warning sent her attention away from it and through Janbi's eyes to the tactical display.

Mira's head felt like someone was hitting it with a hammer, but somehow she could see through the boy's eyes as if they were her own. He was too busy working the controls to pay conscious attention, but the part of his mind that was always scanning and cataloging everything around him still worked just fine. The red danger of the debris field was well behind them, but five green triangles moved rapidly through it on an intercept course.

Outside the shuttle's forward window, a beautiful blue and white planet hung against a star-studded sky. Mira sensed the words forming in Janbi's mind right before he said them aloud, and felt elation from Katra, Jantine, Crassus and Artemus as they heard them.

"We made it, everybody. Welcome to Earth."

KOŁODZIEJSKI

1419 SHIPTIME, SDF *INDOMITABLE*

WITH ONLY FOUR PEOPLE WORKING, *Indomitable*'s usually cramped command center seemed cavernous. Horace didn't mind the illusion of space—the tunnels he and Caroline explored as children on Mars had inoculated him against any incipient claustrophobia. But what did disturb him was the alienness of the place.

This should be the beating heart of my ship, and I've sent all the life out of it, in hopes of saving my own.

On his screens, he watched as the gennies abandoned their position by the bay doors and ran across the compartment towards their captured shuttle. When they arrived, the taller of the two gennies Horace had seen earlier was walking unsteadily down the ramp, helmet off and with spots of blood on his pale face.

The others filed up the ramp, but the tall one stopped at the base to talk to a slight, apparently female gennie. The helmet-less killer stumbled, crashing into one of the piston assemblies used to retract the ramp. The second gennie took half a step forward, but injured one waved her off, then pulled himself together.

Despite her best efforts, the securecams Monahan had used to create the holo couldn't pick up what the gennie was saying, but Horace suspected it was a mission summary.

Probably something along the lines of "I killed all the humans, sir. What atrocity should I commit next?"

Then the tall gennie pulled a weapon seemingly out of his chest, and pressed it into the other one's hands. It looked like the shorter one gave him something in return, but again the holo was limited by the positions of the securecams. The two embraced for a few seconds, then the shorter gennie walked up the ramp while the other one staggered out into the transfer bay proper.

Caught up in the tableau, he almost missed Caroline's voice shouting at her remaining troopers over her comms.

"Get in there! Don't let that shuttle launch. I want prisoners and I want them now!"

Horace's eyes widened, as he realized what she'd seen. The ramp was closing, and the shuttle's running lights were on. He recognized a pre-flight sequence in progress, though whoever was piloting the shuttle seemed to be skipping a few steps. It lifted from the deck just as weapons fire erupted in the bay, and several externals disappeared under heavy fire.

Then a new sound filled the air, that of terrified screams. Monahan went back to a wide shot, just as the black-suited gennie dove into a firing line of armored troopers, seemingly unconcerned by the new wounds he was taking. Incredibly, he punched through the faceplate of a trooper's hardsuit, while at the same time his free hand relieved them of their weapon. The move was so fluid it almost didn't seem real, and when the injured trooper's helmet exploded a second later, it only added to the madness.

The blast took out several other troopers, but the gennie didn't stop to admire his handiwork. He was busy jamming his captured weapon under the chin of another, blowing off the trooper's head before kicking them into two more armored figures.

Six more troopers died messily in half as many seconds before the gennie finally went down under a pile of hardsuits. But by then the damage was done, and the shuttle was moving toward the still-closed bay doors.

The pile of troopers exploded, sending fragments of armor, weapons, gennie and humans alike across the bay. The shuttle rocked briefly as the bay doors cracked open, and all the air and loose materiel in the compartment fought past its hull for escape into the blackness of space. Right before it would have crashed into the still opening doors, the shuttle flipped on its side and sailed through without a hitch.

They're getting away. They're fucking getting away, and there's absolutely nothing I can do about it!

Caroline was apparently still monitoring the situation, and her strident voice called out the order Horace should have given himself.

"Tepes, disable that ship by any means necessary. Ram it if you have to, but don't let it get away."

Horace looked up at the complicated display of firing solutions over Senior Chief Kirk's targeting computer, noting that he'd added the rogue shuttle to the mix. As if sensing the captain's interest, he glanced back for permission with his hand over the launch button. Horace nodded approval, and two green triangles indicating Geyser spreads broke away from *Indomitable* and rocketed across the plot.

Kirk's fingers deftly guided the missiles around tumbling chunks of *Valiant* and space rock, but there were just too many of them for even Horace to keep track of. Plus, whoever was flying the shuttle was weaving erratically through the debris field, reversing the ship's direction several times and pulling accelerations no sane pilot would attempt.

If the consequences of their escape weren't so personally dire, Horace might have let them go just to continue the thrill of the chase. But every second they weren't in custody was another nail in his coffin, to borrow an Earth metaphor.

All too soon they'll be out of our weapons envelope. And I can't have that.

"Whatever it takes, Chief."

A full spread of Geysers launched from the dreadnaught without delay, flying at the edge of the field parallel to the shuttle at first. Kirk kept their drives running at half power, not wanting to overrun the shuttle and waste his shots.

When the pilot finally made a mistake, Kirk was ready, boosting the missiles to maximum acceleration as the shuttle made another nonsensical course change. Kirk detonated one missile half a click in front of them to blind their sensors, then sent two more from behind to take out its engines. Horace lost sight of it on the plot, and then a massive explosion temporarily wiped the display.

When it came back, the shuttle was gone, as were the remaining two missiles. Kirk's apology was not what he expected, but the end result was the same. "Sir, they're gone. Impacted a chunk of space rock, I guess. I'm sorry."

Horace wanted to scream. Wanted to grab Kirk and shake him until the shuttle came back, but his artificial blood was on fire, reacting poorly to the massive adrenaline rush triggered by the chase. All he could manage was a choked whisper, and his vision was beginning to dim.

"Find me a body. Find me...anything"

The odds of any viable DNA surviving the triple assault of impact, radiation, and hard vacuum were beyond incredible, but Horace had nothing left to hold on to but hope. He leaned forward in his chair, head in hands, wondering if he shouldn't just transfer command to Caroline now before he completely lost his resolve.

I can't lose now. I can't...

ANNAHKO

1421 SHIP TIME, PINNACE IDX-02

"ALL RIGHT, Cadet, you heard the captain. Whatever it takes."

Illyana Tepes killed their acceleration and flipped the ship on its nose to give them a better view of the tiny shuttle still boosting hard dozens of kilometers away. An occasional drive plume wasn't the only sign of their quarry—her partner Kurt Currano had them dead to rights on sensors. But visual confirmation was always a good thing, and Caroline found herself leaning forward as if she was about to snatch the tiny ship from the field herself.

With Tepes and Currano at the controls, there wasn't a lot for Caroline to do but stare ahead and will something to happen. Standing just behind the cadet pilots with her boots locked, she alternated watching on instruments and peering into the black as *Indomitable*'s Geysers weaved their way through the debris field towards their prey.

You gennie freaks think you can steal my kill? Think again!

With two full squads of troopers ready to deploy, and a couple hotshot cadets keeping them on station, it was only a matter of time before they ran the escaping shuttle to ground and boarded it.

Then we'll see if this was all worth the effort. I for one will...

A miniature sun flared to life in front of a large chunk of black rock, and died a second later. Currano's feed went blank, and when it came back up the shuttle and three of the Geysers were gone.

There wasn't anything she could do to make the analysis go faster, but Caroline had to say something or she'd explode.

"Status!"

Currano's response wasn't the one she was hoping for, but in the time it took him to speak she saw the shuttle reappear on his plot, and a flash from its faraway drives deep in the field passing below them.

"Huh. That's odd."

"Care to elaborate, Cadet?" Caroline unlocked her boots and tromped over to Currano's station. She knew the pinnace's boards better than anyone, and the power readings beside his targeting plot didn't make any sense.

"I wish I could, ma'am. The first explosion was a Geyser to be sure, but even in a vacuum, the blast dissipated too early. Our bogey juked during the flash, and two more shots detonated where he should have been.

"But those weren't as effective as they should have been either, and that rock—sorry, this rock," he said, highlighting and tossing an irregular image into its own holo, "has somehow doubled in mass in the last thirty seconds. And now there's some kind of...I don't know what it is, to be honest, but all the rocks around it are...humming."

Caroline turned to stare at the wide-eyed cadet, who met her gaze with a helpless expression. He opened his mouth to say something, but whatever it was died in his throat as another flash filled the flight deck with blinding light.

"Shit, *shitshitshit*." Tepes voiced the sentiment all three officers felt, but Caroline's heart sank when her eyes cleared and their plot was completely empty.

"Find me something, Cadet. Anything. We're not heading home empty if we can help it."

"Aye aye, ma'am." Tepes shunted the ship again, this time

inverting them relative to the expanding debris field. Bits of *Valiant*, its destroyed tenders, and the black rock rolled over and over above their window, but there was no outward sign of the shuttle.

"Mr. Currano, show me the whole field. This head-on view isn't working for me."

As the cadet constructed a larger holo, Caroline wished for the thousandth time that she had some of Horace's Simak processing. Her brain and body were wired differently than his, and this was the kind of analysis at which he excelled. Her merely human mind needed a lot more context to make sense of what she was seeing.

"Okay, Commander, this is the best I can do." Tiny images of debris appeared before her, and Currano swiveled his chair to face the center of the flight deck with a holo-emitter in his hand.

The simulation ended just shy of the pilot and co-pilot stations, but otherwise filled the compartment. The big rock which fascinated Currano so much was the first foci of the field, and the tumbling corpse of the *Valiant* the second.

"Ms. Tepes, we could use another set of eyes on this."

"Just a second, ma'am, I've got some confusing readings of my own."

"Okay. Can you extrapolate this backward, Mr. Currano?"

Currano didn't respond, but the furious tapping on his panel was just as good as a verbal confirmation. The holo shuddered, then contracted into a roiling series of red and blue images on one side of the flight deck.

"And forward again, Mr. Currano. Ms. Tepes, how are you doing over there?

"Almost got it, ma'am!"

The simulation propagated across the flight deck as expected, And Caroline stepped into it to track a small, regularly formed object as it moved away from *Valiant*. Unlike the rest of the debris, its path was far too precise, and when the holo was back to normal it hovered a few centimeters in front of Caroline's eyes.

"What are you..." The words where a whisper from Caroline's lips, but at the same time Tepes's very similar "What the hell is that!" echoed around the compartment like a thunderclap.

"Ms. Tepes."

"Ma'am!"

"Find me this. Now." Caroline poked a finger into the holo, pushing the incongruous object this way and that trying to make some sense of it.

"Don't have to, ma'am. I've already set a course."

Caroline snapped her head around fast enough to hurt, and saw a much more detailed version of the same object floating in front of her distant cousin with a rangefinder in motion beside it.

What the hell, indeed.

KOŁODZIEJSKI

1426 SHIPTIME, **SDF** *INDOMITABLE*

EVERY CHIRP, click, and beep in the command center was fresh torture on Horace's already abused nerves. Seconds of comm silence became minutes with no news, and Horace felt his life slipping away with each one.

"Sir, I have Commander Annahko for you. She's found something...strange."

His throat tight, Horace looked up into the Caroline's projected face. Her eyes widened slightly, and he could only imagine what he looked like right now.

"Captain, we've located something at the edge of the debris field that is neither rock nor Fleet standard. It's presenting some strange readings, and we've moved to intercept."

Now it was Horace's turn for surprise, but there had been too many emotional reversals in too short a time to let himself believe.

Still...

"Show me."

His voice was still weak, and he hated the sound of it. Caroline's face was replaced by a large, rectangular metal object, which against all logic appeared to be under power. It took him a second, but as Caroline's shuttle approached, Horace recognized it as being of the same construction as the compartment where Bob had found the two gennies.

Where he died.

The shuttle matched velocities with the object, then fired magnetic grapples. A few seconds later Caroline had it completely under control, and the real-time image was replaced by a deep scan of the interior.

At first, Horace couldn't believe what he was seeing. Instead of the single stolen gennie sleeper unit he'd chased halfway across the solar system, there were rows and rows of them inside Caroline's mystery object, each containing another chance at life.

And nobody knows what they are but me.

"Commander, get back here with that container as fast as you can. I'll meet you in transfer bay one with a security team."

"Yes sir. We should be back in ten or so minutes."

Caroline cut her transmission, and Horace's mind raced through possible outcomes of this discovery. Watson needed new test subjects, of course. But with new gennies to work with, of all different shapes and sizes, could give the Fleet an unbeatable advantage in the war to come.

It's not just me with a new chance at life, but the entire human race.

"Ms. Monahan, send a withdrawal order to both battlegroups. We'll regroup minus three million kilometers, then set course for Luna."

"Yes sir. And *Valiant*?"

Horace allowed himself a thin smile before giving the order. For the first time in months, there was a chance of a cure, and no one was going to jeopardize that. Not Watson, not the Fleet Council, and certainly not a bunch of half-dead mutineers on a floating scrap heap.

"Abandon in place. We got here too late to save *Valiant* and its tenders from the actions of rogue agents. Lieutenant, I'll thank you to prepare our official report to reflect that, using *Valiant* footage only. Most of it, anyway. I'd like to curate our encounters with the gennies, at least until we figure out why they were here in the first place."

"Yes sir. I understand. I'll do my best."

"Get it done, Monahan. We're on the right side of this, and you're going to make sure that stays true. Mr. Henderson, let me know as soon as all our shuttles are back aboard. I want to be underway for Echo Base within the hour."

"Understood, sir."

Horace settled back into his chair. After so long, after so much pain, there was finally some hope for a cure, for a future.

For us, anyway. Not so much for the gennies, though, and that's fine by me.

JANTINE

"WE MADE IT EVERYBODY. WELCOME TO EARTH."

JonB's voice was as smug as ever, but for once Jantine didn't mind.

You jerk. You stole my line.

Jantine was staring at the Earther woman when the shuttle's wild flight came to a halt, but after JonB's announcement she turned and watched as the big blue planet swung into view. Despite everything that had happened, seeing it she finally had some hope that they'd live to see another day. A real sunrise, on a real planet. The planet— the only one that mattered.

Earth was humanity's home, and though they'd exiled the mods centuries ago, just to make it this far was still a dream come true.

Then a white hot knife of pain stabbed into her brain, and she couldn't get her helmet off fast enough. She pressed her hands tight against her ears, but nothing stopped the searing agony.

≈Oh shit!≈

The pain was momentary, and after blinking away tears Jantine recognized the voice in her head as that of the Earther.

But that's not possible...

"You idiot! Take evasive maneuvers! There's a Geyser spread closing in on us!"

Jantine turned her head to look at the shouting prisoner. She was floating free from her restraints and held in place by one of Artemus's hands. The Omega was still hovering in the corridor, and Jantine wished she had a support Gamma present so she could get an answer to her earlier question, or maybe tell her how the Earther was now able to talk inside her head.

The Omega. It did something to her, but what? And more importantly, why?

"Oh, those?" JonB hadn't seen the Omega's actions, and his smug tones were as annoying as ever. "Don't worry, I took care of them."

"What the hell are you talking about?" said the Earther. "You're just a kid, do you even have a clue about what's happening? We are all. Going. To die. Get us away from here!"

The prisoner twisted around in Artemus's grasp, and the Delta dealt with the problem by simply letting go and stepping back. Free from the stabilizing influence of Artemus's personal gravity field, she spun around an internal axis for a moment until small jets fired from her hands and feet. She rocketed forward to the control console just ahead of the Delta's grasping hands and pulled a very surprised JonB out of his chair with one hand while grabbing the edge of the console with the other.

"Missiles. Missiles! If I don't get us out of..."

The woman's voice trailed off as she stared at something on the small holographic readout in front of her. She'd been about to press a button with her free hand when the look of panic on her face was replaced with one of astonishment.

Light flashed in the corner of Jantine's vision, but she didn't shift her focus from the woman, who made no move to resist as Artemus stepped forward and shoved her down into the pilot's chair. If she noticed Jantine, Katra, and Crassus pointing pulsers at her, she gave no sign.

JonB cleared his throat and took a tentative step forward.

"Like I was saying, I took care of them. We got some excellent scans of your missiles when you were firing them at the cargo slug.

Malik's data feed recorded their maximum acceleration, targeting systems, and destructive capability."

Careful, JonB. Don't overplay your hand.

"Those, 'Geysers,' was it?" he said.

The woman in the pilot's seat nodded dumbly.

He continued: "The Geysers use a combination of mass detectors, microwave laser targeting, and ion sniffers, right? All I had to do was find a fragment in the debris field about the same size as us, dump some fuel, and lead them to it. This shuttle has fairly good sensor capabilities. It was easy."

JonB leaned forward until he was a few handspans away from the seated Earther.

"And I'm not a kid. I'm nearly fourteen standard."

Just then, the shuttle shifted again, and Jantine felt a deep vibration. The Earther's face went back to panic in a flash, and when it did the pain in Jantine's head was back. It was a gnawing, sinking feeling, and even though she knew the compartment wasn't spinning, she dropped her weapon and used both hands to grip the edges of her chair.

JonB's reaction was more evident; he grabbed his head with both hands and sank moaning to the floor. Katra was slapping the sides of her face, trailing lines of blood as her fingers moved back and forth. Even Artemus was affected, the normally stoic Delta's lips flattening into a tight grimace.

≈*nononono just a bunch of kids we're all going to die what the hell am I going to do have to get out get away get free let me go Let Me Go LET ME GO!*≈

Jantine shut her eyes tight and tried to force the words out of her head. She had enough anxiety of her own without an outside voice adding more troubles to her plate. She focused on her heartbeat, trying to reduce the universe to one sound she knew better than anything.

She heard a soft thump, and then the hiss of escaping air. Fearing the worst she opened her eyes and grabbed for the pulser floating in front of her. The pilot's chair was empty, and Jantine swung her arm to the left trying to cover the prisoner's escape path.

She'd almost forgotten about the Omega at entrance, but it was as good as a wall in stopping the Earther's trajectory. Two big hands came up and caressed the sides of the woman's head, and as she stopped struggling, Jantine felt the fear and doubt leave her mind as suddenly as they'd arrived.

Katra was already in motion, weaponless but no less deadly. Her hands were up and formed into claws, and the look on her face was pure rage. Artemus tried to intercept her, but he and Crassus both appeared to be having difficulty coordinating all six limbs. Jantine didn't know how to react to anything she was seeing but decided that firing her weapon was definitely the wrong call. She couldn't stop the Gamma's snarling attack, and, in any event, part of her wondered if it was even the right thing to do.

She can't be. It's just not possible...

Just as Katra was reaching to tear the unresisting Earther from the Omega's grasp, a massive orange hand let go of the woman's head and made a fist. Katra's breath left her in an explosive, bloody cough as the punch landed in the middle of her chest. She fell into a gasping heap, then toppled over onto the deck.

Jantine and JonB reached her at the same time, both desperate to help but not knowing what to do. Jarl said she'd survive her injuries, but that was before she'd suffered even more damage to an already compromised system. Jantine had felt the strength in that hand herself, had seen how terrible it could be when set to destruction. If the Omega had killed Katra, turned on one of its own in favor of the Earther, who would be next?

Katra let out an almost inaudible wheeze, and tiny bubbles of blood formed on her lips. JonB looked up from her at Jantine, and started shaking his head.

Jantine was on her feet and two steps toward the Omega before she realized what she was doing. But the big fist was gone, and the Omega was turning away from her to press its back against the bloody corridor wall. It still filled most of the available space, but there was enough for Carlton to shove past shouting "Make room. Make room!"

Jantine felt him brush by her, still not believing her eyes. The Omega was staring at her as if nothing had happened, seemingly unconcerned with the Gamma dying on the deck.

"What do you want?" Jantine shouted. "Damn you, tell me what you want!"

"They're sorry. They didn't mean for any of this to happen. I'm sorry too, for what it's worth."

Jantine added hearing to the list of senses betraying her. The answer to her question was clear and calm, and coming from the mouth of the human woman.

"It's Carlton, right? Katra's left lung collapsed in the fighting, and her breastbone is cracked and pressing in on the other one. You need to re-inflate—"

"Shut up, Earther. I know what I have to do!"

The anger and pain in Carlton's voice combined with a wet tearing sound as he stripped away Katra's encounter suit. Jantine heard JonB gasp, and she used every bit of her will to keep her eyes on the Omega, instead of turning to watch.

This isn't happening. This isn't happening. This can't be happening. The humans on that ship were virus-free...

The human woman winced, shaking her head as if trying to dislodge something in her ear. She then raised a gauntleted hand and pointed at the Omega, who was slowly edging back down the corridor.

"I don't know how this is happening, but he—I guess it's he— wants you to know that none of this is your fault. The—look, is it okay if I just use my own words? She's smart, she'll understand. No, I don't think your way is better. What just happened was wrong, and you know it. Now let me do this, my way."

The impossibility of the situation was overwhelming, and Jantine sat down on the floor and took her head in her hands. Though she didn't want to, she could see the human woman's booted feet sink three centimeters to the floor and settle into place. There was a humming sound, and then the knees of the hardsuit bent until she was kneeling in front of her. The look of compassion on the woman's face was too much to take in, and Jantine closed her eyes and wished the world away.

It's not real. This is a dream. A horrible nightmare. Everyone is still alive, none of this is real. Wake up, wake up Wake up!

"I know you're afraid; I am too. This day just keeps getting crazier and crazier. An hour ago I was a junior officer wondering why in the worlds my captain was hiding out a few light minutes above the ecliptic. Then I was second-in-command of a dying warship, and then minutes later I was running for my life from my own crew to save the life of someone I've never even met."

She spoke loud enough for everyone to hear, but what Jantine objected to most was the warm feeling inside her head that accompanied them. She opened her eyes and saw the woman's strange face hovering in front of her.

Her expression was a mixture of concern and amusement, and there was something different about her eyes that Jantine couldn't quite place. They still had the same hardness about them Jantine had seen earlier, but they were a deeper brown somehow, and the corners were turned up in a way that made her think of home. Her cheeks were flushed, and sweat was beading up on her face.

It wasn't until she formed her lips into a lopsided smile that Jantine decided to punch her in the nose. There was a sharp crack, and when the first spots of blood began pooling under her gauntleted hand, Jantine stood and turned away.

"JonB."

At the sound of her voice the Beta looked up at her from the floor, where he was holding Katra's upper arms while Carlton inserted a small tube into the left side of her chest. There was blood everywhere, and Jantine saw at least a dozen ugly holes on her bare skin.

"You bith. You fuggin bith!"

The warm feeling in her mind was gone, replaced by a simmering anger Jantine knew all too well. If the Omegas wanted to play games with all of their lives, so be it. She still had a mission to complete.

Carlton bent forward and blew into the tube, and Jantine watched Katra's chest expand. The Gamma's eyes snapped open, and she gave a strangled cry while trying to sit up. Only JonB's genetically enhanced strength kept her from injuring herself further, and whatever Carlton injected her with next kept her from trying again.

"JonB, help me get her into one of the sleeping areas. There's a lot more I have to do if we're going to save her."

Jantine shook her head.

"Artemus can do that. I need JonB here."

JonB crawled away and let the Delta reach in to collect Katra in a gentle, cradling embrace. Jantine didn't turn to watch Carlton leave, keeping her attention instead on the blood-stained scientist. She assumed there would be some shuffling of positions behind her to allow the Delta access to the corridor, but she just didn't care how the other mods worked it out.

Jantine sat down in the second pilot's chair and examined the controls. "Which one of these can I use to find the sleepers' container?" she asked. "And why are we spinning?"

The last sliver of Earth's cool blue sphere slipped above the forward window as JonB reclaimed his seat and started studying the panel. He was silent for almost thirty seconds then pulled out his handheld from a thigh sheath. He frowned, and started tapping.

"Well?"

"I just need to…but that's not…Commander, it's gone!"

"Explain." The sinking feeling was back, but this time Jantine was fairly confident it wasn't forced on her by the Earther.

"That's just it. I can't. I mean, a fragment of the slug must have hit us when the decoy exploded, and that's what set us to spinning. But the container, it's just gone! We—I mean, the Omegas—tracked it clear of the debris field, and I should be able to pick up its trail from here. But there's nothing. No wreckage, no bodies, no trace whatsoever!"

"Scientist JonB, could the container have landed safely while we were escaping the Redstone dreadnaught?" Crassus's unexpected question focused Jantine's fear into something she could work with.

"No. If it was out here, the shuttle's sensors would pick it up. I'll need a few minutes to input Malik's pilot program into their core, but I don't have any idea of where it could have gone. I just don't know."

Jantine's patience ran out, and she got up out of the chair and walked over to JonB. He gave out a small cry when she spun the pilot's chair around until he was facing her, and she saw her own fear reflected in his eyes. But she didn't have time for fear anymore, or for any of his hypotheticals. She needed answers, and she knew of only one way to get them.

"Don't tell me what you don't know, JonB. Tell me where they are, and where we're supposed to be going. Crassus?"

"Commander."

The Delta was a solid presence at her side, and the pulser he had trained on the Earther captives gave her something solid to focus on.

"Have Artemus prepare a secure location for our prisoners. I don't care if the Omegas interfere, they can rot alongside them for all I care right now."

"But Commander Jantine, the Builders are—"

"I also don't want to hear any more about 'the Builders.' I am commanding this mission, and I will see us safely down to the surface without any more 'help' from them. Am I clear?"

Crassus was silent, and she could almost hear the thoughts forming in his head. When she started to feel a warmth building inside her mind, her hand weapon came out and was leveled at the female captive before she could even blink.

"None of that. Not now. If you have something to say, use your mouth!"

The woman nodded, and pulled her hand away from her bloody face. The Omega was still crouching in the entrance to the compartment, face impassive. She'd seen them angry before, and what passed for their smiles. But whatever this expression was, she didn't trust their new "voice" enough to believe anything they had to tell her.

"We haff to leaf."

"What?" It took Jantine a moment to understand what the human woman was trying to say with her broken nose, but after a few words it was easy enough.

"We have to leave. Now. There's enemies out there trying to kill the Alpha. You have to—"

"Boss," JonB interrupted. "I found something, I think. There's a flight plan in the core for someplace called the Harrison Institute, in Central North America. Oh, and I can confirm the impact earlier. There's damage to our primary drive systems, but everything should hold together during reentry."

"Are you crazy? North America? You'll be shot down in seconds. Mars. Set course for Mars..."

The human's voice trailed off when Jantine waved the hand weapon in her face. But Jantine was still waiting for the rest of JonB's report, and when several more seconds passed without it, she prompted him.

"And the sleepers?"

The lights in the compartment came back up, and Jantine felt the shuttle's engines kick in. There was a momentary adjustment as the compartment's gravity returned, and Jantine wished JonB had maintained a stronger sense of his environment as she wiped falling body fluids away from her face.

"Still no trace of them. But with more time, and better equipment..."

Jantine turned back to the front of the cabin and saw the stars swing by until the planet was back in sight. The second part of what the Earther had said finally fell into place, and with great effort, Jantine released the firing studs and lowered the pulser.

Alpha. She said enemies are trying to kill the Alpha.

"JonB, get us down to the planet as fast as possible, but at least one hundred kilometers away from any population center. I don't care how close it is to this Harrison Institute, just make sure that we aren't observed."

"You got it, boss. Plotting an insertion now."

Jantine turned and left the compartment, and she heard Crassus fall in behind her. She pointedly ignored the Omega's questioning stare, thankful that she was small enough to squeeze by without having to touch it. Crassus wedged himself through as best he could, but Jantine was too busy retracing her steps down the corridor to care.

By the time she reached the bottom, the shuttle was shaking as it reached the outer fringe of Earth's atmosphere. But even this momentous occasion was dwarfed by the sight of the second Omega sitting in the cargo area, staring with longing eyes at the small figure floating in a blue-green suspension matrix inside the sleeper unit.

From the reverence the Omega was showing, Jantine knew what the prisoner said had to be true. Jantine took a step closer, and then another. She couldn't quite bring herself to touch the gently humming sleeper unit, but seeing an Alpha in person for the first time, under these conditions, shook her worse than the violent motion of their descent.

What am I supposed to do now? Someone, please tell me what I'm supposed to do.

The acrid smell of burning plastic stung her nose, and JonB's excited shouting was barely audible over the much more immediate sound of Crassus's basso.

"Commander Jantine, I think something is wrong."

The shuttle lurched, and Jantine pitched forward into the sleeper unit. She hit her head, then fell to the deck as if pushed there. Then the shuttle stood on its nose, sending her sliding back up the blood-slick ramp.

Discarded micro-slugs scratched her face as the sounds of JonB's screaming came closer. Another change of direction slammed her into the wall, and then she was tumbling head over heels back down into the bay.

"COMMANDER!"

She tried to turn her head toward Crassus, but her neck was made of rubber. All she could manage was a pathetic gasp, and then the sound of tearing metal filled her ears. Hot air washed over her, and Jantine felt herself sliding again until a big orange hand grabbed her arm and she jerked to a halt. Something popped in her shoulder, and Jantine flopped her head over enough to see the Omega holding on to the oversized sleeper unit with its other hand, wincing as the crates of supplies it had carried the length of the *Valiant* broke loose and shattered against its broad back.

Shelters, ration packs and spare energizers rained down on them both, and Jantine tucked her chin into her chest to shield her eyes just before something hard and heavy hit the back of her head.

Her last sight before everything went black was of a tiny, six-limbed figure sailing away from a ragged hole in the hull, arms waving madly as it fell.

AUTHOR'S NOTE

It's all Mark Teppo's fault.

Five years ago I took a rare night off from writing the final act of *Homefront* to attend a promotional event for one of our other collaborations, the *FOREWORLD SAGA*. At drinks and dinner afterward, Mark mentioned that some of his media contacts were sniffing around the book, based on the sell copy we'd prepared when there were only a few chapters in the bag.

Then he dropped this bombshell on me.

"They like it better when there's a sequel. You're planning on a sequel, right?"

As always, my response was succinct and to the point.

"Yeah, I can do that."

In fact, I was deep in the middle of the novel's big spaceship battle climax, and it wasn't that hard to beef up a couple characters for a hypothetical second book. My contract stipulated an option on a second book, I certainly wanted to write a second book, and since we were seven months out from publication, we certainly had plenty of time to get started on one.

Until we didn't.

After a couple rounds of editing, the very scenes Mark had requested to set up a second book were the last ones to go. I managed to keep in the telepathic space aliens (SPOILERS), but the spaceship battles broke up the narrative flow of an already long final act, and I reluctantly agreed to cut four chapters totaling some twenty-two thousand words to tighten things up.

My editors (all three of them) were right, of course. It was a bit bloated, and starting a new plotline that late in the book was always a risky proposition. But in working up those characters, I created their lives in my head, and that level of detail is hard to let go. Especially since the cuts left exactly one line for Lieutenant Marya Andreison, and some fairly cryptic dialog from her wife in response.

Of course, they weren't married at the time. And she didn't have robot eyes, or a tragic backstory, or any of the things that make Marya Marya. All of that came to me a couple years later, but she was always the person I thought would continue the series, and more importantly, she was always unapologetically queer.

As I get older, and the world is more accepting of people like me, having queer voices in fiction is more and more important. Every book I've ever written has had at least one queer character, and *Homefront* is absolutely lousy with them if you know what to look for. But my one regret about that book (minor typos aside) is that I left it as subtext, rather than the text itself. I was afraid that our target demographic would reject a Big Gay Space Opera, and I had a lot to prove with my first published novel.

So about that. *Homefront* did reasonably well in pre-orders, but a $25 hardback book released in November is a hard sell for anyone, and January returns absolutely crushed us. The paperback version we did the following summer was cheaper, sleeker, and wonderfully visible from across the room, but nobody bought it either.

Why is this relevant? When the first returns came in, Mark asked me to hold off on writing that sequel until we had a better sense of the book's future. When he handed me my author copies of the paperback version, he mentioned the sequel and where it might fit into the next year's release schedule, but I wasn't ready to start writing again. In particular, I didn't think I could pull off a good story in the 80k words Mark was asking for, without cutting—again—the stuff I really wanted to write.

It took a while for me to get there, actually, and Marya's first scene in this book was in my head for well over a year before I got it out. The words came slowly at first, and her tumbling in a pod to start the show was a fair distance away from the chapters we cut to get *Homefront* out the door.

After eight months of fumbling around, I only had 20 thousand more words in the tank. It was not going well, and I considered scrapping the whole thing and starting over with new characters. But a weekend writing retreat helped me bust through a big wall of

NOPE, and in the weeks that followed chapter after chapter fell to my relentless assault.

By the end of July 2017, I had Mark's 80k sequel, and a week later was another 30k into a third volume. I turned the book over, patted myself on the back, and waited for his reaction.

By December 2017, Mark knew he had some hard choices to make about his publishing imprint, and told me it would be another few months before he could accept new books. In March 2018, we talked about folding the sequel into a trilogy, which I thought was a fine plan.

And in June of 2018, he offered me the rights back to *Homefront* at a party, about ten minutes before I could work up the courage to ask for them myself. The trilogy was still a go, and he happily agreed to help me edit it. But it meant that now I was the only person in the worlds responsible for the 30k words needed to pull it all together, especially the five additional chapters necessary to complete the book you now hold in your hands.

I'll talk more about that in my next author note, but what you need to know now is that absolutely none of this would be possible without Mark's patience, experience, and general good egg-ness. Especially since twenty-four hours ago he handed back an edited manuscript that's absolutely the best thing I've ever written, and the book I should have written in 2014.

Or in 2016, 2017, or 2018.

So blame him for everything you liked about this book, and me for all the rest.

Mahalo.

Scott James Magner
January, 2019.

P.S. If you're wondering what happened to Marya, turn the page for a sneak peek of *Landfall*, the next book in the *Homefront* trilogy. Mark hasn't edited it yet, but I think it's still all right.

From the ARUS Entertainment release *Landfall*, a novel of the Transgenic Wars.

ANDREISON

1650 STATION TIME, L6 STATION

MARYA RAISED HER GLASS, admiring the cascade of bubbles as her beer settled. Lagrange 6 wasn't exactly the end of the line, but after her unceremonious exit from *City of Lights*, it might as well be.

It was a good dream while it lasted, but it's time to face facts. Even if they let me live, I'm finished in the fleet, and nothing I can do will change that.

Her drink tasted just as good as had the three before it, but even after thirty hours in a jumpseat and with a few beers in her Marya still had no idea of her next move.

She set glass back on the counter next to her tunic. Unlike the rumpled mess of her flight suit, her mess tunic was nearly pristine, a silent reminder of all the things she had yet to accomplish. After seven years of active duty, its main distinctions were the combat pilot's wings she'd never officially got to use, and the Distinguished Service Medal she'd earned the day she lost her eyes.

And if I could reverse that trade, I'd do it in a hot minute. The only reason it's there at all is that I'm required to wear it as part of any display.

In theory, the medal entitled her to a salute from other officers and a bump in pay. In practice, Marya was the only serving officer to have earned one since the Reclamation—*hell, in the last 200 years*—and in any event her reputation made the award mostly moot. She didn't regret her actions, either that day or since. But since her records always took a few bureaucratic detours when she moved between postings, the other commendations she'd earned never seemed to find her.

My real crime was getting caught. And, of course, refusing to quit after the trial.

Marya could have chosen a civvie bar to think in, but her feet took her on autopilot straight to the wardroom and she hadn't felt like moving since. Her only companion was the steward, a pleasant-enough NCO with old-Earth features and a slight limp. The man had noticed the medal as soon as she'd come in, and kept shooting it an occasional glance to make sure he'd read it right.

Besides, bartenders ask questions. This fella knows enough to keep the drinks coming, and how to disappear when necessary.

She took another sip of her beer, half closing her eyes to savor it without distractions. When she put it back down, she narrowed her eyes further to zoom in on the liquid itself.

Drinking out of a glass was a luxury in space, one only possible under constant acceleration or artificial gravity. Lagrange 6 had both, and the interplay between them made the bubbles take a slanting path up to meet the head. The bubbles themselves were interesting, undulating pockets of gas rather than the perfectly round ones people enjoyed down the gravity well.

There's probably some metaphor here for my situation, but I'm so thoroughly screwed I can't think of anything clever.

She finished her drink and signaled for another, and the steward hesitated before taking her glass away. He didn't flinch away from her stare, but also didn't start pouring.

"What?" The word was loaded with all the frustration of the last two shipdays, along with more than a little of the last few years.

"Most officers who choose this mess for lunch order food, ma'am. Are you sure you don't want anything else?

I want another fucking beer, damnit. I want the fucking universe to make some fucking sense. And I want some goddamned respect for once.

"I'm fine, thanks. Just beer for now."

Nodding, the steward pulled her another glass, and swapped it for the empty one before retreating to the prep room.

She turned her attention back to the tunic, and let her fingers brush over the flight wings. They were among the first things she'd seen after the implants healed, right after Mira's face and a bunch of investigators with questions about the accident. Mira had done a good job of shielding her from the inquest, but there was only so much a fresh sub-lieutenant could do in the face of a superior officer's demands, and Mira had a lot more to lose by bucking the system than Marya ever would.

At least she got the truth out. One of a million reasons I'm thankful she's still in my life.

Thoughts of Mira always led to thoughts of Deb, and that more than anything made up her mind to resign. She still had no idea what to do about the out-system transmission that ultimately led to her stowing away on a shuttle, or the fact that her superior officers had probably tried to have her killed on *City of Lights*. But at least this was a problem she could solve.

Maybe Deb will design me a sweet little sub-orbital to ferry bigwigs around in. Because the odds of me getting back to space in any meaningful way just dropped from slim to none.

Maybe I won't blow my brains out from boredom inside a month.

Resigning her commission would be as easy as registering the decision, especially since no-one really wanted her in the Fleet anyway. But Marya was tired of dealing with uniforms and bureaucracies, and she certainly didn't want to wait around in some office with a head full of drunk.

"Steward, can you bring me a handheld, please? I need core access."

There was a brief delay before the man appeared, and the look of fear on his face nearly killed Marya's buzz entirely.

"I'm sorry, ma'am. I can't do that."

Give me the damn handheld, you pissant sonuva...

"And why is that, exactly?

"Because I told him not to, Lieutenant. And around here people obey orders."

It was a man's voice, deep, resonant, and accustomed to command. Part of her wanted to jump to attention and spin around with a hasty salute, but unlike the steward she was through with people telling her what to do.

Instead, Marya picked up her beer and took a long pull at it, setting it back down with a smile.

"It's probably a good thing I won't be around here much longer, then. Listen, whoever you are, this day's been the latest of a long string of bad ones, and I'd really like to get it over with. If you can help me with that, I'm happy to talk. Otherwise, I've got things to do."

"I was told you were smart, Andreison. Too smart to be pulling stunts like this, and definitely too smart to mouth off to a senior Fleet Captain. But by all means, please, finish your drink. I'm sure the rest of my day can wait until you realize how much trouble you're in."

Marya swallowed hard, and eased out of her chair. Determined not to back down, she turned and put a face to the voice, and once again regretted letting her mouth run.

She'd only seen the man standing before her once, during her graduation exercises. But Fleet Captain Samuel DeMarco wasn't the kind of person you could forget.

DeMarco's body was matched well to his voice. He was the kind of man that had to have everything he wore tailored, since normal clothes would look ridiculous on so large a frame. Marya was no slouch herself, but pulling herself up to her full height only brought her eyes to DeMarco's third blouse button, and the bottom of his impressive set of ribbons. And unlike the peacockery of Ethan Phillips, none of DeMarco's ribbons were participation prizes.

Well, shit. This day just keeps getting better and better.

"I was in the process of resigning my commission, sir, so if you can see fit to expediting my request, I'll be off your station and out of your hair as soon as I can."

"Two more mistakes. First, your request is denied, so get back in uniform right now or we'll complete our conversation in the brig."

Marya reclaimed her tunic from the bar and sealed it over her jumpsuit as fast as she could, careful to smooth it down according to regs. DeMarco's slight nod of approval gave her some hope that she could salvage the situation, but his frown did not budge as he spoke.

"Second, this isn't my station, but I was understandably curious when half the ship's complement of *City of Lights* showed up out of nowhere, with one-way transfer orders and nowhere to go but 'away.' Even more so to get a call from Rivers here about a shavetail who walked straight off the transport into the wardroom and started tossing back beers on a stolen credit chip. An officer, I might add, who was not only missing from the shuttle's manifest, but also not listed as part of *City of Lights*' crew.

"Care to explain? Or should I call for station security and let them sort you out after all?"

Marya pressed her lips together, wondering which of her new problems to be angry about first.

"The chip's not stolen, it's mine. I just haven't had to use it in some time, and must have forgotten to update it."

Because my pig of a father did the worlds a favor and died a few years back, and left me enough credit to build one of these stations for myself. I just didn't need any of it until today.

"But as for the rest, sir, yes, I can explain."

"Good. Come with me, Andreison. I get the feeling that whatever you have to say isn't meant for public consumption."

Marya nodded, and turned back to settle up with the steward. Her beer had been replaced on the counter with a glass of water and a couple sobriety pills, as well as her inherited credit chip. She looked up at the steward, who surprised her by offering one of the crispest salutes she'd seen in years.

Although Captain DeMarco was waiting, and she was under no obligation to do so, Marya returned the salute, holding it a few seconds longer than necessary as a thank you for the wordless respect before turning to follow the captain.

ABOUT THE AUTHOR

Scott James Magner has held down many jobs over the years, including circus promoter, warehouse manager, dog-sitter, professional role-playing gamer, and writer. He currently resides in Seattle with his partner of many years and several cats who don't understand why sitting down to write is not an invitation for lap-time.

You can catch up on all things him at his website:

scottjamesmagner.com